THE PRINCE AND THE ASSASSIN
Carentan – Book 3

FG and DC Laval

THE PRINCE AND THE ASSASSIN
Carentan – Book 3

DOUBLE DRAGON

Dedication

In memory of
Derek Clive Laval

For Derek Laval, who was my writing partner for years and whose ideas and thoughts live on in this third book in the series. This one is for you, Dad.

PROLOGUE

It was some time after his coronation when Gereinte Andolin, the King of Carentan returned, incognito, to the small village of Cannan. The wife of the swordsmith, Jael, looked surprised yet dignified as he strolled into Jael's workshop as though he had only been there three weeks before.

"This is an unexpected surprise," Jael said, eyes flicking to his wife. His wife rolled her eyes at her husband, then turned and curtsied with her head bowed.

"Your Majesty," she said. Jael flapped about apologetically, all of a sudden making the connection between the King and the many stories that had come his way about a legendary blue sword. His face flushed as he bowed. Gereinte kept his own counsel.

"I promised to return with fair payment for your gift, though I can hardly repay you in kind for the magnificence of this weapon and the part its craftsmanship has played in my journey," Gereinte said. Gereinte nodded at his companion, Etienne, who produced a bag heavy with coin.

"Oh... no, no. I did not expect this," Jael said. "In fact..." he wandered off to the back of the room. "I have something for you." Jael came back with a magnificent, jeweled scabbard. "I said three weeks, but in fact it has taken me longer to produce something that would really do justice to the sword."

Gereinte accepted the scabbard with a look of

wonder.

"This is much more than what I was expecting. But please accept my coin if only to assuage my own conscience and believe me... it would make me happy to recompense you at least in coin." Jael bowed his head in acquiescence and somehow Gereinte felt that the playing field had been leveled. He glanced at Jael's wife. There was still something about that woman that he just couldn't put his finger on.

Weighing up his gaze, Jael's wife excused herself, reminding them that her son was alone in the yard and quickly made her apologies.

Satisfied with the outcome of his visit, Gereinte turned his back on the little cottage that housed the smithy of Cannan and walked back to where the horses had been tethered. His companions waited patiently beside the King's mount. They appeared be laughing and waving at something to the side of the cottage. When they saw Gereinte emerge, they straightened themselves to attention in preparation for the journey home. Gereinte glanced in the direction of their attention and was stopped in his stride.

What he saw brought a spine tingling spark of recognition to him, which caught him momentarily off guard. It was the image of himself as a boy staring back at him; hair ruffled, mud on his shirt and a lively inquisitive sparkle in his emerald green eyes. They stood at a distance, boy to man and stared at each other for an uncanny moment, before the boy lifted his hand and waved at Gereinte, breaking the spell. Gereinte waved back, turned and walked on towards his companions. He looked over his shoulder again at the boy, then turned and shook his head, dislodging an uncomfortable thought. The royal party mounted their horses and rode away without a backward glance, though Gereinte could sense more than one set of eyes watching his departure.

Chapter One

From an early age, Allan had learnt how to blend into the background. It was a useful skill, growing up as an only child at the smithy in Cannan, often open to speculation from the village children within their friendship groups. Now at sixteen years old, Allan wrestled with the transition from boy to man and all the associated emotions that came with it. Blending in enabled him to observe in relative obscurity the alluring young woman who had just walked into the room on the arm of the King of Carentan.

The forge was in a small, but well ventilated stonewalled room, tucked into the back of his father's, workshop. It was easy for Allan to remain concealed behind the huge black anvil while they murmured and discussed prices with his father in the workshop.

"Your Majesty," Jael dipped his head in deference, "the price is no object."

King Gereinte shook his head with a knowing smile. "Maester Jael, you know I always pay my debts," he said.

"No amount of money can match the debt owed to you by this family, your Majesty." To which, the King scoffed and shuffled his feet, reminding Allan of himself when his mother reprimanded him for some altercation or other. Allan knew the story of the Sarlatian nobleman who came to an untimely end at the hand of the King. Before he became king, he had sought to commission a Jael sword on the strength of the smith's reputation. By happy coincidence, at least for Jael and his family, the King's intervention saved their lives. By way of thanks, Jael had presented him the sword, meant for the Sarlatian. Rumour had it that the sword's Damascene steel glowed a faint blue when the King touched its hilt.

"And so the sword always chooses its master," his father was wont to say whenever Mother told the story. Since that day, the smithy at Cannan had received a steady stream of business from royalty down to the lower levels of gentry who on reputation alone 'just had to have a Jael sword'. It went without saying that Allan would carry on the tradition of skilled smithing; the magic of the craft passing from father to son.

The heat from the hearth sent ripples across the room, making the girl fade in and out of focus. A trickle of sweat ran down Allan's forehead and he hefted the hammer, his muscles bunching in response, then struck the sword with a precision born of experience. The metal on metal made a satisfying ring and sparks flew to the tune of the weapon. Each strike with the hammer chimed a different note and to Allan's ears, it was the sword's very own song. The song that determined its master. He lost himself completely in the moment; the breath-taking heat, the background murmur, the stench of hot burning coals and the song of steel.

It wasn't until he put down the hammer and returned the sword to the hearth that he realised he had not quite managed to blend into the background as well as he had hoped. The sense of being watched made his skin itch. He took up the bellows as an excuse to turn his back on inquisitive eyes. He tried to concentrate on the heat of the coals, but his interest got the better of him and he turned. She was standing in the archway between the forge and the workshop. Her green cloak was trimmed with ermine, quality cloth of noble cut. Her hair wound down her shoulders in red ringlets, framing a freckled round face with eyes that sparkled with curiosity and mischief. By his judgement, she looked about the same age as him. He didn't know why she was watching him or what she wanted but only that his heart started up a steady drum beat in response to the intensity of her gaze.

"Countess Del'oro?" A woman's voice from the workshop.

The young woman looked around and the King's sister, Princess Alliane stepped into view. She was dressed in riding attire that played down her royal status; brown leggings and a green jerkin. She clapped her hands together in barely concealed exuberance. "Come and see these weapons. There is sure to be one for you here." The Countess glanced back at Allan, a smile twitching at the corner of her mouth. Her eyes darted towards Allan's left hand and he turned his back enough to hide the ugly stump of his little finger. But not before she had seen it and judged him. She whirled around and strode back into the workshop.

Allan drew the steel from the heat and laid it aside to normalise. It was a fine piece of work, one that would earn the reputation of a Jael sword. Wielding a hammer had become more difficult for his father in latter years, but Allan was proud to maintain the legacy on his behalf.

There was a clash of steel on steel and voices rose in alarm from the other room. Allan watched the scene from the shadows of the forge. Princess Alliane was wielding her sword against the Countess, who stumbled backward raising a clumsy two-handed broad sword. The King looked on with an amused expression on his face. Allan had often wondered at the regularity of the King's visits to the smithy. Perhaps he still felt there was a debt to be paid for the sword that had forged his reputation. The King's eyes flicked over to the forge where Allan stood. Allan willed himself to blend into the background. But it was almost as though the King saw beyond the apparent, his reach seeking Allan's presence and urging him forth. Allan sank back further into the shadows.

He still had a good view of the Countess, who had given up on the broad sword and picked a one-handed long sword from the display. She began to cut the air in front of her with long slow arcs, testing the weight and feel of the weapon. She was clearly no novice to the art of swordplay, despite her initial choice of weapon. Alliane responded to the advancing Countess with measured caution. The cut and thrust of the Countess's strikes pushed the Princess back towards the forge, and every time the Princess moved forward, the Countess leaned into the attack, further cutting down her distance. Allan was all but ready to catch the Princess as she came two steps away from tumbling into his space. Then she found her feet and started to parry and hold off

14

the Countess with just enough finesse not to lose face in front of the King and company. The Countess was no novice indeed.

Jael was flapping his arms on the periphery conflicted between the need for safety and interrupting this royal game.

"Ladies, your Majesty… please. We do have a practice yard. My son, Allan, will show you a veritable assortment of swords to choose from. Allan," he called into the forge. Allan stepped into view. The Countess dropped her guard and continued to swish the blade experimentally to and fro while the Princess sheathed her own sword.

"Well," Princess Alliane said. "Perhaps your son might be good enough to provide the Countess with more of a challenge." The King was laughing.

"You give up far too easily, Ally," he said. "Just because a young woman took you by surprise." Alliane scoffed as though it meant nothing to her, to be disgraced by a girl nearly half her age.

Allan was staring at the Countess, who was testing the weight of the sword, transferring it from one hand to the other.

"Not bad," she said to no one in particular, "but it's still not quite right." She spoke in Etanese, the most widely-spread language of the Western Isles, but with a Langan accent, native to the Southern Lands. It gave her voice a hypnotic lilt.

Silently, he chose a selection of swords from the display, and then exited by a side door into the yard without waiting to see if anyone followed. He strode to the far end of the yard, kicking up a dust storm. The sun beat down with relentless heat, giving him no respite from the sweaty oven of the forge. He set the swords down on the wooden rack. They would soon see which design best suited the Countess and her unique brand of swordsmanship. He wondered where she had learnt to lean into the attack like that. It was a move not many seasoned warriors would have the confidence to pull off and she applied it with the ease of someone born on the battlefield. There were only two others he had ever seen fight like that: The Queen of Carentan, Jehanna Mantar and her twin brother, the King's Chief of Staff, Jehan. They were renowned for their fighting skill, particularly for delivering deathly blows from horseback.

Allan lifted the eastern scimitar. He gripped its hilt and walked through a few patterns, slicing thin air and stirring a breeze in the still heat of midday. His parents had insisted on his training in the art of swordsmanship. After all, how could he hope to forge the perfect weapon without first knowing how to wield it? The scimitar was a single-edged blade that tapered to a point with a slight curve on the end. With such a weapon, you could apply cutting and thrusting techniques with equally devastating effect. Perfect for fighting from a mount.

As he turned and levelled the blade in front of his body, his eye caught movement to his left. He turned his back to the entrance, making a play of exchanging weapons, but not before he had seen the Countess speaking to his mother. Was it his imagination, or did they already know each other?

How he wished to be invisible. Better still, a pesky fly, unseen to the unsuspecting human eye.

He laid the scimitar aside and lifted the bastard sword, one that could be used equally well as a one-handed or two-handed weapon. He suspected the Countess was more comfortable with a one-handed sword, but it wouldn't hurt to try all options. If she were looking for a balance between the broad sword and the long sword, the bastard sword could be just that. He felt its weight and wondered about the conversation going on behind his back.

Returning the sword to the rack, he finally lifted the third sword he had picked. The hand-and-a-half sword. This one was a beautiful balance between the two-handed and one-handed preference. It had a cruciform hilt that was leather coated with a cord wrap. Its blade had a flattened diamond-section, giving it perfect precision as Allan weighed the weapon in his grip. He felt certain he could fashion a perfect blade for the Countess based on one of those.

"Good selection." She peered over his shoulder at the choice of blades. He put the sword back and turned, finding himself face to face with those piercing azure eyes. Without a thought, he pulled the string that kept his own hair from his face and offered it to her.

"You might be needing this," he said. Her eyes twinkled with mischief as she nodded without dropping her gaze, then turned her back.

"Perhaps you would be so kind?"

Allan drew her curls together into a long tail down her back and took his time to tie the string in

17

place. Without meaning to, he brushed a thumb across her skin at the nape of her neck and her body shivered in response. It stirred the most curious feeling inside him; an inexplicable sense that he had been there before. That he and the Countess had known each other a lifetime ago, though he barely knew her at all. He pulled the string tight and let his hands drop. The Countess turned and smiled.

"Thank you." Then she was once again looking at the swords, while Princess Alliane and the King strolled into the yard, laughing at something. His mother was staring at him with that look he knew would only mean trouble for him later on. His father fussed around the King and the Princess, finding them stools to sit on, but Alliane refused to be seated. She insisted on continuing with her sword practice in preparation for the try-out of the swords for her esteemed guest.

King Gereinte looked at him with a curious expression on his face and he waved a hand to the Princess, beseeching her to stop her activity. Alliane came to an abrupt stop, holding her sword hilt in the hanging guard position, point sloping down.

"What? Are we taking training now too?" Alliane said.

"I am thinking that perhaps the boy would indeed be better placed to put the Countess and her swords through their paces. He will be the one, after all, to forge the final piece." King Gereinte was staring right at him and as if he wasn't overheated enough, Allan still found the capacity to blush under the King's level gaze.

18

Princess Alliane dropped her guard with a deflated exhalation of breath.

"Very well," she said, taking up a stool next the King. He gestured towards Allan, who dipped his head in response, wondering if that was deep enough to satisfy the kind of royal etiquette his mother had instilled in him. He looked over to where she stood and saw that she was smiling. At least he had got that bit right. Quashing the desire to find any excuse to touch the Countess again, Allan watched her remove and fold her cloak before joining him in the centre of the yard. He took up the bastard sword and offered it to her hilt-first, then selected the scimitar for himself.

They bowed to each other, then he had barely straightened from his guard position when she was upon him with the speed of a wild leopard. Fortunately, the scimitar was a beautifully designed weapon of stealth and a flick of the wrist brought its dull edge in line with her attack to parry the thrust of the bastard sword.

Mother of Fire. He had not been prepared for the strength behind her slight build. He noticed the ripples of well-worked muscle down her arms and across her chest. His distraction was almost his undoing as she pushed him back further with that disarming lean. Where had she learnt such confidence? By the gods though, it worked and Allan had a hard time parrying each thrust as she weaved forward and back, sidestepping and moving off line, only to come in with another deadly blow.

The scimitar was bearing up under his experienced hand, but was not the right weapon to be pitted against anyone in one-to-one combat on the ground. He felt it give whenever she did that tilt with her shoulder. He tried to second-guess her moves by watching her body, but she was practised at hiding her intent and even tricked him a few times with her feints.

Sweat poured down his face now, as he began to make ground and take the fight back to her. She didn't like it and a small frown creased her brow when he delivered an inside thrust with just a fraction of a drop, imitating her signature move.

"Enough!" King Gereinte's voice rang out across the yard and the Countess dropped back, withdrew and held her sword in front of her body, point down, head bowed in deference to her opponent. "I think we get the point. This is not a tournament after all, no need for any bloodshed." There was amusement in the King's tone. Allan dropped back, bowed and replaced his weapon on the rack. He relieved the Countess of the bastard sword, noting her nod of approval as she handed it back to him.

"Your choice this time, my Lady," he said.

Chapter Two

Allan wasn't sure if it were the heat of the forge or the memory of the Countess that made him so hot and bothered. After several bouts with equal exertion on both sides, they had reached the conclusion that a made-to-measure version of the bastard sword would best serve the Countess' needs. They had all withdrawn to the relative comfort of the parlour to discuss particulars. The King discussed money with Jael, while Allan discussed aesthetics with the Countess. He measured her grip and the length of her arm while she watched, barely taking her eyes from his face as though she were afraid of forgetting what he looked like. It was quite unnerving and Allan avoided her gaze and continued with the job at hand as though nothing were unusual about her attention.

"Have you always lived here?" she said.

"No." He continued to measure the inside of her arm, tracing a line from her shoulder to her wrist with a piece of tape. "I mean, I wasn't born here if that's what you mean, my Lady," he added, remembering his etiquette. A smile twitched the corner of her mouth.

"Where were you born?" Her directness was as unnerving as her scrutiny. He looked up and smiled at her, hoping to hide his discomfort.

"I don't know, my Lady. I was adopted."

"Your mother has taught you the manners of a gentleman, I see. I wonder what else?" Before he had a chance to unpick the meaning of her words,

21

she took hold of his hand and raised it to eye level. Embarrassed by the fact that she had chosen the hand with his mutilated little finger, he snatched it away. She paused, watching him.

"How did you lose your finger?" she said.

"I don't remember. It was a long time ago, before my parents adopted me." His cheeks reddened.

"Where did they find you?"

"If you don't mind me saying, my Lady… I find your questions rather unsettling." He often asked his mother where, why and how, but never received a satisfactory answer.

"Does it feel awkward?" she said, making another play for his hand.

"No." He put his left hand behind his back. "I have never known any different. May I continue with the measurements?" She puffed her cheeks out with an exaggerated sigh, then shrugged.

He longed to ask her where she came from and what she was doing in Carentan in the company of the King and where she learnt how to fight like a warrior. Her face had a bewitching femininity and her eyes were deep pools of ocean blue.

He sensed another pair of eyes on him and knew without looking that his mother was around somewhere. Hidden from view, as she often was. He returned his attention to determining the accuracy of the Countess' grip and the length of her arm.

When the deal was done, they agreed on a day two weeks from then for Allan to deliver the sword to the Countess at Castle Helmstedt.

***

Two days before his trip to the Castle, Allan was in the workshop, polishing the sword, when his father and mother came in together. He knew something was going on by the way they both stood, pretending to admire his work, idly finding chores to do around the workshop which they both knew he had already completed. Yet he continued to run soft strokes up and down the blade with his cloth, caressing the weapon with the care only a Jael sword deserved.

"Be careful, lad. You'll be polishing the steel back down to its core if you carry on like that. A good smith knows when to stop," his father said.

Allan sighed and put the sword down.

"Rubies or emeralds?" he said. Jael raised his bushy white eyebrows. "For the scabbard."

"Amethysts perhaps," his mother said, "to match her eyes."

Allan thought about this for a moment. "She has blue eyes," he said.

"Sapphires then," his mother said, narrowing her own eyes. Sometimes she just saw right through him.

"I know what you're thinking. She is above my status, I understand that."

"Well, there are plenty of nice girls in the village," Mother said, sounding rather insincere.

"And they all think I'm a freak," he said, waving his left hand in the air. His mother looked away with sadness in her eyes and his father busied

23

himself, pretending not to hear. Jael always maintained a distance from Allan where girls were concerned, claiming that his expertise lay in forging swords not relationships.

"There is something you need to know, Allan." His mother returned her gaze to him and his father stopped what he was doing and stood with his hands behind his back, as though on guard duty.

"Your mother is going on a trip," Jael said. "She has been commissioned to complete an assignment of great importance." Allan looked from one to the other. His father had a resigned look on his face, his mother stoic. Allan knew something of his mother's past. She had once worked in the higher ranks of society, serving barons and princes. Quite what she did, he had never managed to ascertain.

"What kind of a trip?" he said. "Can I go too?"

"Son, you have other business to take care of here in the forge and not least the trip you have to deliver this sword." Jael said. His parents exchange a guarded look.

"What about Lorcas? I'm sure he could do with the extra work." Lorcas was Father's latest apprentice from the village, who came in two days a week to help out. Particularly when there was a commission from the garrison.

"There will be plenty of work for both you and Lorcas, have no fear of that," Father said. But Allan knew he was stalling. It wasn't even that Allan was that desperate to go with his mother, he was just curious to know what was so important that she had to go away on a so called 'trip'. It was clear they were not going to reveal any more than that.

"All right, then," he said. But he knew there was something they were not telling him.

He returned to the forge to continue his work. The emotional undercurrent from his mother was hard to unpick. Anger on the surface, though laced through with fear and a sense of loss. What was it that she feared to lose?

He heard their voices, raised in discussion. Then as the evening wore on, the light busy shuffles of his parents preparing for sleep. They didn't bother him and he worked into the night, letting the hypnotic movement of his hands free his thoughts.

Later, he turned in for the night himself, lying atop his pallet and falling into a dreamless sleep. He awoke in the deep dark of the night, the room illuminated by a faint glow from the forge leaking in from beneath the crack at the bottom on his door. He sat up. That was odd. He was certain he had banked the fire, so the coals should not still be glowing so brightly. Unless someone else was using the fire.

As silent as shadow, he slid from the bed. The door made an audible clunk and he cringed. So much for stealth. Opening it a crack, he peered out, but there was no sign of life. A quick check of the workshop and forge revealed no intruders, so he turned back towards his room. A lick of flame caught his eye and he glanced with curiosity at the forge. There was something flat and square nestled in amongst the coals. It looked like a notebook with a hide cover and parchment pages, which were

25

curling up at the corners with the heat. One corner of the book had caught a flame, which was creeping up the front cover. Allan grabbed a pair of tongs and lifted it out, slapping it down on the worktable to extinguish the flames. The book smouldered and the corners turned black with soot. He shook it a few times, then when he was sure it had cooled, flicked through the pages. He recognised his Mother's looping script. It was written in an old version of Etanese, clearly not meant for the eyes of a commoner. He could speak the older language, but had to concentrate to understand its written form. His name jumped off the parchment in several places, so he took it to his room and stashed it beneath his bed on the stone floor. In the morning he would make up his mind what to do about it, as clearly its owner, his mother he presumed, had not wanted the content to be read.

Chapter Three

Allan slid the Countess's new bastard sword into its scabbard. The sapphires glinted in the sunlight and reminded him of her eyes. He wrapped it carefully in sackcloth and buried it in his saddlebags. It was a two-day ride to Canrac and Castle Helmstedt, where he was expected to deliver the sword to her. Beside the sword, he tucked the book he had rescued from the fire the previous night.

The uncommon heat of mid-summer began its daily oppression, despite the early hour. His mother and father came to the door to bid him farewell and he still sensed an undercurrent of uncertainty when his mother wrapped her arms around him. She pulled away and looked him up and down.

"I've packed some provisions, but if you run out, your father has also packed some coin in the inner pocket of your bags," she said. If he didn't know her better, he might have said there were tears welling behind those deep soulful eyes. But his mother never cried. He grasped his father's hand and shook it.

"Son. Take care and may the gods speed you."

"I'll be back in a few days," he said, looking from his father to his mother and wondering why they were making such a big deal about a simple goodbye.

"Will you be gone by the time I return?" he said.

"Most likely." She nodded and looked wistful.

There it was again. That feeling that they were holding something back. He was impatient to get away and start deciphering whatever it was his mother had wanted to burn. With no further delay, he swung himself into the saddle. His parents waved him away as he nudged his docile chestnut horse, Dilla, into a slow walk. He looked over his shoulder and gave them one more wave before turning Dilla onto the track and heading off towards the river Caren, which would lead him all the way to Canrac. His parents disappeared behind a screen of trees and undergrowth.

By midday, the sun had reached its full height and was threatening its revenge on mortals. The nape of Allan's neck was itching with heat and his legs clung to Dilla's sides in a sweaty embrace. Their pace had reduced to a slow walk, in part due to the heat, but also the river path was narrow and precariously close to the bank. He had been tempted at one point to pull out the book and allay the boredom of the repetitive clop of Dilla's pace and the unchanging scenery. Then he dismissed a brief twinge of guilt and continued to stare at the sky waiting for a copse of trees under which to take a moment's rest in the shade. Before long, he came across a large willow tree that overhung the river and gave him ample room to sit on the bank and rest his sun stroked limbs.

He led Dilla to the water's edge and found a shallow enough part to allow her to drink, then hoisted his saddlebags onto his shoulder. Positioned within sight of the horse, he settled his back against the tree trunk and after slaking his own thirst, let the cool shade of the willow calm his thoughts. In his mind's eye, he was back in the workshop, measuring the Countess, while she watched him. With women you could never really be sure what they were thinking. There was a girl called Erika in the village that he once thought was interested in him, but it hadn't turned out so well. She had seemed like a pleasant girl and encouraged his attentions, but he misread her so badly, he began to question his ability to make a sound judgement where girls were concerned.

The sun peeped through the canopy of leaves, warming his skin and resting his soul. Perhaps the Countess was the sort of person who was curious about everything. That was the way of a true warrior. Someone brought up to fight the way she did could not afford to dismiss the minutiae of everything around her. You had to be ready at a moment's notice to leap into action. That much his mother had taught him. But then, when he thought about the Countess, he felt a strange warming sensation inside, as though his thoughts were being answered by an external presence. Perhaps they were. He wondered then if she were thinking of him and flushed under the sun's embrace, though no one was there to see it, save Dilla and an array of chattering birds and river fish. This was ridiculous. He stirred himself up and dug into the saddlebags to see what his mother had packed him to eat.

As he pulled out a chunk of bread and cheese wrapped in cloth, the book tumbled out and lay on the grass in front of him. He chewed on a hunk of bread and nibbled the cheese, taking measured

29

gulps of watered down ale from his water skin. He watched the book with suspicion. It was taunting him, the pages turning in the breeze of their own volition. Gods be damned, if he didn't know better he might have thought his mother had bewitched it. He reached out a finger and turned the parchment to the start. A flake of charred parchment fluttered on the breeze. Fortunately for him, the fire had only taken the corners, without reaching the words. He flattened it out so that he could read and eat at the same time. No point in wasting the moment, he thought, squinting at the writing and reading slowly to get the full meaning of the language.

***

My dearest Son...

His mother's long, script sucked him in. It was written for him. She knew there were few who could read the old language – poetic as it was in style. A friend and mentor had taught her, she said, and it was she who had taught Allan. So it was meant for him, but not meant for him to read. When he was a child and had got into arguments, she always told him to write a letter to the person in question telling the whole truth about how he felt and then to burn it. It was good for the soul, she said. He continued to read.

"For many years I have wished to tell you this truth. A truth that you may find incredible, a truth that you may indeed hate me for in time. In my defence, I can only say that I kept this from you for your own protection and hope for that you will

30

forgive me. Your father has always known and kept his own counsel at my request, so please don't blame him for his silence. Now that you have turned sixteen, it is time for you to know your true parentage and with this knowledge make your own decisions about your future. Both your father and I decided that to keep you in continued ignorance was a cruelty neither of us wished on either you or your true family. I hope that they will understand that what I did was to protect you from an evil that would have destroyed both you and the country. My own conscience is clear. Here is my story and I hope that you understand and make the right decisions for yourself.

***

Allan slammed the book shut. Perhaps she meant for him to find it after all. Did he want to know the truth? He wished he could know how it would change his life before he continued to read. Then he could make the decision whether or not to read the rest, based on the final outcome. That was ridiculous and he admonished himself for his own procrastination, wondering if Countess Del'oro would have been struggling with herself in the same way. Perhaps not. She seemed far too pragmatic. Perhaps then just a little flick through, to see if it were worth reading after all. If the ending was good, he might read the rest. He slipped his finger between the covers and flipped to the back and stared with horror as his mind struggled with the translation. Right. He needed to know the full story

31

before he could even begin to comprehend what he thought he had just read. So he went back to the beginning where his mother's script began her story.

***

My true name is Delyth Lanner. To my knowledge, my only living relative is Renn Lanner, my elder brother, who serves at the Court of Baron Issoire and has done from a young age. I never knew my brother very well, we were separated and he now believes me to be dead. Renn followed his lifelong dream of becoming a knight and I have watched his progress from a distance, happy to know that he exceeded even his own expectations and went on to become Issoire's Master Knight-at-Arms, his right-hand man.

***

Allan looked up for a moment, lost in the hypnotic swirl of water and the gentle rustle of Willow leaves. He had an uncle. Not only that, he had an uncle who was a knight in one of the largest and most influential houses in Carentan. Perhaps he should visit. But what would he say? I'm your dead sister's adopted son, oh and by the way, she's not really dead. He didn't think that was the best way to begin a familial relationship. He put his head down and continued to read.

***

I lived my early life in the small village of Wellspring, just by the southern end of the Forest of Dreams. I was born and brought up in the village, it was my home and I loved it as such. Never did I have any notion of leaving the village like Renn had. As far as I was concerned I would live out all my days there and was happy to do so. My father was the local blacksmith and my mother, the herb mistress. So, as you can guess, I picked up a lot of my combined talents from them. My skill with the herbs delighted my mother and established my right as the village herb mistress, once my parents passed away. It was inevitable that one day they would pass their family business on to their children. To that day, it disappointed father that Renn had not wanted to take up the role of owning and running the smithy, but he was compensated by the fact that I took his apprentice, Arban, to be my husband.

Arban was a sweet and gentle man who loved me from the moment he set eyes on me as a young girl. And so it was only natural that he would take over as the local blacksmith once my father had died. He supported me through the tears and transition of my bereavement. Until that time, my parents had been my entire life and they passed on within days of one another. Then when our son arrived, it felt like the skies had opened up and poured joy down onto our simple existence. We named our son, Allan, after my father.

***

33

Allan frowned. Now he was confused. Was Arban his father? That would mean his mother, was indeed his real mother. According to her account, he had grandparents he never knew existed and a village, somewhere near the Forest of Dreams, where he was born. Why would she not tell him this before?

The sun had begun its afternoon descent and the pull of completing his journey and finding a suitable inn to rest overnight, won over the allure of his mother's unfolding story. He packed the book away. Now he had an incentive to get Dilla moving a little quicker. The sooner he found an overnight place to stay, the sooner he could sit down with this book and unravel the truth.

* * *

Chapter Four

The river path widened, steering Allan and his horse, Dilla, away from the banks of the Caren and towards the first signs of civilisation. It was late afternoon by the time they rode into the village of Ashwra feeling hot, sore and tired. Dilla dipped her head with every dogged step; he guessed she was also done for the day. The stench of latrines hung over the place, mingled with the fading scent of riverweed. The people of Ashwra were friendly enough, directing him towards the local inn, where he handed Dilla over to the stable boy, then carried his bags into the public room to negotiate lodgings for the night.

"Where are you heading, young messer?" the innkeeper said with a curious glance at his saddlebags. Allan glanced around the room. An elderly man with grey travel worn robes sat with his head hovering over a tankard of ale. Two bearded travellers were staring at Allan and the innkeeper with interest. Allan guessed they must have come from the Helm, judging by their thick muscled build, which northern Carentans inherited from their Klagenstill ancestry. Although not nearly as forbidding as a true Klagen warrior, they still made Allan nervous.

"I have business at Castle Helmstedt," he said, keeping his voice low. The innkeeper's eyes flicked over his shoulder and back to Allan.

"Good weather for travelling. Keeps us busy, for sure. That'll be two silvers for supper and board." Allan handed him two silver crowns. The innkeeper nodded and squirreled away the coins. "Bread and mutton stew, ale included, no food or drink in the rooms and my good lady wife will take you up. Latrines in the back, behind the stables." Allan wrinkled his nose. Yes, he had already gathered that.

He followed the innkeeper's wife, who chatted all the time about the weather, the price of butter and the summer fayre in Canrac. Allan nodded politely and made the appropriate listening noises and she seemed happy enough with his attention. He returned to the public room and ate quicker than was comfortable for him, as he noted with a twinge of anxiety that the northern men were no longer there. On his return to the room, he checked the sword, which was still there and intact. A sudden and inexplicable jolt of panic made him upend the saddlebags and he only felt reassured when the parchment book dropped out onto his bed. He let go of the breath he had been holding.

Curling up on the lumpy hard pallet, he tried for at least a modicum of comfort before opening the book and turning to the page he had left off.

***

I was picking herbs in the forest, on the day that changed my life forever. Since the passing of my parents, I spent a lot of time wandering, thinking, enveloped by the smell of wild flowers and the scent of the forest greenery. I can tell you, my son, that even now, when I recall that day, I smell the tree bark, the grass and the sweet underlying fragrance of heal-all violets. For a long time after, I couldn't touch the little purple flowers. It was just too painful. That day, a whisper of something sinister carried on the breeze. There was an acrid smell despoiling the wind. I looked up and there were great curls of smoke snaking into the clouds.

I stood still and silent. It was surreal. As though the entire flora and fauna paused for breath. Then it hit me as though someone had opened the door to a crowded inn and the noise just flooded out to me; screams of agony and cries of the desperate.

I snapped out of my daze and bolted towards the village with a sick tingling sensation in my feet and my hands, heart hammering against my chest. By the time I reached the outskirts of the village, the noise had abated and a silence shrouded in death hung over the area like a veil. The only life remaining was that of the animals that shared our land.

I could barely breathe through the smoke and my eyes were streaming. There was a lump in my throat and I felt sick in the pit of my stomach. My dearest Allan, you have to remember that this was my village, my life, and my family.

***

Allan paused and took a deep breath. His throat constricted and the threat of tears stung the corners of his eyes. He had heard stories of this kind of thing happening, although it was less rife in Carentan, particularly since King Gereinte's coronation, nine years ago. He had heard whispers of villages destroyed in the Southern Lands by raiders, but nothing so close to home. He turned back to the book.

***

I walked down the winding path of Wellspring towards my house. Bodies littered the scene, bloodied and battered. I stumbled in a daze looking around at the carnage of death and destruction. Most of the houses were on fire and those that were not had a trail of blood at their doors. A stray chicken ran across my path, squawking and flapping. I leapt to one side and crouched down. The air was rich with an acrid smoke and the pungent smell of burning flesh. I ran then. Ran, like I had never run before, pounding down that village path ignoring the sights and smells with only one thing in my mind; Arban and little Allan.

I rounded a corner and stopped when I saw the smithy on fire. Dreading what I might find inside, I peered in and reeled back at the stench of human flesh. A body was slumped over the forge, knife protruding from its midriff, reddened flesh peeling and crackling as fire licked its way around the small room. I stumbled out of the doorway and retched in the street. After several deep breaths, I wiped a hand across my mouth and peered around the doorway, forcing myself to look at the burning mess. I had to see, I had to know. The body was long with a slim waist - it couldn't have been Arban, who was built like a tree with big hands and feet. This long limbed burning carcass could only have been his young apprentice; Stefan. I was appalled at my own sense of relief and then I felt guilty and sad in equal measures. I set off up the path towards the only other place that Arban was likely to be - at home with our baby son, Allan.

***

Allan put the book down. He sat up and put a hand over his mouth. His skin quivered and tingled with the pain of his mother's words. He thought he knew what was coming next, but couldn't bear to read it. Obviously, Arban must have died. But the baby. The baby had his name, so the baby must have survived. Is this how he lost his little finger? Perhaps it had been mangled in a fight between his mother and whoever the perpetrators were of this crime. Or perhaps it was so badly burnt that it had to be cut off. Why had she never told him this before? He rubbed the stump on his left hand, which had a habit of aching in remembered pain. He yawned and lay back. He really needed to sleep, as he had a long journey ahead in the morning. Perhaps just one or two more pages...

***

As I approached our family cottage, I slowed down, coming to a stop just outside the door. All was quiet. There was not a sound other than the distant crackle of fire. The smell of death hung limpet-like to my little haven. My beautiful home.

My family. I wanted to turn and run, not daring to face my fears inside. The door hung askew, as though it had been rammed with something large and heavy. It made no sense. Arban was more than capable of taking on a few brigands; there was nothing he would not do to protect little Allan. Then as I edged my way past the broken door, I realised that was exactly what he had done. His body was pinned to the far wall of the living area, the shaft of a spear protruding from his chest. A trail of blood ran down his front and his head slumped awkwardly on his chest.

I was numb with grief. Where was Allan? Frantically I ran from room to room, daring to hope that he was still alive, lying hidden somewhere. But there was no sound; nothing but the drip and trickle of blood pooling around Arban's feet. Then I stopped in front of my dead husband. He would have done everything to protect our son.

With both hands, I grabbed the spear and pulled as hard and as quickly as possible. Arban's body collapsed to the floor and there behind him lay the tiny body of our beloved son, Allan, caught by the spear that had taken the life of my husband. In a fit of disbelief, I grabbed the baby and held his limp body up, shaking and shaking. But the body stayed as limp and lifeless as I had found it. I sobbed and screamed, held him to my chest and squeezed him close, hoping that my very proximity would squeeze the life back into him.

As I sat there, cradling and sobbing, my mind turned towards the people who had done this thing and my grief turned to anger. My eye caught sight of the skinning knife, laid on the table, which I often used to collect herbs. I had to act now, before the moment was lost. Carefully, I laid the bodies together and wrapped them in a blanket, before grabbing the knife and heading out towards the forest at a run.

***

Allan's eyes stung with the pain of his mother's grief. He could not bear to read another word. He closed the book and laid it on top of his saddlebags before dropping back onto the pallet and closing his eyes. His mind kept churning over and over this question about the baby Allan. If the baby had died, then who was *he*? Perhaps it was true then. He was tempted to flip to the end and re-read the last page, but he was too tired. Sleep took him, but it was troubled by images of burning cottages and bloodied villagers and at the centre of it all, the sad aching heart of a young woman who had lost everything.

Chapter Five

There will come a time in your life, my son, when you are driven by a hunger that is bigger than you can contain. A hunger that you cannot ignore and will sap your energy, reducing your life to dust. This is what drove me. My husband and my son were gone. Perhaps if Arban had lived, he might have pulled me from the edge of the precipice, but without him I had no anchor in the world, no rock to cling to in the raging seas I faced. This you have to know above all else. Only then can you begin to understand what motivated me to do what I did.

As I ran towards the forest with no idea of what I might find, I knew it was a turning point. The fire in my life had been put out and surrendered to a cold, hard exterior. At that point, all I had to cling to was a single-minded determination to exact revenge. It was the only thing that kept me going. I could have laid down beside my family and died of a broken heart. I could even have weighted my pockets with stones and leapt into the river; the thought had crossed my mind. Or I could find a new purpose.

There were three laggards, who had left an obvious trail through the forest. I caught up with them before too long, but held back to watch. I had enough sense to realise that if I just attacked I would end up as dead as my family and I wanted to hurt them. Hurt them as much as they had hurt me.

Hidden behind a tree, I watched as two men appeared to be locked in combat with a slight, middle-aged man. The speed with which the older man fended off the attackers was swift, as though he were swatting flies.

A third man popped up with his sword drawn. I barely had time to think, so dropped to the ground and kicked low, taking the man off his feet. I had seen the village boys do it in play with each other and was so shocked when it actually worked, that I just froze there in a crouching position. The outlaw hit the ground with a thud and then all pretence to reason left me, as I leapt on top of him like a wild cat. I hardly remember making a conscious decision, so driven by anger, but I stabbed him again and again with my skinning knife. I surrendered to the sweet release of unleashing all that rage, seeing only the image of my dead son. It wasn't until the man lay still, staring lifelessly up into the forest canopy, that I stopped. The blood pooled around him and I rolled away and retched into the bushes, sickened by what I had done.

I staggered towards the clearing. The middle-aged man was still parrying strikes, playing with his opponent. He glanced in my direction, made three quick passes with his sword and the other two laggards fell dead to the ground. He had hardly broken a sweat. He studied me for a moment, then looked over at the dead man behind me.

"Hmm. You are quick and savage, I'll give you that." He held out his hand. "Arabus Castan."

"My village..." I choked back a sob, then the cold stark anger returned and any sense of remorse for the dead man dissipated. "I swear to follow *every single one of them, hunt them down and kill them all. That is my life now, I have nothing else."*

"Well," Castan said, dropping his hand. "At best, you might kill one or two of them before you are overwhelmed by numbers."

"Perhaps then, that would be a welcome end to it. At least I can take a few out with me. My life is already over."

"These men are only tools," Castan said. "Wouldn't revenge on the toolmaker be more sweet?"

"Yes, but…"

"Look at these men." Castan cast his hand across the scene and for the first time, I opened my eyes beyond my own rage and took in the quality of their clothing and the weapons they carried. I moved forwards and stood over one of the dead men, felt the cloth of his tunic and caught sight of my own reflection in the blade of his sword. A woman I barely recognised. Then I understood.

"But why?" When I glanced back at my reflection, I saw a deluded and frightened young girl staring back from her blood-stained face.

"This is part of a local power struggle, involving a Lord who seeks to discredit his adjacent Lord, so that he can take over the land with a claim that his neighbour cannot control the local outlaws."

Then my anger came back, bubbling in my veins. "I'll find him and kill him myself." I turned and strode back to the man I killed, placed a foot on his shoulder and plucked free my knife.

"Hold your anger for one moment. I have a contract for the assassination of this Lord who is responsible for the destruction of your village." I stared at Castan, studying his face for the first time. In any other situation, I would have passed him by on the pathway without a second glance. He looked just like an ordinary middle-aged man. But then I recalled the rigour with which he had dispatched the two outlaws.

"Who are you really?"

Castan paused. *"I may go by the name of Arabus Castan, but I am known in the trade as the Executioner."*

My skin twitched. I had heard stories told of this man; a deadly assassin who operated in the shadows at the highest levels of society, took on few assignments, charged fabulous sums for his services and had, according to the stories, never missed a kill.

"But I am now paying the price for my success," he said. *"Too many clients are coming to me with tempting offers. I do not have the time to do the background work required in order to ensure absolute success. My reputation will suffer if I do not deliver the result required each time, but it will also be damaged if I start to turn down work."*

I listened in silence to Castan's words, unsure of why he was telling me this and where it was leading. He surely didn't think I would stand in the way of him completing his contract?

"Put simply, I need an assistant," he said, *"to undertake some of the menial tasks, leaving me more time for the tricky work. After completing this*

contract, I will train you and reward you beyond anything you could have imagined in your previous life."

"But, we are complete strangers. You don't even know my name. How do you know I would not betray you?" I said.

Castan smiled. "Betray me? To who and why? You are alone in the world and I am offering you a future over which you have some control. Which is more than you had and more than most people will ever have."

An emptiness gnawed at my insides, but I dared not think back to what I once had. Driven by impulse, I held out a hand and Castan shook it firmly. "My name is Delyth Lanner," I said, "and I accept. You have my word that if you deal honourably with me, that I will respond in kind." So indeed, I would have my revenge.

***

Allan flung the book aside. An assassin. His mother was an assassin's assistant. Well that certainly made a lot of sense. Everything she had taught him was beginning to fall into place. He always knew that she occasionally went off on special assignments. Now he knew the truth of it. He shuddered. What kind of assignment was this latest trip, he wondered? Who was she being commissioned to help assassinate?

He left the village of Ashwra shortly after sunrise, hoping for a good start before the midday heat slowed their progress. Long before the sun had risen to its highest point, his curiosity got the better of him and he found a suitable spot beside the river to let Dilla graze and take a mid-morning break. The book called to him like a spit roast over an open fire. He wanted so much to believe that she was truly his mother, that he persuaded his imagination to cook up all sorts of reasons why she might have lied to protect him over the years. But then none of his invented scenarios made any sense either. Where did his father fit in to all this?

Angry and disillusioned, Allan packed up his things and shoved the offending item on top, making little effort to tie the flaps back, hoping that the book might just fall out on the way and that would be the end of it. Conflicted by the need for security in his life and the need for truth, he turned back and made sure the tie was secure before nudging Dilla back onto the river path.

He focused his gaze into the distance, pushing thoughts of his mother's clandestine identity as far as possible from the front of his mind. A lone rider appeared on the horizon, trotting at a leisurely pace towards him. The track was just big enough for two riders to pass and Allan thought nothing of it as he gathered his thoughts and continued along the way. He was keen to make good time and deliver the sword to the Countess Del'oro early the next day as agreed. He shot a glance over his shoulder and was troubled to see two more riders bringing up the rear. He plodded ahead, but the rider reined his mount in across the path in front of him causing Dilla to react by skittering to a standstill. Allan tried to turn Dilla only to see the two riders behind him pull up and dismount, their horses forming a barrier. Then he recognised them. The bearded northerners from the inn in Ashwra.

Chapter Six

The three men drew their swords. They looked confident enough, so perhaps they thought Allan was just a village apprentice out on an errand for his master. Close enough to the truth. He rummaged around in his saddlebags, until he had the hilt of the sword within easy reach.

The man in front gave him the twitch of a smile, brigand speak for *you don't have a hope in hell, so give it up now before we get nasty*. The kind of smile that sends most people off and running in the opposite direction. Except Allan had nowhere to go, other than into the trees, which was not a great idea. He glanced at the two behind him, who wore mismatched tunics and trews of inexpensive cloth. The one in front had slightly better attire, though Allan noticed a rip in the seam of his surcoat on his sword-hand side. All three had unkempt beards and hair that was bordering on Klagen standards, making feeble attempts to braid itself with no help from its owner other than long-term neglect. They clearly didn't see him as a threat.

The man in front dismounted and nodded his head. His nose had a rosy glow – was that just a propensity for too much wine, or a disagreement with the southern summers? As though in response to Allan's scrutiny, the man rubbed his nose and a flake of peeling skin fluttered away on the breeze. The sun burst through the clouds and the man winced, blinded by the sudden impact of the dazzling light.

Allan could bolt for the trees, but the two behind him were blocking the way. He took out the Countess's sword and drew it from its scabbard. The man in front flinched and his eyes widened in surprise. Perhaps he wasn't expecting a mere apprentice to have the skill or audacity to draw a weapon. Allan dropped the scabbard and silently apologised to the Countess with a promise to make good any damage. It was ironic really that the sapphires in the scabbard alone would probably make these three northern thugs very rich men. He leapt to the ground to meet them face-to-face.

"That's a fine sword for a smith's apprentice to be wielding," the man said. Was there a faint twinge of uncertainty in his voice and his exaggerated grin?

Allan stared at him, hoping the man might think Allan was too dumb to actually use the weapon. He was confident that he could match him in a one-to-one fight, but with two men bringing up the rear, he couldn't be sure of a positive outcome.

"Well you didn't get those muscles from serving tables at the local inn," the man said. Oh, so he was watching, sizing Allan up. The odds shifted. The man moved his feet, changing his line of attack to the right, at the same time as revealing a tiny flick of the wrist. Enough for Allan to predict the speed and direction of the attack even before he moved.

Allan parried the attack, shifting his footwork to put his body in on the inside of his opponent's line. The man was so committed to the power of his thrust that he couldn't recover in time and stumbled past, only just regaining his feet in time to meet

Allan's counter attack. The man's northern build shouldered the weight of Allan's strike and sent a sharp pain up Allan's arm as their swords clashed, ringing out to the empty afternoon countryside.

The man's eyes betrayed his surprise as he tried to reassess his initial impression of Allan's capability. Allan could see the conflicting thoughts running across his face and affirmed that he was indeed dealing with amateurs. This conflict would have been over in seconds if he had been dealing with real mercenaries; they don't get it wrong - they just go in for the kill. These barbarians would do their very best to draw this out for as long as possible, hoping to pluck the sword from Allan's grip and make off with their spoils.

One of the others jumped straight into the fray, launching an attack just as the leader was recovering his composure. The third man disappeared into the trees and Allan didn't have time to speculate what he was up to before he was forced to parry two simultaneous attacks. He spun away from the first thrust, redirecting the force of the blow using the edge of the bastard sword. The man's frustration only served to unbalance his stance as he veered off at an angle, while Allan sidestepped, narrowly missing a killing slice to the neck from the second man's sword. He recovered and turned to deal again with the first man.

It was difficult to dodge the attacks with no let up from both directions, although the swordplay was clumsy and desperate. Before long the third man would surely come back and despite Allan's superior skills and weapon, his chances of surviving a three-on-one frenzied attack would be somewhat improbable. The sweat trickled down his brow, stinging his eyes and blurring his vision. The northerners puffed with exertion and Allan wondered how long they had left in them if they continued at the current pace.

The bigger of the two, the leader, swung his sword for another head blow grunting with the effort. The second man had dropped back a few paces and was breathing heavily, his head hung low. Allan evaded the slow moving attack and parried the man's sword, stepping through the centre line so he ended up with both men facing him and backing up towards the trees. With both men in his sights, he was confident to be able to hold them off. The second man drove forwards with another attack, which Allan fought off and then the first one looked up at something behind Allan. Distracted, Allan turned, looked over his shoulder and saw the fresh-faced rugged grin of the third man burst into sight. He stepped into Allan's path swinging something huge, something…

His legs gave way first, and then there was an almighty explosion of pain across the side of his head that travelled through his skull as though a nail had been driven into his brain. Then the light slid from his eyes and he collapsed into a deep, dark dream.

Chapter Seven

There was a sharp rap on the door and Demaris Del'oro took in a deep long breath. This was it. She was about to meet the man she would spend the rest of her life with. She was in the receiving room outside her guest chambers at Castle Helmstedt. Her heart thudded softly against her ribcage and she ruffled her long red curls into some semblance of normality, then adjusted the bodice of her jade gown. Princess Alliane had insisted she wore her best for this meeting.

Although nervous and at the same time intrigued, she had a nagging irritation about the whole arrangement. She felt as though she were a piece of property being sold to the highest bidder. She pushed the feeling to the back of her mind. Gilbert Amand, her father's sergeant-at-arms, her sole guardian and mentor had arranged this match. It was political, he said. It would establish her future and her fortune across continents, he said. She trusted his judgement and despite her nagging doubt, Gilbert always had her best interests at heart.

"Countess Del'oro," King Gereinte entered the room with a flourish and a train of attendants, whom he shooed away with a harassed smile in her direction. One or two of his advisers looked ready to argue with him, then thought better of it when he graced them with his emerald glare. Prince Edwyn, at three years old and the youngest of the next generation of Andolin children, trotted in and held his chubby little hands up to her pleading for a swing in her arms.

"Oh, my," she laughed, "he's a little young don't you think, your Majesty?"

Gereinte chuckled. "Oh, I don't know. Only thirteen years difference. How do you feel about marrying a younger man?" There was a small cough from behind the King and he moved to one side revealing a tall, rather austere looking man with dark hair and a beard. His pointed nose gave him a look like a weasel and his eyes were far too close together. "Countess, may I introduce Colton Barra, youngest son of Count Barra, advisor to the King and court." He eyed her up as though he hadn't seen a woman since leaving the protection of his mother's skirts and Demaris shuddered inwardly. Oh dear. She bowed her head with respect.

"My Lord. A pleasure," she said extending her hand. He took it readily and she gauged his nerves by the clamminess of his palm. Give him his dues though, he didn't attempt to kiss her hand.

"Well and good," King Gereinte said, lifting a squealing Prince Edwyn and carrying him outside. The door swung shut behind them and she was left alone with Colton Barra, but for the guards outside the door and the maids who scurried in the background. She silently begged the King to forget something and return.

"Well," he said.

"Well," she said.

"So…"

"So," she said, massaging her fingertips against her temple.

54

"Are you all right?"

"Yes... yes. It's just a small headache."

"Shall I call someone, my Lady?" Lord Barra said.

"No, no. I'll be fine." She sat down. It was starting to clear, but she was left with a vague sense of frustration. No, desperation. Where did that come from? And then it was gone. Nothing. She shook her head, perplexed. "I don't usually suffer from headaches. I assure you my Lord, I have a very strong constitution." Lord Barra was nodding with approval. She shifted the lace veil to her shoulders in a self-conscious attempt to cover the less-than-feminine shape of her upper arm muscles.

Another thing that Gilbert had insisted upon during her upbringing was to teach her how to wield a sword; perhaps not the best attribute for a potential wife. She had better keep quiet about the meeting arranged with the smith's son tomorrow to take delivery of the bastard sword. The image of the smith's son made her smile and feel warm inside. He moved like the sea; fluid, strong, capable of engulfing you in waves. Something held him back, though. Perhaps it was too much respect. Despite his lowly background, he had been taught well and knew his court etiquette.

"Did I say something funny?" Colton Barra said sitting opposite her.

"Oh. No. I'm sorry," she put her hand over her mouth, "I was just thinking about something else." Someone else. A faint twinge of the headache lingered like a fading memory. But the smith was not for her. She must dismiss him from her mind at once and concentrate on getting to know Lord Barra.

"Only, I thought I might have missed something. You know, culturally. I don't know many southerners," he said.

"Oh, we are much like you. You know. Culturally."

"Except for the language and the accent, of course," he said. She frowned at him and he continued quickly. "Not that you have much of an accent. I mean you speak Etanese like a native. And I understand you like to play around with swords."

Play around with swords?

She frowned. "Indeed," she said, drawing a line beneath her words. But he didn't seem sympathetic to her mood.

"I mean, I'm sure we can come to some arrangement. After all, Sir Fulk allows his lady wife, Alliane to play about with swords from time to time. Under his guidance, of course. We wouldn't want the little lady to come to any harm."

Demaris stiffened. Every hair on her neck bristled with irritation. Little lady? Allows? This was not going at all how she expected.

"Have you ever tried to tell the Princess Alliane that she is not 'allowed' to do something?"

Colton Barra paled.

Hmm. Thought not. This was going to be interesting. She was either going to have to disabuse this man of his notions about female subservience or try to put him off the idea that she might be an appropriate match.

"Besides," he said, trying for a recovery, "you won't have too much time for swordplay once the children arrive." Demaris stared at him, her mouth ever so slightly open. She snapped it shut, not trusting herself to say what she really thought.

"You don't spend much time around court, do you?" she said, wondering whether he had actually met or spent any time with King Gereinte and his warrior Queen. He shook his head.

"This is my first time at court in Carentan, although I have travelled around to some other countries with my father."

Hmm. She would like to wager that he had not visited the Queen of Sarlat or indeed met Princess Jessamine of Dern.

"Well. We have some catching up to do then," she said, rising to her feet. Colton Barra offered her his arm and she took it reluctantly. If nothing else, at least she could find him something to do over the next day whilst waiting for her sword to arrive.

As it turned out, she didn't have far to turn for inspiration on how to get Lord Barra tied up into knots while she planned her exit. They opened the door and little Edwyn was left standing, looking up at them with soulful eyes while his sisters, Karla aged six and Evgenia aged seven, disappeared down the passage in a whirlwind of skirts and laughter. Demaris knelt down to Edwyn's level.

"Where is your nursemaid, your Highness?" she said, raising her palms in question. Edwyn raised his palms even higher than hers in parody and shrugged his shoulders.

"She coming soon," he said, stretching his arms up to her then opening and closing his hands demanding to be picked up. She lifted him into her arms, then turned and dumped him onto Lord Barra, who floundered to hold onto the royal prince, managing to look both surprised and disturbed at the same time.

"You can get some practice in for this family you are planning," she said, then strode off down the corridor in search of the princesses. Edwyn should keep him busy, at least until the nursemaid arrived in search of her errant charges.

Demaris caught up with the princesses in the receiving room of their quarters, where they were ensconced in a window seat, huddled together reading stories and for all the world as if they had not been anywhere else all morning. She stood in front of them with her hands on her hips.

"Your Highnesses. Much as it pains me to admit that you are so mean to your poor loving and utterly devoted little brother, you are also a pair of evil geniuses," she said. Karla and Evgenia looked up from their book, gazing through their mother's almond shaped eyes at Demaris. Their eyes were not the only characteristic they had inherited from the Queen. They also had her beautiful chestnut skin and long dark hair to frustrate even the most diligent of nursemaids. Not to mention a feisty temperament.

They looked at each other, back at Demaris, then burst out laughing. Laughter descended into nudging, each trying to attribute blame to the other that descended into an intricate display of hand

58

pushing, which to an outsider might have looked something like a slapping contest, but Demaris had seen how the Queen had trained her children to defend themselves.

They had grown up with a propensity for fighting like a pair of cubs brought up on the battlefield. That, and the amount of time they spent out with their mother in the company of the King's guard and the Forest Rangers, had turned two potentially sweet little girls into potentially dangerous female warriors. Demaris sighed. She liked their culture and should have been brought up as an easterner herself. It was a shame that it had been left to her to teach the southerners what it really meant to defend oneself and one's family.

The older princess, Evgenia, managed to twist Karla's wrist into a lock and they both stopped, Karla acknowledging her defeat with a curt nod. Demaris admired their restraint. If that had been two boys, they would have been at each other's throats by now, threatening all manner of revenge. And the gnawing insistence of revenge was something Demaris was all too familiar with.

"We told him to run, but he just stood there like a silly little boy," Karla said, rubbing her wrist.

"You're supposed to look after your little brother, not leave him like that. Lord only knows what he is doing to poor Colton," Demaris said. The girls looked at each other and burst out laughing again. She tried to keep a straight face, but she kept hearing Colton Barra say… *you won't have too much time for swordplay once the children arrive.*

Then the parting image of him wrestling with a wriggling Prince Edwyn in his arms was too much.

Alliane had told her that Edwyn was so much like his father as a young child; he would not sit still for more than a moment and his curiosity often led him into situations that warranted rescue from his over-indulgent elder sisters.

"And what did your royal highnesses hope to learn by listening at the doors of your visiting guests?" The princesses stopped laughing and looked at each other, then back at Demaris, both shrugging their shoulders in annoying semblance of Edwyn.

"We didn't hear anything," Evgenia said in earnest. Demaris let out a sigh.

"Well all right. I suppose it doesn't matter then."

"Please don't tell father," Karla said, "he might stop us from watching sword practice with Alliane and Sir Fulk."

"Maybe not. As long as you come with me now to rescue poor Colton," she said. The princesses jumped up and led the way back out of their quarters and down the corridor to Demaris' rooms.

"You're not really going to marry Lord Barra and have his children, are you?" Evgenia said. Demaris stopped, opened her mouth to say something then thought better of it.

"Walls really do have ears," she muttered to herself.

"That's silly," Karla said, "walls can't have ears."

"I always said the castle has secrets, didn't I say that, Karly?"

"Yes Evi, but how do we get it to tell? Walls would have to have mouths and that is even sillier."

Demaris was keen to avoid getting drawn into one of princesses' absurd debates and strode ahead, rounding the corner to the spot where she had left Colton with Prince Edwyn. But the passage and indeed the rooms beyond were empty. The girls smiled at each other.

"Can we go to sword practice now?"

Chapter Eight

Allan was being chased through the forest. Not the forest he recognised, but a dark and deep maze of grey trees with branches bereft of leaves. He sneaked a look over his shoulder. The animals were gaining on him fast. Big brown bears with teeth lined maws that dripped with the blood of their victims. He could tell that they were closing in, as their growls grew louder and louder and the thundering of their paws seemed to shake the ground beneath him. The trees didn't want him to leave and they whispered his name over and over; Allan, Allan, Allan.

He burst into a clearing and found his mother fighting two more brown bears, which stood on their hind legs, claws extended like needle-sharp daggers. She was whirling and dancing around them wielding her skinning knife, but unable to get past those lethal claws.

"Oh good. Allan, you came. Where is that bastard sword?" she said. Allan looked down at his side, but the sword was no longer there.

"I had it a moment ago." Bewildered, he swung around looking for evidence of where the sword may have gone. But all he found was the deep forest beckoning him back and the rumbling of the ground beneath his feet, as though an army of mounted soldiers was bolting towards him.

He opened one eye. The ground was his bed with a pillow of dead branches and leaves tickling his ears with the promise of tomorrow's sun, low in the sky with trees darkening in the shade of the approaching night. His head thumped and Dilla was raking dead leaves with her hooves, lacking the will or the intellect to do anything else. For a moment he lay still, not daring to move his head. Events caught up with him; the fight with the bearded northerners. The third man, swinging something big, like a tree branch. They must have left him for dead or they didn't care, now that they had what they wanted.

The bastard sword.

He touched a hand to his head and felt the lump. His fingers came away flaked with dry blood, congealed and matted with hair and dead leaves. So the forest floor had acted as a compress, a poultice. His mother would be proud, he thought with sour resignation. Slowly, he raised himself onto his elbows and looked around. A bloody stump of wood had been discarded nearby and there were odd bits of his belongings strewn about. No sword in sight. He wondered if they had backtracked and found the scabbard as well. He hoped not. That at least would give him enough collateral to buy himself a bed and a meal before he made his way home. The thought of turning up at the smithy, without having fulfilled his duty and having to explain the loss of this sword made him shudder. Not to mention the loss of business with the King on top of the loss of his dignity. Then he remembered something else.

The book.

He scrambled to his feet, then crouched back down as his head went dizzy and darkness crept around the edges of his vision. The pressure eased a little as he kept his head down and willed himself not to black out. In time, he lifted his head up and wobbled to his feet. With a spiralling sense of shame, he began to sort through what was left of his belongings.

Not only had he managed to lose a priceless weapon that he wasn't sure if he would have the skill or energy to replicate, but he had also lost the key to his past. His mother's story. His story. The answers to the mystery that was his life. He tried to console himself that he could re-forge the sword and just ask his mother to tell him, but as he picked through the remains of his discarded food packs and assorted paraphernalia, his cheeks burned with the thought of having to do so. He would have to admit to stealing her private account from the fire. Which, although written to him, she clearly had not intended him to read.

Countess Del'oro trusted him to deliver her sword the next day. Or was it already the next day? He had no idea how long he had been unconscious. As though in response to his curiosity, his stomach rumbled and he groaned, picking up a discarded piece of jerky. The meat was tough as old leather, but he chewed nonetheless, thankful for anything to stave off a collapse back into the abyss of unconsciousness. Either the northerners had taken all the bread, or Dilla had chewed her way through it, waiting for him to wake up.

He picked up a few discarded smallclothes and started to pack things back into his saddlebags, which had been upended close to the edge of the river. Dilla looked at him with soulful eyes.

"Just don't," he said to the pony. "As if it's not bad enough, I won't have my mare feeling sorry for me." Dilla shook her tawny mane and snuffled his hand, looking for treats as he took her reins. Allan picked up a half mangled apple and fed it to her in small pieces, coaxing her out of the wooded area and back onto the main path. It seemed pointless now to worry about brigands since they had taken everything of worth in his possession.

In the twilight, he searched the area where they had fought, hoping that he might find the scabbard, but to no avail. He cursed aloud, then swung up into the saddle and nudged Dilla into motion.

Unable to bear the thought of returning to Cannan, he let Dilla take him forwards, following the path of the river towards Canrac and his now ill-fated meeting with the Countess Del'oro. The path was dark, only lit now by the light of the moon, which revealed the recent tracks of horses. As they trudged along, Allan looked at the fresh tracks and his bitterness turned a shade sweeter as an idea began to form. He smiled to himself, sat up straighter and started to pay more attention to where he was going, studying the hoof prints on the path whilst nursing a growing headache.

They kept doggedly to the river path until the river began to veer off towards the east. They must have been close to Lake Mariac. The northerners would not have wanted to ride straight into Canrac on the south side of the lake, carrying stolen goods. No one would believe they truly owned such a magnificent weapon, not judging by the look of them. Allan guessed they would most likely want to find somewhere secluded to rest before avoiding the town of Canrac altogether. Unless they meant to try and sell the sword.

He could steal it back from them while they slept. Or if he didn't catch up with them in time, alert the King's Guard to the theft. If they made as far as Canrac and tried to trade, he would have the added complication of trying to persuade the potential buyer that the sword did not belong to the northerners. But the King would believe him.

Allan followed the tracks as they left the river path and headed away from the lake, which shimmered with reflected moonlight. In the distance he could see the turrets of Castle Helmstedt. His mother had brought him to see the castle and the town of Canrac many times as a child. They never stayed long, but she always had stories to tell of the history of the Andolin dynasty and the battles at the great Helm. Seeing the castle gave him a profound sense of belonging.

As a child, his biggest ambition was to serve in the King's guard. But his mother had always dismissed it as unattainable.

"You have to come from a well-connected family and be recommended as a squire. Even then, you have to serve many years before moving up the ranks. It is not a life I would wish for my only son."

The tracks became harder to follow as the ground gave way to woodland, carpeted with fern, twigs and dead leaves. In the distance he caught the faint flicker of light and wondered if they had been foolish enough to light a small campfire. Allan dismounted and crept further into the copse on foot.

He tied Dilla to a tree, so she wouldn't wander off, then followed the tracks on silent feet. As a young child, he had boasted to his mother that he had the skill to make himself invisible and she often chided him.

"No one has that ability, son," she said. "Besides, it would be dangerous to believe it true. You never know what kind of danger you are walking into."

She misunderstood his way of thinking. It was merely a process of putting himself in the right frame of mind. She used to call it *going into the spirit* in the same way that warriors in the east perform a ritual dance before they go into battle. When Allan became *invisible*, his heartbeat slowed and his senses became acute. He heard every murmur, every screech and scratch from the wildlife, the smell of meat cooking and light of the campfire flickering orange in the distance. His head began to throb with the exertion of concentration. Not a good sign, but he was so determined to retrieve his belongings that he ignored it and pushed further towards the location of the northerners.

They had indeed started a campfire, right in the middle of a small clearing. If they stayed there too long, the forest rangers might come to investigate. Maybe he should just sit tight and wait for that to happen, but curiosity got the better of him. To get a better view of the situation, Allan climbed the nearest tree. The boughs were strong enough to take his weight and the canopy green enough to disguise his presence.

There were five of them. Great. That was going to make it more difficult to sneak in and back out without being seen. Three of them were sitting around the fire, poking a roasting wild animal that looked like the remains of a scrawny squirrel, and the other two were walking the perimeter of the clearing, scanning the surrounding undergrowth. What were they looking for? An army of marauding squirrels, come to get their revenge on nasty northern appetites? Or perhaps they were looking for a few more to roast. Judging from the way the three were looking into the fire, the rations that they had stolen from Allan had not gone very far. His stomach grumbled in response to the cooking meat. His concentration was beginning to falter the more his head throbbed.

They didn't appear to have any belongings beside the fire, so Allan could only assume that the sword and his book were wrapped up in the saddlebags of the horses that were tied to a tree on the far side of the clearing. Damn. He would have to sneak all the way around to the other side, which was going to be tricky since the two perimeter guards were walking to and fro with alarming regularity. He would just have to wait until they went to sleep.

The guards started to expand outward and subsequently disappeared into the undergrowth. The leader looked up from their meal and pointed a meagre squirrel leg after his compatriots.

"Bring me something with more fat on it this time," he said, throwing the carcass to the other two who devoured it like they hadn't eaten for a week.

68

"The sooner we can sell that sword, the sooner we can get something decent to eat and a place to sleep." Ah, so he was right. They were just brigands looking to cash in on a poor travelling smith's apprentice. He wondered if they even realised the value of what they had stolen.

Allan settled back. He guessed it would be a long wait before the opportunity arose to get down from that tree and recover the sword and the book. He leaned his head against the tree's central bough, his eyes heavy and his head still singing with the repercussions of the blow. Nausea and dizziness crept around the edges of his consciousness and he swayed as the wind rocked the tree. He could just shut his eyes for a moment, while he was waiting for the northerners to go to sleep. He felt himself slipping back into the darkness when a gruff voice caught his attention, then the sight of Dilla being led into the clearing brought him back to full awareness.

"Look what I found," the man said. They had eaten his food supplies and his apples, they couldn't possibly mean to eat his horse too?

"Don't be a gobshite, Ren, that there horse will fetch us another few crowns to share. Tie it up with the others and find me some fecking squirrel. Or rabbit. I could eat a rabbit." The northerner glared at his leader, then took Dilla over to the other horses, where he tied her reins to a tree, then slipped back into the undergrowth, grumbling.

"Wait a minute," the leader said, looking up and frowning at the horses. "How did that bloody mare get here so quickly on its own?" Not the brightest of the bunch, but nonetheless, a worrying conclusion for Allan. The remaining three stood up slowly and started peering into the darkness beyond their campfire.

One of the men came stomping through the undergrowth just below Allan's tree, then a thin grey squirrel scurried up into Allan's space, gave him a marble-eyed stare and a piercing screech before darting up into the canopy. Allan slipped from his bough and fell down into the undergrowth landing on his back, the breath driven from his chest. He just about held his head together, before a large, bearded man loomed above him.

"Oh no, not again," he thought, before being plunged back into darkness.

Chapter Nine

"Is he dead?"

"I thought he was already dead."

"He looks dead now."

"He was supposed to be dead the first time."

"Well the dead don't just get up and follow you, do they?"

"They don't if you've just whacked them over the head with a large stick."

"Well you didn't hit him hard enough then, did you?"

"Must have a thick skull or something."

"Do it properly this time."

"Right you are."

Allan braced himself as best he could whilst floating in a sea of fog.

"Wait!" Reprieve.

"What?"

"Tie him to the back of his horse. I've just had an idea."

He felt the ground move from underneath him. Or was he moving along the ground? Rough hands hoisted him up and he lay face forward, slumped across Dilla's back. He could tell it was Dilla. She smelt of stables and home and she didn't complain at the extra weight, just whickered at him gently. Good Dilla. At least he was in familiar company. He drifted back into unconsciousness.

The next thing he knew, his stomach was being gently pressed and his head and legs lolled from side to side. He squeezed open one eye and noticed the ground moving again. The early morning light peeped through the grey of day and the ground had a grassy dewy smell to it. His lips were dry and cracked, his thirst overwhelming, and hunger pains churned his stomach making him feel nauseous. His arms were over his head and tied at the wrist. His feet were tied at the ankles. On the plus side, his head didn't feel so bad although if he continued to ride face down like that, his stomach might just decide to empty its meagre contents onto the path beneath him. He should politely ask his captors to at least let him sit up.

"Urggh…" The horses stopped, the ground stopped and a rough pair of hands hauled him up. The northerner, who he recognised as the one who had wielded the large stick, cut the tie on his ankles and let him ride upright on Dilla's back.

"Why couldn't you have just stayed dead? Would've made things much easier," he muttered to himself.

"Wha… what do you want with me?" Allan said. The northerner looked up, surprised. Then one of the others leaned over and dumped a cup of water over Allan's head. He lifted his face towards the source and tried to get as much as possible into his mouth, like a fish flopping from side to side, bereft of its glorious river.

"Give him some more. We need him in a fit state to strike a bargain with the buyers," the lead man said. Oh, so that was it then. They meant to have him sell his own sword for their unprincipled profit. That was new. How did they think that was going to work?

A knife appeared at his throat.

Right, so that was how it was going to work. The man forced his head back and tipped a canteen of water down his throat. He had to swallow quickly to avoid choking, gulping down mouthfuls of water and air that made his belly swell from trapped wind.

The man finally stopped when the canteen was empty and Allan spluttered a mouthful of water all over himself and sneezed snot down his tunic. He coughed and his eyes watered, but at least his thirst had been slaked. He burped loudly and found his breath.

"Don't… suppose… any jerky left?"

"Unless you can tell us where you hid it. All we got was fecking roast squirrel," the lead man said, then turned his horse and beckoned his men to continue. Dilla followed meekly. Allan wondered what day it was and whether he had missed his appointment with the Countess. Not that he would be in any fit state to present himself at the court of Castle Helmstedt.

His cheeks burned with the thought of not presenting himself to deliver the sword. By his reckoning, they must be close to Canrac. Probably would arrive by midday at least. He kept churning thoughts over in his mind, trying to work out how to get himself free, take back the sword and deliver it to its owner.

"Hello there!" A voice from the trees. Allan's heart leapt. Had the forest rangers found them? But it didn't sound like a ranger. This voice had a strange southern lilt to it, not unlike that of the Countess Del'oro. Then his heart began to skip in little panicked beats. It might be almost as bad to be caught like this by the Countess and her men-at-arms. He might rather fight the brigands or die trying. He squirmed in the saddle, finding the strength to wriggle his wrists enough to loosen the ties. Foolish men couldn't even tie a knot properly. That was their second mistake. The first mistake, of course, was letting him live at all.

A rider stepped into view in front of the brigands. The lead man raised a hand and halted the party. A few moments later, Dilla came to a stop. Allan continued to twist his hands and work on loosening the knot whilst the men were distracted. Then a second rider came into view from the right and a third backed up the rear. These were definitely not forest rangers. They wore red and green tunics, shot through with bright yellow pinstripes and large lacy collars. It reminded him of pictures his mother had once shown him of the fashions of the southern lands. Their hair was worn long and untied with looping moustaches and long thin beards. They seemed comfortable on horseback, like they spent a lot of time in the saddle and their weapons were sheathed, giving them a lazy confident air. But the fact that they had surrounded the northerners with such precision was an overt threat in itself. The lead man of the northerners felt it too, his hand resting on the hilt of his sword.

Chevaliers. That was it. They looked like chevaliers; the infamous knights of Arrontierre. The one in front leaned forward in his saddle and scrutinised the scene.

"What is this?" he said.

"None of your business, is what it is," the northerner said. "Now if you don't mind." Allan had a funny feeling that the chevaliers did mind and were about to make it their business. The chevalier twirled the end of his moustache in thought, then nodded to himself.

"There are laws in Carentan, no? Have you heard about the peoples' charter?" The northerners looked at one another with blank expressions. If they hadn't, they weren't about to admit to it and if they had, they certainly didn't care. "No? Well, let me enlighten you."

"Just a moment," the leader of the northerners said. "Who are you? I don't remember the King having southerners in his employ."

"Ah, well you see, we are visitors to this great nation. And as such, we have an agreement with the King. In our country, we are known as the watchkeepers. My name is Tavorian. I am most pleased to make your acquaintance." Tavorian nodded in lieu of a bow. "And these are my compatriots, Abendigo to your right," Abendigo swept the hat from his head in a flourish and bowed. When he looked up, he caught Allan's gaze and winked at him. "And to your rear, you will find Brutas." Allan glanced over his shoulder, following the gaze of the northerners. Brutas was indeed a brute. The musculature on his arms stood out, rippling in the rising sun and his legs were like tree trunks. Brutas didn't bow. Brutas didn't even smile.

"Good Sire," the lead northerner said, trying for a modicum of manners. "If you let us pass, we will

75

pay you handsomely, once we reach the trading town of Canrac and can sell our goods." Tavorian narrowed his eyes.

"And what wares might they be?" He made a show of looking around, eyeing up each and every one of them and what they carried. His eyes lingered a little longer on Allan. "As far as I know, the trading of people was outlawed in Carentan two decades ago." The lead northerner laughed nervously and looked at Allan.

"Oh… you surely don't mean the smith's apprentice? He is just a boy, along for the ride. Estranged from his family and looking for adventure. Ha, ha… pay him no heed."

"I see," Tavorian said.

"And what a merry soul he is," Abendigo said, walking his horse leisurely forwards and closing the gap between the northerners and the watchkeepers. "See Tavorian, what an adventure he is having tied to his horse like so." Allan barely blinked in the time it took Abendigo to draw his sword and use the tip to flick away the ropes holding his hands. Allan held his hands to his chest and rubbed his wrists, trying to get some feeling back into his hands. The moment the northerners saw that a sword had been drawn, all five of them drew their own weapons and Allan didn't know whether to run, hide or fight.

Five on three hardly seemed fair and the option of running or hiding was too craven for him to even consider. Especially now that Abendigo had freed his hands. He felt obliged to even the odds.

The northerners kicked their horses into action and scattered. The two to the rear were chased down by Brutas who engaged them both from horseback. Allan could not recall seeing such speed with the strength to match. The northerners were being forcefully driven back, blow upon blow weakening their line of attack, which was a thing to say for two northern men built like ancient oaks themselves.

"Brutas, stop playing with your foe, we have work to do here," Tavorian said. He unseated the leader of the northerners and leapt down from his own horse to engage him in combat.

"Let the man be," Abendigo said, parrying the attacks from the fourth northerner, as though walking his mount through a patch of prickly thorn bushes. "This is the first piece of action he's had in weeks."

Allan was knocked from his horse by the fifth northerner, who barrelled into him sending the horse skittering away. He rolled over backward, using the momentum to get himself up into a standing position. His legs wobbled and threatened to give way, having been tied up and then sat on the back of a horse for the best part of a day. The fifth northerner leapt from his horse and advanced. Allan just found his legs with enough strength to dodge the sword thrust as it came sailing towards him. He used his forearm to deflect the blow at the hilt and redirect the attack at the same time as taking control of his opponent's wrist. With a twist and a lock, he managed to force the man to release his sword, just as the man fell into a heap at his feet. Good timing. Even for a half starved, thirsty prisoner fuelled only by the heat of the moment.

As the man scrambled to his feet, Allan, lifted up the sword and held it in a guard position. He held it with enough strength to look threatening but secretly hoped the man didn't want to fight; he wasn't sure he had the energy, even with the advantage of being in possession of the weapon. But the man turned and ran into the cluster of horses that stood around braying like donkeys in the middle of the path.

"See, Tavorian," Abendigo said, parrying a brutal but ineffective thrust from his opponent, "told you the boy had some fight left in him." Tavorian had his opponent halfway into the trees, backing away and making alarming noises. Allan wondered how long these watchkeepers had been following and observing them.

"They're not so clever, these boys," Tavorian shouted to his compatriots. "They haven't even tried to negotiate for their miserable lives."

Brutas batted away an attack like swatting a fly, then with bored determination, drove his sword through one of his opponents. The man slumped to the ground with a grunt. Brutas switched his sword to his other hand and continued to drive back his second opponent, stepping over the other body as though it were nothing of consequence.

Allan was so bemused by this outlandish display of superiority, that he hardly noticed the fifth man who had run off until he loomed up from behind the horses with another weapon in hand. And not just any weapon. It was the countess' bastard sword, albeit a little grubbier than it had been but all the same, glinting in the morning light. The scabbard lay forgotten at his feet.

Allan's legs shook and his sword arm wavered as he wondered if he could hold it together long enough to face his snarling captor. Unlucky for Allan, he had just survived being clonked over the head several times, dragged through the woods, tied to his horse and nearly starved of food and water for a day and a night. So it was all he could do just to remain on his feet. He had managed to salvage an inferior weapon from one of Brutas' dead men, but was well aware of the mismatch in size and weight. He made a few exploratory passes, aware of his clumsiness in comparison to the sword he faced, which sliced through air with ethereal majesty. He could not help but admire his own work as it threatened to reduce him to ribbons in the hands of this rank amateur.

The man made a sudden feint, then sliced left, right, up and went for the thrust. Allan saw it coming, but the fogginess in his brain and his weary limbs made him slow to react. The tip of the sword just nicked his upper thigh, tearing through his tunic. On the retreat, he didn't take the full force of the blow, but a crimson pool blossomed on the fabric of his leggings and he staggered, left leg buckling beneath him. The Countess' sword had a mind of its own despite being wielded by a barbarian with no skill. Was it the sword that made the swordsman or vice versa?

Any experienced swordsman would have taken the advantage and moved in for the kill, but this man hesitated long enough for Allan to scuttle

79

beneath the next slice and counter with a thrust to the joint beneath the man's armpit. The man screamed and dropped the bastard sword, clutching his now limp arm to his side, eyes darting to and fro as though he could not quite believe that this almost dead boy had risen to defeat him.

Where did they get this man? Was he just brought along to tend the horses? Despite the man having been responsible for tying him to his horse, Allan did not want to hurt him any more than he needed to make an escape.

Allan grabbed the discarded sword and slipped back out of reach. The man looked at him through bewildered eyes, weaponless and bleeding. He kept his eyes trained on the man, lest he make a final ditch attempt to attack. The man's eyes then shot open wide just as Tavorian stepped up behind him and drove a blade right through his middle.

"Really, my boy, a good soldier always finishes the job," Tavorian said with a jovial wave. He pulled his sword clear and gave the northern man a shove. The man fell in front of Allan, eyes rolled upward to the heavens, screams silenced.

"I...I'm not a s...soldier," Allan said, "I'm a smith."

Chapter Ten

Wilhelm dropped from a tree overhanging the stockade of a little camp in the darkness of night. He had been watching two children, whose boisterous play had prevented him approaching without being seen. Even by Klagen standards, the two tubby children should have been fast asleep. A fair-skinned woman with straw-coloured hair and a formidable bone structure, dumped the little ones onto their pallets like two large sacks of grain.

"If you nay go to sleep, Wilhelm of the Forest will come and get you and take you away," the woman said. She was rewarded with squeals and shrieks, then reluctant silence. She stood for a moment, one ear pointed in the direction of the children, before nodding to herself and stalking off into the night.

Wilhelm stared ahead without blinking. Really. After all this time, they were still using that old story to scare the little ones. He slipped past them and into the heart of the Klagen camp, which lay in the foothills of the Ventrikken mountain range. As he crept away, he just caught a whisper of a child's voice.

"Here comes the dagger to open your head and here come his spear to put you to bed." This was followed by succession of growls and giggles. Whether or not the children believed the nightmares their parents fed them, he wasn't sure, but it certainly kept them in their beds long enough for him to creep past unnoticed.

Over the years, Wilhelm had developed a lithe physique, but he still owed his formidable strength to his Klagen heritage. The Klagen lived in makeshift camps in the country of Klagenstill, far to the north of Carentan. The camps ran along the length of the river Hakken and gave the Klagen warriors easy access for marauding clans to the coastlines of the Western Isles and the oceans beyond.

His ice-blue eyes and musculature he got from his father, which allowed him to move freely amongst the Klagen without undue attention. Only when viewed up close, did people wrinkle their brows in confusion over his darker skin tone, and his mousy-coloured hair that clumped into locks and draped like rat tails down his back. His darker complexion, he owed to his mother. Each time he returned to these camps, he stood in silent contemplation, thinking about her. As a boy, on nights like these, he had stolen away to the slave pens, always to find her tied to the same post. He was ten years old when he stole the Clan Chief's dagger to cut her free. His stomach stirred with the sickness of the memory when he finally lifted her chin to discover her sightless eyes, her breath and her life sacrificed to the Aesir Gods. Blinded by his own tears, Wilhelm escaped into the forest, making his own vows to the Aesir and the Vanir.

He looked back at the tree, an enormous beech, with boughs overhanging the camp. It had been easy enough to drop down without being seen. He had spent a great deal of his early manhood in the forest, but where trees were concerned, coming down was always easier than climbing up. The river might be a good adventure. He could stowaway on a schooner bound for the coast, then hop off before they reached the southwest. But not before he had completed the task he came there for in the first place.

The children's giggles subsided and Wilhelm heard a faint moan at a distance. He stood still in the dark and listened, watching for any movement. On the near most side of the river, he could see the outline of a wooden pen. The night was thick with the scent of horses and the wicker of resting palfreys and pack animals. For sure, they had recently returned from a marauding trip with yet more captives faced with a future that would make Odin's toes curl.

The river water glistened in the moonlight, sending shards of reflected light to illuminate the outline of people slumped against the wooden poles inside the pen. Wilhelm sniffed the air and caught the scent of urine, stale sweat and faeces. But that could just as well be coming from the Klagen tent just a few hundred yards away, where the merry sounds of an arak drinking contest filtered across on the breeze. It would be a long night for the Klagen, which would most likely result in more than one sacrifice to Loki by way of arak. This thought only fuelled Wilhelm's fervour.

It was the perfect opportunity and while the Klagen were distracted with their drinking game, Wilhelm flickered into motion. To anyone watching, it might have looked like a blur as two Klagen guards at the entrance to the stockade slumped soundlessly to the ground, victims of his legendary spear. The people inside the stockade shrank back, as far as their binding permitted, approached by yet another warrior with a weapon. A quick flick with his dagger and Wilhelm released each of them from their bonds. Without further pause, they fled towards the trees on the edge of the camp, scrambling and climbing over the stockade and into the forest. A young girl with dark hair and burnished skin stood behind the wooden bars of her pen staring at him, lit up by moonlight. Was she immobile with fear or indecision? She looked like Arianna had when he first freed her and he stalled, overwhelmed by the memory of his wife who died at such a young age.

"Shoo! Go!" he said in snarling Jarvik. The girl did not understand his words, but it was enough to terrify her into action. She slipped out into the night, but paused looking back at him. Not fear then. She had Arianna's boldness; perhaps that was a trait from the Gaullians. He pointed his spear in the direction of the forest and she scarpered after the others. He watched as they each made their escape, helping each other to safety.

Though not his original intent, Wilhelm couldn't resist the temptation to take a detour via the drinking tent, just to see if he could glean any clues as to the plans for the next raid. The more of these he could stop from happening in the first place, the fewer occasions he would have to sneak about releasing the unfortunate prisoners. The night was young, the arak may not yet have claimed its first victim. Concealing his spear in some undergrowth so as not to appear a threat, he moved with purpose through the camp. His bulk stirred no outward signs of suspicion until he reached the tent with all the noise and was then caught up in the throng of movement.

In the centre of the tent sat a ring of Klagen warriors, heavy bearskin cloaks and thick long blonde tresses keeping the chill of the northern evening at bay. The tent was lit up by torches outside, held in metal sconces spiked into the ground. Wilhelm recognised the Clan Chief at the head of a makeshift table made from upturned oaken barrels. Upon the table sat an earthenware jug from which he was ladling a dark, treacle-like liquid into small clay cups. He barked commands at his brethren in a guttural dialect of Jarvik. The Clan Chief's name was Ullr, named after the god they were apt to invoke before either a fight or sea voyage. He wore a curtain of braids, knotted and tied with bone fragments, here a tooth, there a forefinger. A trophy for every conquest and every fight he had won to maintain his standing. He was Chieftain of the clan of clans. But Wilhelm was not impressed. He looked just like any other lowlife clan chief. And perhaps tonight was his turn to die, judging by the way he was knocking back that arak.

"I salute you my fellow warriors on a raid well executed," he said, raising his cup and spitting chewed up berris leaf across the assembled throng. Not so well, thought Wilhelm, as he willed the freed slaves to expedite their escape. Those closest in the circle growled in affirmation, knocked back their own drinks, then slammed the cups down on the upturned barrels. One or two cups didn't make it to the next round, and shattered to clay fragments on impact. One of the warriors made a grab for the jug, but Ullr shot out his hand and grabbed him by the throat. Wilhelm watched the warrior's face turn red, blue, then slowly grey before Ullr released him only moments before he would have passed out.

Someone swept away the broken cups, along with the throat-choked warrior and a new Klagen was shoved into the circle from the outer reaches of the tent to fill the gap. Wilhelm was jostled forwards, as each man pushed and shoved to join the Chieftain's game. There was nowhere to go, he was surrounded by warriors left, right and behind. The only way was into the circle at the centre.

"Ugh," the warrior beside him grunted, "Plenty to go around," he said.

"You!" Ullr bellowed across the tent, pointing a finger in Wilhelm's direction. Wilhelm ducked his head and shrank back, trying to blend in. He could get away with being in such a crowd but close up, Ullr might recognise his difference.

"By Odin, yes," the warrior beside him bellowed, forcing the crowd to part with the use of strategically placed elbow strikes. Wilhelm let his breath go and sank back into the crowd.

"I think he means you, my friend," a thick voice grumbled beside him.

"I meant that one," Ullr jabbed a finger into the crowd and slapped the usurper aside, but Wilhelm had already disappeared into the mix and was manoeuvring back towards the exit. Ullr was determined and his brothers, though slow to react, were quick enough to intercept Wilhelm before he made it out of the tent. Several sets of meaty hands, clasped around his shoulders and upper arms, turning him back towards Ullr and forcing him to the centre of the circle. A chant of indecipherable grunts started up from the crowd, punctuated by a steady thump of fists on the overturned crates. Wilhelm thought with regret about his spear left outside in the undergrowth, and his dagger, which was burning a hole in his left boot. His arms were pinned to his sides and from somewhere, one of the warriors had produced a hunting knife, which was being waved with drunken abandon in front of his face, as though its keeper was asking permission from the gods to cut something off. Perhaps for the time being, his own knife was better left where it was.

Then he was shoved in front of Ullr and left to explain his presence, but not before Ullr himself had filled one of the clay cups and shoved a measure of arak under his nose.

"Drink," he said. Wilhelm smiled. The arak was sharp like gooseberries and slid down his throat. He swallowed and then braced himself for the burn as the liquor went down into his stomach. Ullr grabbed a handful of berris leaves from the table and shoved them into Wilhelm's mouth. "Chew," he said. The leaves were bitter like crab apples and Wilhelm winced in response but dutifully chewed, knowing the consequences if he refused. When finally, he had got rid of the muddy cake of forest leaves in his mouth, he drew a long breath. Ullr looked at him expectantly.

"Hello Father," Wilhelm said.

Chapter Eleven

The Countess Demaris Del'oro stepped out of the training ground and sat down on a bench. Her sparring partner, a young squire with a propensity for cutting down her distance then dancing out of reach, soon found his match in a knight who surpassed his speed and agility with sheer strength.

She clasped a hand to her chest as the pain once again radiated out in waves, filling her with nausea. Princess Alliane, who was taking instruction from her husband Fulk, glanced at her from the other side of the ground with a frown. Demaris made a reassuring wave in her direction and Alliane resumed her drills, casting her the occasional look.

Demaris had to admit, it was unusual for her. There was very little that distracted her from a fight; focus was one of her strengths. She thought about Colton Barra. Maybe it was the thought of having to marry him that was affecting her. Yes, that was much more reasonable an explanation; nausea, pain and a nagging desperation. Desperation to run to the hills and never return. No, she must not think like that. She owed something at the very least to her dearest Gilbert, to give this match a try.

The pain dulled and then dissipated. She let out a long sigh and pulled the tie from her hair, letting the curls tumble down her back. She turned over the tatty piece of string in her hands and smiled to herself, remembering the curious young smith to whom it belonged. Then she looked up at the sun, which was reaching its apex in the midday sky.

Where was the smith? It was well past the time they had agreed upon for delivery of the sword. A sudden spasm of pain shot through her chest and she stood up, dizzy and rocking unsteadily on her feet. Something was not right.

She made straight for the stables and waved down the stableboy, who hurried off to prepare her mount. While she was waiting, Alliane burst through the stable doors.

"Countess, where are you going?" Alliane said, her voice breathless. Demaris looked back out to the training ground beyond the stable door where the knights and squires continued their daily practice.

"I have a bad feeling, Alliane. I can't explain it, but I think something has happened to our smith. I'm taking a ride out to Canrac, to see if I can find out anything." The stableboy appeared leading her palomino mare and Demaris led her out of the stable, mounting with ease. She settled her sword by her side.

"Wait. I'm coming with you," Alliane grabbed the stableboy and pointed at the chestnut horse in the end stall. "That one will do, quick as you like."

"Yes, your Highness."

Demaris walked her horse towards the inner gate and before long, Alliane trotted up beside her.

"And what do you think you are going to achieve if you do find the smith?"

"I don't know, I'll work that out when we get there." Demaris felt uncomfortable with the Princess trailing along behind her. For all her training and bravado, Alliane was still bound by the etiquette of the King's court. Her husband Fulk, who was Captain of the King's Guard, would surely not approve of her taking off like this. She glanced over her shoulder and recognised the purple regalia of the King's Guard. Two riders were bringing up their rear. "I might have guessed we wouldn't have been able to just head out alone," she said. Alliane looked behind them.

"Well," she said, "it is an extra pair of sword arms, should we need it. It's market day in Canrac, so at the very least people will give us a wide berth."

Demaris could see the sense in that, but she had hoped to go alone. If it was nothing at all but her overactive imagination, then she was going to feel stupid having dragged along Princess Alliane and two of the King's best men.

They rode in silence. Demaris urged the palomino into a trot as they passed through the inner and outer circles of the castle grounds then onto the track in the direction of Canrac. Demaris kept her focus ahead, but noticed that Alliane kept glancing sideways at her.

"I didn't realise you were so wedded to the idea of a Jael sword," Alliane said. "I mean, most people are impressed when Gereinte draws his sword, and once he tells the story of how he came to own it... well, most people want one."

Demaris cast a sideways glance at Alliane. Should she tell her that it was not the sword that interested her? But she kept her own counsel.

"Why do you always wear that grubby piece of string in your hair? We can buy some proper ties at the market. I know a vendor who makes them from velvet in every array of colours," Alliane said.

"It's only for training." What was all this scrutiny; did Alliane suspect something? As they continued down the track towards Canrac, the tops of the vendor stalls became visible in the distance and the road swelled with people; young, old, some leading ponies piled high with wares, others trailing carts, and well-to-do folk looking to spend their fortunes.

"I know it is probably not my place to say this, but may I make a suggestion?" Alliane said.

"Princess. You know I value your opinion. Since coming here and getting to know you and your family, I have come to think of you as the older sister I never had." Alliane smiled at her comment. In truth, Demaris had no idea what it might have been like to have siblings and Alliane's real sisters were leading their own lives.

"If ever I had a little sister, I would have wanted her to be like you." Alliane had a wistful look. "In fact, I did have a little brother who would have been the same age as you now, had he lived."

Demaris kept her silence. She had heard the story of their brother, Josselin.

"So what do you suggest?" she said, bringing Alliane's attention back to the present.

"Colton Barra," Alliane said. Demaris' heart sank. "Don't look at me like that. I know he is not perfect, but what you did to him was very cruel."

She tried to look suitably shame-faced. After finding him missing, Demaris had sent the twins on a mission to bring him back to her quarters on the promise that she would take them out to sword practice afterwards. But the twins had found something far more entertaining to occupy them with that afternoon.

Eventually, Demaris went in search of him herself and found Lord Barra being led around the nursery by a makeshift donkey lead, braying on command and carrying little Edwyn on his back. On further inspection, he had undergone his transformation by way of a pair of floppy ears that were once a dampened wash cloth, a felt nose kept in place by a string tie, oversized shoes which came from who knew where and a painted face that looked more like some ghoul from a childish nightmare than a real donkey. She was just waiting for some visiting dignitary to start complaining about missing footwear and ladies' face paint before admitting that it was all her fault and apologising profusely. She afforded herself a little smile at the memory. Poor Colton Barra had not looked very happy.

Alliane cast her a disparaging look.

"I'm sorry. It was cruel. But he kept going on about having children and I just thought he might like to get some first-hand experience."

"If you do marry him, you won't have a choice. That is the way of the world."

"It is easy for you to say. You married for love. What are you supposed to do if you don't love your husband?"

"Then it becomes duty. Both my sisters had to marry for duty. You might even fall in love."

Yes, thought Demaris. Just as long as it is not with somebody else.

"It may be the way of Carentan and the Western Isles, even admittedly Arrontierre, but in some places it is not a duty," she said.

"I see you've been spending time with the Queen," Alliane said.

"Is that such a bad thing? I would rather not marry at all and be Countess of my own land and holdings, than marry someone I don't love."

"I'm just saying that you should give Lord Barra some time. He is a sweet and caring man. Don't be so quick to dismiss him," Alliane said.

Demaris kept her eyes forward, focusing on the path. It was fair comment. She would give Colton Barra a chance to redeem himself. Though she had a few other things in mind that might put him off the idea of marrying the Countess Del'oro. In the meantime, she had an errant smith to find.

The path ahead forked in two directions. One would take them towards the market and funnelled most of the traffic in a cloud of road dust, the other led beyond Canrac to lake Mariac and the river path that took travellers on the northern road. Her feeling of angst intensified, just as the two riders from the King's Guard shot past them in a flurry of purple up the northern path. They followed in trepidation, Demaris wondering what had sparked such an instant reaction. It wasn't long before she found out.

The path lead to a small clearing, surrounded by trees, with several mounts wandering aimlessly. The ground was fresh with the scuffles of a fight, patches of dark mud, which could have been blood.

A little further into the trees, they came across some bodies. Demaris dismounted and walked over to where one of the King's men was turning them over, while the other kept a keen eye on the path.

"Northerners, by the look," he said, "and freshly killed. There are five of them. Looks like an ambush." Demaris moved to each body in turn, taking in their faces and dismissing them in her mind one by one. The smith wasn't there.

She needed to get away from there, to see, feel and hear what had happened to the smith. A seemingly honest man had made a promise that for some reason he had been unable to keep. Demaris wanted to know why.

She studied the corpses; brigands all. Garbed like those who would stick a knife in you just to strip the clothes from your back. These were not men to take on lightly. She studied their wounds. Most carried clean thrusts but there were two or three who had been disembowelled, judging by the piles of innards decorating their corpses. Someone liked to play with their prey. Either that, or these men had done something to upset their opponents. However great the smith's skill, this was not the work of one man alone.

Something glinted blue in the undergrowth, reflecting the sun and catching her attention. Placing a boot underneath the shoulder of the nearest corpse, Demaris rolled the body over and revealed a muddy, jewel-encrusted scabbard.

"Look," she said. Alliane came up to her side, as she prised the object from where it had been pinned by the weight of the dead man. Taking a cloth from her belt, she wiped away some of the dirt and admired the scabbard. Sapphires. And beautifully inlaid.

"That," Alliane said, "looks as though it belongs to something magnificent." Demaris looked at her and Alliane held her gaze. "I think we need to find your smith," she said.

Chapter Twelve

In the drinking tent, Wilhelm reflected on his life as the muddy bitter leaves clogged in his throat. The Berris leaves worked their magic to disperse the worst effects of the arak. Ullr slapped him on the back and the surrounding men took up the chant.

"Wilhelm, Wilhelm, Wilhelm…"

It was Arianna who had first saved Wilhelm. Not the other way around, as she would often have him believe. Perhaps they had saved each other. In some ways, the girl he had freed earlier that night reminded him of Arianna. It wasn't just the long dark hair, the soulful brown eyes and the burnished Gaullian complexion. There was something about the girl's bold attitude that so reminded him of his wife.

"Shoo! Go," he had said. And just like that girl, Arianna stood there staring at him with little comprehension of the Jarvik he spoke. But there was no mistaking his meaning when he pointed his spear first in her direction, then at the forest. But Arianna, unlike the girl that evening, would not budge. In the shadows of the moon, she had walked with calm reassurance to his side and took his hand, urging him to join her. Her touch was like a shot of energy, a call to action that he had no strength to fight. But fight he did, as the snarling Klagen rushed to the scene, raised by the alarm of the night time activity. He swept Arianna into his arms and sprinted with her pressed to his chest like a child with a ragdoll until he reached the perimeter of the forest. There he set her down with only just enough time to turn and face his pursuers.

"What is your name?" Arianna said, still refusing to budge. He had learnt a little Gaullian from his mother, before his father had separated them forever. "Arianna," she said with her hand pressed to her chest. His heart warmed at the gesture.

"Wilhelm," he said and she smiled. Then he turned to face his angry compatriots.

"Wilhelm, I shall return for you." Then she disappeared into the forest. He had little time to ponder on her parting words, as he was overcome and outnumbered. He had been ready to fight to the death and had no illusions that death was what now faced him, given his crimes against the clan. But under his father's instructions, they just locked him up in the pens, as though his presence in some way was recompense for the slaves he had just freed. That was the first time he had been caught and he had no doubt that Ullr would devise something suitably grisly and fatal to serve as an example to every clan across Klagenstill.

Such interference had to be held to public account and swift justice enacted. It was precisely this kind of bloody-minded thinking that had stirred Wilhelm up in the first place. Perhaps he had inherited a little too much of his mother's Gaullian empathy. Ullr might be set in his ways and would remain so until the next eligible chief challenged his authority, but Wilhelm believed in the spirit of the Klagen and their capacity for change. All they needed was the right leadership. He had witnessed it over the last ten years, as interbreeding became more prevalent, the closer they got to the borders of Tennengaul and Malvas.

But the ideology of change might be pointless now. Now that he had been caught. Now that Ullr had a chance to extract the thorn from his side. As a young boy, it had been easy enough to flit unnoticed in and out of the camps, his main purpose to free those that were innocently caught up in the evils of the clans. As a man, this was proving more difficult.

Arianna did return for him. That very night. Returning to him the gift of freedom, with just a skinning knife and a sweet smile of seduction to divert the guards. He was so angered by her blatant disregard for her own safety that he almost refused to go with her. Almost. But then he fell into the deep well of her eyes and he could never again distrust or deny his beloved Arianna. Once at a safe distance from the Klagen camps, they made their vows to the Aesir and the Vanir, Arianna acknowledging her northern ancestry. For a while, Wilhelm left the Klagen camps alone and for the first time in his life found true happiness when Arianna gave him his girls; first little Ruby and then just a year later, Opal. They were his jewels. His three girls were all that he lived for and everything to die for.

Their worst enemies were the cold dark northern nights and the occasional forest cat that slinked around looking for small animals to poach. Wilhelm would tuck up the girls in the black velvet pelt as they slept, oblivious to how close they had come to being the cat's next meal, rather than sleeping in the comfort of its coat.

The trees became their friends. A hiding place from the clan members who had wandered off camp, shelter from the storms and a place to just be. To be a family. To be loved and to live a life of freedom from the trappings of convention and the interference of the clans. It was idyllic.

They learnt how to live off the land, hunt small animals for meat and fur, harvest nuts, seeds and by trial and error, which plants to eat, which ones to use as medicine and which ones to leave for the wildlife. In the end, it was the sleeping sickness that took Arianna and their two little daughters, just babes in arms. Wilhelm had raged for what seemed a lifetime and spiralled down into a deep dark place, from which he thought he would never find reprieve. Only the memory of his mother kept him going. Her and the vengeance he had sworn to take on the Klagen.

The rising chant of his Klagen half-brothers alongside the bitter taste of Berris, brought Wilhelm's thoughts back into focus. It was always the same when they caught him. They felt a need to punish him, but at the same time had respect for his unorthodox ways and tried their very best to bring him around to the traditional Klagen way of thinking. Which to Wilhelm, was no way of thinking at all. In fact, the whole ethos of the Klagen was centred around the self and the capacity for non-thought. Still, they didn't look like they were about to chuck him into the pens for his unconventional infiltration of their camp. Then again, they hadn't yet discovered that the pens were now empty. There was still time to make a timely exit.

"Father. It has been a long time since we last had occasion to cross paths," Wilhelm said, thinking back to the last time he had set fire to their camp after one of their particularly fruitful raids.

"Perhaps we need to show the baby warriors that they need not have such fear of Wilhelm of the Forest. An example of how not to piss off your father might not go amiss." Ullr's smile was anything but friendly. In fact, Wilhelm often wondered why the children were so taken in by the story of Wilhelm, when they had a living, breathing nightmare in their very camp every day. He supposed it was all a question of perspective. He looked around at the warriors crowding in for a better look at the legend that was the son of Ullr. The one that got away. The thorn in their side. Realistically, there were too many for him to take alone. It was all a question of biding his time. A bit like his life on the whole.

The air was thick with the scent of arak, mingled with the sweat of too many over-sized men in a confined space. The more Wilhelm thought about the prospect of being hauled back to the pens, the more he thought about the knife concealed in his boot. His heart thrummed a steady drumbeat to match the crescendo of adrenalin in his veins. As though sensing his state and mistaking it for fear, the Klagen warriors who held fast to his arms tightened their grip.

"Uh uhn," Ullr said with a mean and nasty grin splitting his face. He shook his head and the bones in his hair rattled in response. "The pens are far too good for you, my son."

He wondered how Ullr was able to read his thoughts. Wilhelm supposed he must owe some kind of likeness to that freak of nature claiming to be his father, though it shamed him to even think about it.

"I have a better idea," Ullr said. "I have always wanted a figure-head for the prow of my ship. Something of a likeness to worry all those who would oppose me. It will be a message to all; the Chief of the clans is coming, lock up your wives, your daughters, for we take what we want and destroy what is left."

Wilhelm's skin prickled with disgust. To be strapped to the prow of Ullr's ship. Well, if he didn't die from the bonds they used to hold him in place, then he would certainly die from drowning once they set sail. A grisly reminder to all those who dared oppose the will of the mighty Ullr, Chief of the Klagenstill clans.

Ullr nodded to himself, satisfied that he looked and sounded sufficiently odious and exactly as a marauding clan chief ought. There followed a brief display of joyous grunts of approval and banging of fists on upturned crates, most of which collapsed into splintered tinder with the force of the strikes. The two warriors holding onto Wilhelm, loosened their grip involuntarily, looking for a suitable something to thump before remembering that they were the ones guarding the booty. It was enough for

Wilhelm. Enough to break the grip on both arms, slam into their faces with two back-fist strikes, then grab them both by the neck to bounce their hairy heads off each other.

He dropped down and relieved his boot of its hidden treasure, before cutting and barrelling his way through the mountains of drunken warriors. Their eyes widened as it slowly dawned on their slumbering minds that the enemy they had hoped to crucify to the prow of their ship was making a hasty getaway.

Ullr bellowed and the warriors took chase, but they were no match for Wilhelm of the Forest. He collected his spear and sped away. As he crested a rise just beyond the pens, there was a brief moment when he would be unseen to the eyes that followed. He took this moment to slip into the river, gasping as the icy water filled his boots, his trews and his furs. Using his spear driven into the riverbed as an anchor, he kept below the surface, holding his breath as the men ran around up above, wild with frustration at having lost their quarry. Sight and sound was muffled below the surface, but he fancied he heard cries of anger and imagined that their interest in catching Wilhelm of the Forest had been supplanted by the discovery of the missing slaves from the pens. He smiled to himself, raising his head just enough to gasp another breath, before sinking below the surface and beginning a slow wade down the river length, towards the two ships that were moored, awaiting the next marauding trip down south. It was then that Wilhelm had an idea.

Chapter Thirteen

The watchkeepers looked as though they had barely broken a sweat, whilst Allan trailed along behind, only just managing to stay upright on Dilla's back, trying to piece together what had just happened. They backtracked around Lake Mariac and headed towards a secluded area that Tavorian said was an excellent place to make camp.

"You have a well-trained cut and thrust – where did you learn to spar?" Tavorian said, trotting along at the front of their party. Allan had picked apart his opponent in three easy moves, using the northerner's fear to his advantage. Somehow he had overcome the desire to drop from exhaustion at the man's feet and found a depth to his survival instinct that he had never before tested.

"My father… and my mother," he said.

"Oh my," Abendigo said, "you must introduce us."

"Wait," Allan said, "where did you say you came from?"

There was a moment's silence and a furtive looked passed between the watchkeepers. Brutas shook his head and grunted. Did he ever speak?

"We are the watchkeepers," Tavorian said. "We take care of things."

"Yes, I get that," Allan said, "but why are we heading away from Carentan when we have just killed a rogue band of northerners? Shouldn't we be explaining what happened to the King?"

"Well… yes," Tavorian said.

"And no," Abendigo said. Allan was dog-tired and his brain was working overtime, what with far too much adrenaline pumping through his veins.

"Does the King even know you're here?" he said. Again, the three of them exchanged glances.

"Well... yes," Abendigo said.

"And no," Tavorian said.

It was too much for Allan to take in, so he just followed along thankful at least that the watchkeepers had arrived when they did. Although, he had no idea whether he was better or worse off in the current situation. On the good side, at least he wasn't tied to his horse, so that had to mean something.

Dilla's trot soon slowed to a walk and Allan began to nod away in the saddle, jerking awake at regular intervals each time he nearly fell to the ground. After hours, they found the area Tavorian favoured and clearly they had already made themselves at home, as there was evidence of a camp in place; a banked fire, make-shift shelters of branches laced with bracken, and tree stumps which served as perfect seats. The horses were left to graze on a grassy area which opened out onto Lake Mariac and gave them ample food and water. Somehow, from somewhere, Brutas managed to rustle up some provisions and start a fire. They soon had a pot of bubbling stew filling the air with sweet smells of braised meat, boiled potatoes and herby broth. Allan couldn't decide which he was more in need of; sleep or food, so he just sank to the ground in a stupor and dozed while the watchkeepers kept watch and cooked supper.

After what seemed only seconds but could well have been hours, he was nudged awake and handed a bowl and spoon. Blinking back the clouds of sleep, Allan spooned the stew into his mouth and swallowed, hardly bothering to chew.

"Steady on," Abendigo said, tucking into his own meal, "there's more where that came from. No need to choke on it." He forced himself to slow down, sipping at the tantalising broth, breathing in the scent of stewed meat and onion gravy. He was so hungry that his stomach was twisted in pain and when they offered him a canteen of water he couldn't get it down his throat fast enough and the first mouthful went mostly down his front.

As the sun went down beyond the trees, Allan started to feel a little more lifelike. The fire warmed his toes and fingertips as the night chills descended. For a while he was content to just sit, eat, drink and listen to the watchkeepers babble away in their native tongue, waving their hands and pointing here and there with the occasional nod in his direction. He recognised a few words from Langan, but it was otherwise incomprehensible to him. His mother might have been able to understand it, but she was leagues away on some mission of her own and anyway he would hate to have to explain this mess in which he now found himself.

Abendigo was casting him worried glances, while Tavorian frowned at him with some level of disapproval and Brutas just grunted and scoffed down his stew.

"I'm all right," he said. "And I'm not about to run off and report you all." They looked blankly back at him. "After all, that is what you are worried about isn't it?" He may not speak the language of Arrontierre, but he certainly understood the language of the body and the face. "Where are the sword and my book?" The watchkeepers looked at each other.

"Ah. Well. Now there's the thing," Tavorian said.

The thing? "What thing?" Allan said, his mind beginning to wake up to the possible dangers of trusting three complete strangers.

"What we would like to know," Abendigo said, stroking his long thin beard, "is how you came to be in possession of such a magnificent weapon? I mean, we can understand perfectly why such a band of northern barbarians might be interested in relieving you of such a burden, but what we don't understand is where you got it from."

Allan could see where this was heading. They must think that he himself stole it and they were planting themselves on the side of justice.

"We would also like to know what this is," Tavorian said, plucking his book from underneath a pile of leaves like a court jester pulling a bunch of flowers from his sleeve.

"Please," Allan said, "I should like very much the return of the sword and my book. These things are very dear to me and the sword is not mine. I had an important appointment at Castle Helmstedt to deliver it to its new owner, which I have now reneged upon."

The watchkeepers watched him with curious expressions on their faces. Brutas even stopped sloshing down his broth for a moment to fix Allan with his gaze, an eyebrow raised in question.

"If I am not very much mistaken, that sword is one of a kind," Tavorian said.

"A very special kind," Abendigo added.

"Made by a very special kind of smith."

Brutas put down his bowl and uncovered the countess' sword, lifting it up so that it glinted in the firelight. They had cleaned it up a bit and it looked as though someone had also given it a vague polish.

"Where is the scabbard?" Allan said.

"There was no scabbard found," Tavorian said. "An oversight on our part perhaps. You have yet to explain how you came to possess such a treasure. You were on your way to deliver it to whom?"

"That is my business and I don't see any need to share it," Allan said, regretting his words even as they left his mouth; these men had after all saved him from the barbarians. The watchkeepers looked at him, then at each other, Abendigo narrowing his gaze.

"I see," Tavorian said. "In that case, we shall hold onto these treasures until such a time as we can uncover some truth behind your motivations." Perhaps they thought that he was some kind of notorious thief and that the notebook was an account of his nefarious dealings with other criminals in the Western Isles.

"The Countess Demaris Del'oro," Allan said. That got their attention. Brutas put the sword down with a reverence that seemed out of character, Tavorian's eyes widened and Abendigo almost choked on his stew. "I am just a lowly smith's son,

108

but the sword is my own work and it is indeed one of a kind. It is a Jael sword." A slow comprehension leaked across the three men's expressions as Allan's words hit home.

"And this?" Tavorian said, raising the book.

"Is my mother's story, written in ancient Etanese. For my eyes alone. And I haven't even read it all yet."

Tavorian had the presence of mind to look a little sheepish. He reluctantly passed the book over to Allan. There was a welcome silence around the fire while they finished the remainder of their supper and Allan kept the book by his side, comforted by its proximity.

"For now, we shall sleep," Tavorian said, "and Brutas will keep first watch. In the light of morning, we shall decide how to deliver this magnificent weapon to its rightful owner."

They left him to his business and threw a blanket in his direction before turning in themselves. With relief, Allan wrapped himself up and inched close enough to the fire to be able to make out his mother's script.

***

Arabus Castan, was my trainer and mentor. He was known in the trade as 'The Executioner', renowned for never missing a kill and able to command vast sums of money for his services. You may find this hard to accept, my son, but I was subsequently known as Kali and fast gained a reputation in my own right as his assistant. 'Lady

Death', some called me. Others, the 'Black Widow'. Whichever way you looked at it, all roads lead to death.

I remember Castan watching me with interest, as my knives cut the air with a cool confidence, hitting their target on the tree trunk every time. It felt good, it felt congruent as I retrieved my weapons and turned to meet my mentor's measured gaze.

"You are ready," he said.

From the first day I had arrived at the spacious house belonging to Castan, all domestic chores, such as cooking and cleaning, that had dominated my life in the village became a thing of the past. A grim, taciturn woman named Martha supplied all my meals and clean clothes without fuss or comment.

My focus was entirely on my training. I learnt the covert arts, disguises, surveillance, how to appear short, tall, fat, thin. I discovered to my delight that I had a natural flair for languages and acquired a new level of expertise in mimicking accents. I was taught how to behave like a slut in a tavern or a lady in high society. Please don't judge me too harshly, my son, because remember – I had lost all that was dear to me.

I remember well my first lesson in weapons. The training room was light and airy, the floor was covered with polished boards and the walls sported an array of weaponry from broadswords to hunting knives, from axes to war hammers and lances. I stood on the threshold in awe, while Castan walked around the perimeter of the room, nodding and smiling, proud of his collection.

"Come, come." He beckoned to me and I hesitated before entering the training room. "Let's see now," Castan said, then hefted a sword from its mounting on the wall. He held the blade in one hand, rested the hilt across his forearm and offered it to me. I gripped the hilt and tried to lift the sword, but my tired and overworked muscles screamed in protest. Determined not to look a fool in front of Castan, I held the sword aloft awaiting instructions. Castan frowned and shook his head. "You must hold it like this." He showed me and I duly tried.

He demonstrated the thrust and the parry, but all the time I struggled, clumsy and unwieldy in my movements. After days and days of physical endurance, I had just begun to feel alive and ready to believe I could do this, so you can imagine how defeated I felt. All of a sudden, my hard work seemed for nothing. I knew it would take time to master that weapon.

Castan was oblivious to my tears and grunts of frustration. In the four corners of the room there were thick wooden posts fixed into the floor, which he made me attack with the sword one after the other repeatedly until my arms felt like they were filled with lead and my legs were ready to buckle. My torment was intensified by Castan's repeated command, "Again," as I ran to each post and attacked with slow, clumsy blows, which barely scratched the surface of the wooden dummies.

"Again," Castan said. I screamed with frustration and launched the sword at the nearest

post. The ineffective throw made the sword clatter to the floor to lie discarded. In an uncontrolled fury, I grabbed the nearest weapon on the wall, a set of four throwing knives, not caring any more about protocol or how Castan might feel about me defiling his precious collection. A strange sense of familiarity came over me, as I weighed the knives up in my palms. They felt light, manageable and infinitely superior to the sword. I glanced at Castan, fearful to see him angry at my sudden disobedience, but he had an expectant look on his face.

Then he smiled.

I thought he was amused at my total incompetence with the sword and a flare of anger ignited briefly inside me. Not anger at Castan, but anger at myself, for I wanted this opportunity so badly. What if I had destroyed my chances? What kind of a life would I have if Castan abandoned me? The knives felt cool and yet alive in my hands; an extension of my own energy. I emptied my mind of emotion, then launched them one after another at each of the four dummies in the corners of the room. There was a distinct 'thud' followed by three more as each knife found its target and stood firm in the wooden posts. It had felt so easy in comparison to the stupid, unwieldy sword that lay in disgrace on the floor. Castan was laughing and clapping his hands.

"I was beginning to think we were not going to get there before sundown." I looked at him and frowned in confusion. "So be it," he said without further explanation. "Let the knives be your weapon of choice."

112

Chapter Fourteen

There was a thud and Allan woke with a start. Brutas was chopping logs with an axe for firewood. None of the others were anywhere to be seen. When he noticed Allan watching, the corners of his mouth curled up and a little white line of teeth appeared in the semblance of a smile. Allan panicked and patted the ground around him, lifting his blanket in desperation, then his hand found the comforting flat cover of the book and he let out a long slow breath. Despite the season's hot weather, Brutas was lighting a small fire and setting a kettle of water on to boil.

"Don't you ever speak?" he said. Brutas looked at him and grunted. Then he muttered something unintelligible and Allan realised for the first time that it was just Etanese he didn't speak. "Speak?" he said in Langan, miming a duck's bill with his thumb and fingers. Brutas' head shot up. He understood that all right. "I speak a little Langan," Allan continued, faltering over some of the syllables. The light of recognition lit up in Brutas' eyes. "Where are your friends?" Allan used his arms to sweep the camp and then raised them to the heavens in question.

"They look for way to castle," Brutas said in a rough accent. So, they could just about understand each other in Langan. That was a start. They were looking for a way in to Castle Helmstedt.

"Why not Canrac?" Allan said, wondering why they didn't all just march up to the front gate of the

113

keep. Then he remembered the butchery they had left behind in Canrac. Brutas handed him a steaming cup of broth, shaking his head as though dealing with a wilful child. Allan hunched himself up, knees pulled to his chest, trying to make himself as small as possible in the hope that Brutas would just forget he was there. At some point he was going to have to take the sword to Countess Del'oro and explain his absence, not to mention the pile of bodies in the woods near Canrac and the presence of his newfound companions.

In a bid to distract himself from the rising panic in his chest, he sipped the broth, which had a sweet peppery tang to it, and pulled open his book. The deep dark world of the assassin unfolded on the pages as he read more about the renowned Lady Death or Kali as she was sometimes known. He remembered stories that the village youngsters told to scare each other on dark winter evenings on their way home. If you misbehaved or betrayed one another, Kali would come to take you away and she would feed you to the fires of hell until your skin crisped black or poison you until your head went pop. Allan shuddered. He thought it was all just playful tales, scary stories they made up to hold you in their power. He never for one moment thought that Kali really existed.

***

So there I stood, hooded and shadowed in the corner of the room in a dark seedy tavern, watching

114

that weasel Denzl Charrock pace nervously up and down.

This was our second meeting. In the first meeting, Charrock had identified my target and for an instant, I just stared at him in shock. It wasn't so much that I was surprised by him or his Lord; I could believe anything of them, it was just that I could not fathom why Castan had taken the assignment. It was out of character for him, but it was not my place to dispute that. I named my price.

"That's insane," he had said, "no one will pay that much for any assassination."

I had looked at him for a long moment before saying, "Find somebody else then. But I suggest you check with your principal first."

So there we were. Our second meeting and Charrock had pitched up with one half of the fee, as requested.

"Sir Denzl," I said, moving into the light. Charrock flinched and turned around.

"How long have you...?" he said in a choked voice. "Never mind, I have your gold here. But there is a condition on payment of the other half." He faltered. I raised an eyebrow. "This is a royal prince, we need absolute proof. Josselin has a birthmark on the little finger of his left hand. Bring me that finger and you will get the second half of your fee." A strange ripple of emotion shivered down my back.

"I will send word. Make sure you have the gold. Breaking our agreement would have unfortunate consequences," I said. Charrock paled. He handed the package over to me and I squirreled

115

*it away beneath my cloak. As I blended back into
the shadows, Sir Denzl made a quick and noisy exit,
summoning attention from all corners of the tavern
as he stumbled his way past tables and chairs in his
haste to get out.*

*You might ask, how I had the presence of mind
to do it and I wouldn't blame you. Especially
considering all I had been through and the dull
ache of loneliness that was a constant battle to
suppress. Every day without my son was a millstone
around my neck.*

***

*It wasn't hard to gain access to the child and
build the confidence of the castle staff as Isla,
Josselin's nursemaid. I settled into my new role
with no qualms and prepared myself for the agreed
day of the kidnap and murder.*

*One day, I saw the young Prince Gereinte, just
outside the door to the Great Hall. He paused and a
smile flickered at the corners of his mouth, before
he glanced briefly at me then set off in the direction
of the western staircase. I didn't expect him to
acknowledge me. All he saw was his baby brother's
nursemaid, carrying a pile of clean blankets back
up towards the royal quarters and that was exactly
what I intended. When the time came, he would not
be able to recall any distinguishing features about
me – so complete was the blending of my existence
into castle life. That was my speciality.*

*I climbed the eastern staircase with the care of
a nursemaid carrying a pile of clean laundry. The*

delicate steps I took belied the year-long arduous training I had undertaken to become a professional. An off-duty guard passed by without a second glance at the meek, small woman who struggled up the steps, head bowed in concentration. Despite outward appearances, I saw every face, breathed every scent and heard every utterance within earshot. My muscles longed to take the staircase, two, three steps at a time. My lungs ached for the joy of physical exertion, as I recalled the endless running up and down the steps outside Castan's house. I longed for the fresh air of the foothills of the Helm, which once stung my lungs and throat with the torture of physical practice. But the endurance had only been one small aspect of my training. Had I wanted to, when that guard passed me on the stairs, I could have slit his throat and walked on by before he even registered my existence. Lucky for the guard that he was just a royal guard and not a royal prince.

I nodded to the guard outside the royal chambers and entered with my pile of blankets. Celie, maid to the Princess twins, relieved me of the laundry.

"Goodness, Isla, you do take your time. The baby has been whining for you since you left." Celie sighed and took the blankets into the sleeping chamber. I could hear Josselin grumbling in the next room. The last nursemaid had left abruptly when her milk had dried up; funny that – how a little pinch of just the right substance in the poor woman's food had helped create just the right

opening required in order to carry out the task for which I was being so highly paid.

I reached into Josselin's cot and took him in my arms. He stopped grumbling and focussed his big round eyes on my face as though it were the most interesting thing he had ever seen. I stroked my index finger over his forehead and down the side of his cheek, drawing the outline of his face. The reddening around his cheeks and his raised temperature meant that he was probably teething.

"And who will look after you, little one, when the wolf comes knocking at your door?" I said. Josselin gurgled with delight at the sound of my voice, though he understood not a single word I was saying. I sighed. "There, there. Let Isla fix you something to take away the pain." I bounced him a couple of times on my knee and replaced him in the cot before retreating to prepare his food.

It would have been so easy to just mix a little extra of my special formula that helped him sleep and finish it there and then. But no, that is not how the Lord wanted it. I had to wait, as instructed, and carry out the task as required in order to collect the second half of my payment on behalf of Castan.

Sometimes it was hard to recall the love and joy of family life as I sat, posing as Mistress Isla, feeding the baby prince with a compound of Chamomile flower mixed with oil and potato, to relieve his fever. Josselin made gurgling noises as he ate and stared at me with huge saucer-like eyes that reminded me of that millstone and a time I would rather have forgotten.

The scene was set. There was no going back. I had a task to carry out and one that would inevitably end in death. I sighed deeply as I burped the baby and returned him to his cot. Whichever way I looked at it, every road led to death. Lady Death. How apt.

I watched Josselin lying on his back, trying so hard to keep his eyes open, blinking in vain, and then finally surrendering to sleep. I smiled to myself. It worked every time. The sound of footsteps approaching alerted me, but I kept my eyes on the cot. Celie peered into the chamber.

"Mistress Isla. I don't know how you do it, but you truly have a gift with the little ones." I jumped visibly at the sound of Celie's voice, glanced up at her, then shyly averted my eyes. "Now don't be modest, my girl, you must learn to take a compliment." Celie was gone as quickly as she had appeared.

As I peered at the sleeping baby, a sudden wave of emotion rose up inside me and my heart thudded. With the ease of experience and professionalism that had become my stock in trade, I suppressed it. Very soon it would be time to put the plan into action. A little aconite might do the trick; a poison sometimes known as Monkshood and popular amongst men of the holy orders. In order to aid their own religious advancement, they often needed a clean way to dispose of their superiors. Yes, aconite was a truly effective poison for a job like that.

Most people deserved what they got, I mused, watching Josselin and studying the baby boy's face.

"Will you turn out to be just another corrupt official, struggling to control your loyal subjects by slaughtering innocent villagers?" I whispered. The baby let out a long sigh in his sleep and lightly smacked his lips, searching for food in his dreams. This was going be the hardest test of my time as Kali. It had always been adults up until then. Adults who, for the most part, deserved all they got. Never a child. Never an innocent babe.

Chapter Fifteen

Demaris dreamt she saw smoke, rising in clouds above the chateau. Not even covering her ears or pinching her nose would shut out the sounds of screaming horses and the stench of burning flesh. The air was spiked with the victorious roar of the raiders as they took her life apart, one precious piece at a time.

Her father's sergeant-at-arms, Gilbert Amand, fought until he fell and for a long time she thought that he too was dead. Dead, alongside her parents, alongside the death of her life as she knew it and the death of her childhood dreams.

She was choking. Her breath came in fits and starts, her lungs struggling with the weight of the noxious fumes that filtered into her hiding place in the hay loft, surrounded by screaming animals.

In her dreams, she often tried to change the outcome, forcing herself to get up out of her immobile state and fight to save her parents in the hope that she would wake up and realise that it was all just a dream. However much she forced her dream-self to act, she was only ever an eight-year-old girl and she was forced to re-live the death of her parents again, the outcome in the stark reality of morning always the same.

There was a tap, tap, tapping going on in the background as she saw the collapse of the barn through the eyes of her dream-self. The heat intensified and the tapping grew more insistent and nudged her back over into reality. She opened her eyes into her guest chamber at Castle Helmstedt. Her bed was like a furnace and she threw off the blankets. Who was tapping on her door at this hour? Had they found the smith?

Demaris got out of bed, wobbled a little before her body caught up with her mind. She drew an extra shift over the top of her head to cover her modesty, then peered around the door. The maid was talking softly to someone. She opened the chamber door a bit more to try and get a better look.

It was Colton Barra. Her heart sank. When he saw her, he spoke over the head of the maid.

"My Lady," he said frowning and wrinkling his nose, "the hour is past our meeting time. I was..." he looked her up and down, "...concerned."

Her shift had been caught in her haste and was hitched halfway up her leg, revealing a long muscular thigh. She pulled it back into place and did her best to settle down her hair, which was sticking up at all angles on account of her not having bothered to tie it back at night. Perhaps she didn't need any more tricks to put him off; the sight of his future wife first thing in the morning might be enough to put off any determined suitor.

"Mala," she said to the maid. "Please invite Lord Barra into the receiving room, then help me get ready."

He hesitated on the threshold, casting her a wary look as though she might corrupt him if he took a step further.

Then he was in and settling himself down in the chair in her receiving room. She returned to the bedchamber and let Mala tidy her up, then donned a gown of grey and green cotton. Mala smoothed down her hair and pinned it into a net. When she emerged, Colton Barra was wringing his hands in his lap like a man with the weight of the world on his shoulders.

"I have something to ask you," he said. "And if we are to be married, we must have complete honesty with one another."

"If we are going to be married, I hope you are not going to make a habit of waking me every morning at this hour," she said through a yawn.

He frowned. "Did we not agree a time?"

Did they? She had never been particularly good at sticking to someone else's plan. She had no idea what possessed Gilbert to think that she would make someone a worthy wife.

Demaris sat opposite Colton Barra and tried to look serene, like Queen Jehanna, even though her nerves were jumping. It wasn't so much the idea of being wed, but more what she had done to deserve a man like Colton Barra. Did he somehow think he could tame her? What was Gilbert thinking? At least give her a man with some backbone who she could respect as an equal. She doubted whether Colton Barra had even lifted a practice sword in the yard. Alliane said he was a sweet and gentle man. If indeed they were married, what would they even talk about? As it was, she was struggling to find anything about him that remotely interested her.

He hesitated, a thin line of perspiration beaded his brow. She nodded with gentle encouragement.

"What's that?" Colton said, looking over her shoulder.

Demaris turned around just as the sun lit up the sapphires on the scabbard like the sky had come into the room. Colton Barra's presence began to irritate her, particularly as thoughts about the smith came crashing back to the forefront of her mind. They had spent all of the previous afternoon following a bogus trail of hoof prints around Lake Mariac and back. Whoever's company the smith had fallen in with, they certainly knew how not to be found. She couldn't say why, but that worried Demaris. It had a familiar pattern to it.

"It's a scabbard. My scabbard, I think," she said.

Colton's face clouded over. "Is that really all that concerns you, finding that damn sword?"

She looked at him, startled by the vehemence in his voice. "You wanted to ask me something."

Colton sat up straight, rested his elbows on the arms of the chair and steepled his fingertips. "I am concerned about this nonsense with the sword and the smith. It doesn't become the behaviour of a countess betrothed."

Betrothed. That very word made her skin itch.

Colton smiled like a man victorious in his conquest. "Both the King and your guardian have given their blessing to this match," he said, reading her thoughts. It was just as Alliane had said; sometimes you married for love, sometimes for duty.

"I think I need some time to think about this," she said, standing in the hope that he might take the hint. He did, and she ushered him to the door.

"And the need for honesty," he said at the door, "means no more of that monkeying around with the royal children, agreed?"

"Why Lord Barra," she said wide-eyed, "I rather thought you made quite a fetching donkey. Our future children will be in safe hands."

He blushed like a beetroot and Demaris smiled sweetly before shutting the door in his face. She leaned her forehead against the back of the door. It could not be so decided. Were the King, Gilbert and Barra conspiring against her? Did she not get her say in whether she thought it to be a good match?

She sat at her writing table and laid a piece of parchment flat, picking up a quill and dipping it in ink. Her script scratched across the sheet, as all her thoughts tumbled onto the page in desperation.

"My dearest Lady," she wrote. Then hesitated. What she was about to reveal would send the recipient into a turmoil for which only Demaris herself could be held responsible. Was that fair? But if she did nothing, what would become of the smith? What would become of her life? "I write to inform you that our contact did not arrive according to plan and I now fear for his life."

That would certainly warrant a call to action. "I now find myself at a crossroads and without a sword or companion to complete the contract. My King and Kinsman are pressurising me into a marriage alliance with no future and no desire on my side."

Was it wise to bring Colton Barra into the picture? She almost put a line through those words, then thought better of it. The recipient would think she had something to hide and besides, would no doubt be able to decipher her hidden words. Best to tell the whole story. Demaris had no idea to what extent Colton was prepared to fight for her hand, though the thought of him fighting for anything brought a wry smile to her lips.

"I am quick to learn and have ample motivation for the task at hand and although you once advised me that I was too close to be objective, I find myself now with no alternative. I will leave today for our agreed location and I beseech you, Lady, to teach me all that you know. If the smith is as good as you say, he will not be found in all of Carentan. If he has your sense, he will remain hidden. My Lady, please meet me at your earliest convenience."

Demaris signed the letter simply with 'D', then blotted the ink and folded the letter into a neat square, securing it with a royal wax seal. There was a loud hammering at the door, causing it to rattle in its wooden frame. She leapt up, concealing the small square letter inside the bodice of her gown.

Standing outside the door and to one side of the castle guardsman were three curious looking fellows who strangely reminded her of home.

"Countess," the guardsman said, "these men have been admitted on the King's command."

She looked them up and down, wondering if their attire was an attempt at building an alliance or a cruel joke at her expense. The taller of the three had a doublet and hose, dark in hue but shot through from waist to knee with panes of yellow and red. Quite the fashion at present in Arrontierre and the kind of attire that Gilbert might have worn, albeit not quite as travel-stained. His hair hung loose and his moustache curled at the tips. The second man was slightly shorter but more flamboyantly dressed in a crimson and pea green doublet with a mauve cloak thrown over one shoulder, and a matching hat with feathers. He doffed his hat in greeting.

"Countess Del'oro. We are at your service," he said in perfect southern Langan.

Not a joke, then. Warning bells clanged in her head when she fully took in the sight of the third man, a brute of a warrior who dwarfed the rest of them as he stepped into the doorframe.

Demaris took a step back and then the strangest thing happened. The big man went down on one knee and drew a sword from his belt. She was about to shut the door in his face when he laid it quite deliberately across his knee and dipped his shaggy head in reverence.

"Is that? Oh my," she said.

The smith had made good on his promise to deliver a fine weapon. She reached out tentatively, and the man was even accommodating enough to turn his knee so that the hilt was angled towards her. She slid her palm around the hilt and the sword sent shivers up her arm and down her spine. Taking another step back into the receiving room, Demaris made a few experimental passes through the empty space. It was perfectly weighted and the hilt fit her palm as though it had been moulded to her skin. A tiny blush filled her cheeks when she remembered how difficult she had been when the smith had been trying to take her measurements.

The smith. She popped her head out of the door and took a glance down the passage, but there were only the three southerners and the guardsman.

"I think you had better come in," she said in Langan. The three men stepped over the threshold into her outer hall and the guard settled himself outside the door. After a quick glance up and down the outside hall, she pulled out the letter and pressed it into the guard's hand. A few whispered words into his ear and it was done.

Chapter Sixteen

Wilhelm emerged from the icy-chill river, weeds clinging to his skin like tendrils of creeping vines. He was hidden from view by the two ships moored to the shore, but could still hear the stifled grunts and see the movement in the distance. The Klagen were running back and forth, scouring the surface of the river and the horizon, looking for him.

A rope ladder hung over the side of the ship and Wilhelm was just about to reach up and grip the first rung when he heard voices drifting down from amidships.

"Aye, but Ullr has changed the plan now."

"Would not be the first time. What is it now?"

"We set sail tomorrow for the southern lands. He has his eye on a raid."

"And what about the forest boy?"

"Guess he hopes to flush him out."

"Or he is in a hurry to fill those pens, just to spite the boy."

The two Klagen men guffawed, then the one nearest the side hawked a large mouthful of spittle over the edge. Wilhelm dodged the phlegm but knocked into the rope ladder, which thumped against the side of the ship.

"Did you hear that?"

"What?"

"That noise."

Wilhelm could just make out two large hairy figures with muscle bound shoulders and thick necks leaning out over the side. He slid down into the water and held his breath for as many counts as he could manage, his thick fur jerkin filling back up with water and weighing him down. He floated downriver, using the keel as a guide and popped up again at the aft of the ship.

So Ullr was planning another raid. Unusual when he had not long returned from the last one, but then Wilhelm had deprived him of one his favourite spoils of war, his captives. Or maybe it was indeed a ruse to flush him out. Perhaps there was a way he could use this to his advantage and escape the camps from right under their noses. He drifted to another rope ladder and checking that there were no crewmembers lurking nearby, he hauled himself out of the water and dripped onto the deck. He shook himself like a big shaggy bear, spraying the bulwarks above him with a shower of river water. It looked like Ullr had most of his crew scouring the docks and the embankment looking for him, so he took advantage of the moment and sneaked off to the forecastle, his shoulders hunched and his head down low trying to look small and insignificant. Perhaps he could find a suitable place to hide away before the rest of the crew came back.

"Oi, you!"

Wilhelm stopped in his tracks.

"Yes, you."

Slowly, he straightened up. Damn.

"What are you doing up here? Get back down into the forecastle and finish getting ship shape. The captain says we sail tomorrow."

Wilhelm kept his gaze ahead and without looking back at the speaker he grunted with suitable vehemence and continued on his way down into the forecastle. But the owner of the voice followed along behind, jabbering away in Jarvik.

"Hold on there. Are you new on this brig?" the Klagen said, gripping Wilhelm by the shoulder. He turned around and faced the man trying to look surprised at being questioned. "What? Fell overboard did you?" Then he started to laugh. Wilhelm laughed along with him, shaking his head. *Oh yeah. What a fool I am.* But not half as much a fool as this boatswain who clearly had no idea who or what his crew were searching for ashore. He stopped laughing and shrugged as though he wasn't quite sure what he found so funny. "Get yourself down there and clear those quarters. And you won't be needing no furs where we're going," he said, giving Wilhelm's fur-covered shoulder a quick shove.

The stench in the crew's quarters was a festering combination of, sweat, vomit and urine. Even Wilhelm, who was used to living a rough life, had to stifle the need to gag. Without thinking, he leant over the nearest bunk to try and open the porthole. It was too late when he noticed the mound in one of the bunks. The covers flipped back to reveal an ugly face, all bruised and discoloured; a classic symptom of arak abuse. The man's nose had a distinct kink to it, as though it had been broken too many times and never properly healed. Wilhelm was positioned in exactly the worst spot when the man sat up and cracked his forehead across the

131

bridge of Wilhelm's nose. His nose crunched and then blossomed with blood. The pain split across his face and he instinctively backed up, clutching at his nose. The man in the bunk followed his movement, then wrapped his huge arms around Wilhelm and started to squeeze. Wilhelm's breath came in short sharp bursts as his ribs pressed against his insides. But the man gave him one last burst of energy before collapsing back onto the bunk, eyes rolling into the back of his head.

Wilhelm ripped a strip of cloth from the man's shirt and wrapped it around his head, keeping the pressure on his nose enough to stop the bleeding. He looked at the man, waved a hand across his face, listened for signs of breathing, but he was dead. Whatever final frenzied activity he managed had cost Wilhelm his nose, but the arak had taken the man in the end. Wilhelm caught his own reflection in the porthole and barely recognised himself. He looked at the man and back at his own now mutilated face and an idea formed in his mind.

He lifted the cover and turned the man over, then rolled the fabric over and tied the ends off to fashion a makeshift sling. This body, whatever misfortune had caused its owner's demise, was going to be his lifeline. As he lifted the bundle onto his shoulders, a thick black tongue lolled out of the mouth and a rasp of gas escaped the man's body and filled the small cabin with an even more putrid stench. It was all Wilhelm could do not to vomit. It would take days to restore the cabin to a reasonably smelling place.

Wilhelm checked for the boatswain and when the deck was clear he hefted the body over the side of the ship, relieving himself of his burden and at the same time giving his pursuers something to think about. It might at least take them some time before realising they were not looking at the drowned corpse of Wilhelm of the Forest. The body made a *splosh*, then sank briefly before bobbing just below the surface and floating downstream. By the time they found it, he expected to be on route to the southern lands. He wondered what havoc Ullr and his crew had planned.

By the time the crew returned, Wilhelm had cleaned up their quarters as best he could and availed himself of some of the dead man's belongings to try and blend in as much as possible. Sadly, the Klagen had little desire or use for personal items, so all he had to use as his disguise were a few crudely sewn together rabbit skins, a pair of oversized boots and a collection of arak drinking cups. The bruising came up around his eyes and when he removed the makeshift bandage, his nose had a definite kink to it.

While cleaning up, he had stumbled upon a makeshift table with upturned cups and the spilled remnants of a jar of liquid. Perhaps his dead friend had overstayed his welcome with the god of arak and his own luck had run out. He didn't have long to wait before the Klagen embarked onto their ship and Ullr took his place on the bridge, far enough away from Wilhelm to allow his presence to fade into the background bustle of setting sail. For the time being.

As the Bestla, was made ready to sail, Wilhelm watched the faint glow of a fire in the distance. So, they had built a pyre and set it ablaze. Was that for Wilhelm or their lost crew member? He would have to be careful, as Ullr's men might be stupid but Ullr himself would not be slow to realise what had happened if he got close enough to Wilhelm to recognise him.

Two large and loud Klagen, who he guessed were the dead man's drinking partners returned to their quarters bearing armfuls of provisions, mainly in shape of clay jars, much to Wilhelm's consternation. A slap on his back nearly sent him flying and he just had enough presence to stop himself from erupting into fight mode, although, given the Klagen's propensity for a scrap it might have helped his cover more if he had.

"Lodur!" the Klagen said. He had a large bell-shaped belly and a droopy nose only just visible beneath a mop of tangled hair, matted with what looked like yesterday's supper. "So you finally decided to get out of that pit," he said waving a meaty palm at the now clear bunk that once belonged to the dead man. Well, at least Wilhelm now knew who it was he was impersonating. Another Klagen peered around the massive body of his crewmate and looked Wilhelm up and down with suspicion. This one was not quite so large, but just as suitably unkempt and they both stank nearly as badly as their dead friend, which led Wilhelm to wonder why he had bothered cleaning up at all. The man frowned at Wilhelm.

"You fell on yer nose again, Lodur?" He laughed at his own joke. "We should all do an arak binge and sleep for two days – looks like a new man don't he, Kracaw?" The droopy-nosed Kracaw guffawed and slammed the jugs of unknown arak-looking substance down on the table.

"We'll soon get you back to your old self, Lodur," he said, eyeing him up suspiciously. Wilhelm settled himself down and committed to indulging in an afternoon of drinking. Fortunately, he was very soon relieved of the duty by the boatswain who came looking for suitable candidates for the oars and supervisors for the rigging monkeys. None of the Klagen ever climbed the rigging, as their physical stature would not allow them to make it past the first yardarm. So they trained young boys and sometimes girls from the camps to work the rigging, whilst the rest took care of the oars.

The oarsmaster was a formidable Klagen woman, named Jaanta, who had long blonde braids with beads and shells interwined. There was a clickety-clack noise as she turned her head and a passing crew member ducked just in time to avoid having his face struck.

"You." She had a double-take at Wilhelm when he appeared. "Have I seen you before?"

"See what a night of arak and two days sleep can do to a man," Kracaw said with a little more uncertainty in his voice. Jaanta eyed him up and down.

"That's not Lodur," she said putting her hands on her hips. "Are you blind as well as stupid?"

Wilhelm held his breath for a moment. That was it then. He had been rumbled and now they would toss him overboard at best, or worse - tie him to the prow in keeping with Ullr's original plan.

"I... urg," Wilhelm said, wondering whether to protest innocence, fight or run. Jaanta broke into a wide smile.

"No matter. Get yer arse down here, all I need right now is some muscle to get this baby moving."

Wilhelm let out a long slow breath, leapt down onto the benches and took up an oar with both hands. Kracaw settled himself down on a bench opposite, casting sidelong looks at Wilhelm with alarming regularity. In the distance, they left behind the dwindling spark of the real Lodur's funeral pyre. Kracaw followed Wilhelm's gaze.

"More'un he deserved if you ask me," Kracaw mumbled from beneath his mop of hair. "Shoulda strapped 'im to the prow."

"He was the Clan Chief's son," Wilhelm said, regretting his words as soon as they left his mouth. Kracaw said nothing, but continued to cast disapproving glances in Wilhelm's direction.

"Row, you bastards, or I'll tie *you* to the bloody prow," Jaanta strode up and down past the benches, using a large stick to rap the knuckles of any oarsman who looked to be slacking. In the distance, the second Klagen ship rowed smoothly into the slipstream.

Chapter Seventeen

For a long time after the watchkeepers left, Allan sat beside the dwindling fire looking into the dying embers. He spread the fingers of his left hand in front of him, inspecting the stub. He had always been led to believe it was because of some kind of accident. Could it be true that his mother was really his nursemaid?

No. It could not be true. He had misinterpreted the story. The baby prince was someone different, someone else caught up in the political machinations of the Western Isles. But then, why would she tell him this? Was it a coincidence that his little finger was also missing on his left hand? Perhaps that was part of his mother's plan. She meant to use him for some ulterior motive that related to her past. But that would not explain why she would send him on this trip to deliver the sword to the Countess.

At least that part of the deal had been met, thanks to the watchkeepers. They had freed him from his captors and he had trusted them to return the sword to their countrywoman, who, they had informed him they had come all this way to protect. They were expecting to find him still at the camp on their return, but now he was re-thinking his whole reason for being there in the first place. He picked up the book and was about to dump it into the hot embers, but then he hesitated. No. If it were true, he could not just deny his identity. Or could he? After all, only he and his mother knew the truth and perhaps his father, but Jael would always defer to his mother's wisdom.

May the gods forgive him, what was his mother thinking? He flicked to the end of the book again, to re-read the final passage – just to make sure he had not made some mistake in his translation. The parchment crumpled under his thumb and then he stopped, an angry fist bunching in his stomach. There was a jagged line of torn paper where someone had ripped out the final pages. All that remained were a few inky squiggles where his mother's script ran to the edge of the page.

For a moment he stared at the torn remnants of the missing pages. Was this his life now? Unfinished, unknown and now lost somewhere on the road to Carentan. What purpose would anyone have to steal the end of his story without reading the beginning? He slammed the book down on the ground, wanting to stamp up and down on it but lacking the conviction. Now he was going to have to go back to his mother and ask her to tell him the rest of the story. For the gods' sake, he was hoping to avoid that; he would have to admit to stealing it in the first place.

He could wait for the watchkeepers to come back and question them about the book. After all, it had remained in their custody for a while when he was recovering from his ordeal. Perhaps they had taken the pages, as a precaution in case he disappeared. Or perhaps the northern men had taken them. If that were the case, he might be able to recover them at the scene of the fight. And if the watchkeepers had taken the pages, it would not be wise to trust them further, so perhaps it was time to move on. Could he even trust that they had delivered the sword to the Countess?

On both counts, there was only one way to find out. He saddled Dilla, scrounged a heel of hard bread and some apples from the watchkeepers' food stores, pocketed a few loose coins and headed back the way they had come, towards Canrac. His head throbbed and his wrists ached and he wondered not for the first time that day whether it was the right move to return to a scene of battle where he was one of the perpetrators. In fact, it became more apparent as the day wore on that it was not one of his better decisions. His mother always berated him for acting first and thinking later. Once, she had even muttered under breath;

"Like father, like son."

He remembered thinking at the time that it was an odd thing to say, as his father Jael was a cautious man.

He left the lakeside and before long turned around a bend in the track. The path and surrounding area was awash with the purple insignia of the King's Guard. His first instinct was to pull back on Dilla's reins and run speeding in the opposite direction. But he realised that would only make him look guilty, so he plodded on, head bowed beneath the hood of his cape, hoping that they would let a poor traveller pass without notice. Not so fortunate.

"Hey, you."

He looked up, glanced behind then tapped a finger to his chest. *Who me?* The guardsman was on foot and strode over to him, gathering Dilla's reins in his gloved hands and patting her mane to stop her from bolting.

"Where are you going?"

"To… Canrac?" He didn't need to feign nervousness, as his stomach was as jittery as a jumping bean. They had moved the bodies. The five northern men were lined up in a row on the side of the track waiting to be loaded onto a cart. Cotton shrouds covered them, so it was hard to make out the extent of their injuries but the blood that soaked through left no one in any doubt about the finality of their state. Another guardsman walked down the row, daring any onlookers to cross an invisible border between the bodies and the public track. People milled about, some in uniform, some angling for a closer look with morbid curiosity. The guardsman's boot snagged the corner of the shroud as he walked past the body nearest to Allan. The cotton pealed back to reveal a head of bushy black hair and two eyes, raised to the heavens in surprise.

Despite the encroaching heat of the midday sun, Allan's skin crawled with a cold sweat.

He leaned over Dilla's neck and vomited breakfast and bile onto the track.

"All right, all right. Move it along," the guard said, waving Allan through with a look of disgust on his face. "That way to Canrac."

As Allan walked Dilla past the line of bodies, he scanned the area for any bits of paper lying abandoned, but the track and the clearing did not reveal anything. The two guardsmen who patrolled the turnoff towards Canrac, gave him a wary glance

140

until he was waved on by their compatriot. One of them muttered, "bloody peasants," just as Allan made it through their blockade. He kept his head down and pushed Dilla on, eager to put as much distance between himself and those bodies as possible.

Indeed, he wasn't a soldier. Yes, he could fight. His mother and father had made sure of that, alongside learning the skills of the smith. Fighting was always the last resort; he was not a killer and certainly not a soldier. So where could an out of work smith's apprentice hide away in a town like Canrac? Hide away long enough to nurse his wounds and re-gain some self-respect. He could not face going back to the smithy at Cannan; Jael would cope, he had other apprentices. He could no longer trust the watchkeepers. So that left the smithy at the garrison of Castle Helmstedt. Hiding in plain sight. Well, that was one thing he was good at and one thing his mother had taught him well. It was a plan, of sorts.

As he rode Dilla into Canrac, it was easy enough to get lost amongst the crowds. Every day was market day, so he headed towards the stalls and the shacks and the peasants with their wares, potatoes, beets, apples. Fresh mutton from the surrounding farms and cotton sellers by the dozen. He was jostled along with the melee and no one paid him any heed. He was just a weary traveller, atop his pony, his face covered by the hooded cloak he wore to keep the sun from his eyes. It wasn't until he stopped and dismounted at one particular stall, manned by a stick-thin elderly man who made

141

flatbread boats filled with mutton stew, that he took down his hood. His stomach grumbled at the rich meaty scent and hot baked bread. He fumbled around in his pockets for a loose crown and flipped it onto the counter. But the man wasn't watching his movements, or filling up a bread boat. He was staring at his face.

"Oh, my lord," the man said.

Chapter Eighteen

Allan stared at the man and the man stared back at him with eyes wide.

"Marci... Marci! Get back here and look at this. I swear this boy... is it even possible?"

A woman came out. She had plaited black hair streaked with grey and a weathered face.

"My word," she said, tipping her head to one side and looking him up and down. Allan fidgeted with unease. They recognised him. What if someone had told the King's Guard and they were making their way back to detain him? He was a murderer. Well, not quite, but he was still responsible for those bodies lined up outside Canrac. He swiped up the coin and put it back in his pocket, then flipped up his hood. He would just have to suffer the heat for now. He took Dilla by the lead, hustling through the thickening crowds. As he walked away, the man shouted after him.

"Hey, you forgot your food." But Allan was weaving his way in and out of the market stalls, looking for somewhere to hide. A broad-shouldered man knocked into him, sending him spinning to the ground. He hit the dirt track with a thump and felt the shock of impact ricochet up his spine. His hood fell back.

"You want to watch where you're-" the man stopped and stared.

"I'm sorry. Really, I'm sorry," Allan said extending his hands in what he hoped was a peaceful gesture. Perhaps the man would just accept the apology and let him go. Instead, he gripped Allan, forearm to forearm, then lifted him back to his feet. The man shook his head, as though dismissing his thoughts and Allan decided to try another tack. "I don't suppose you know where I can find the garrison?"

"Garrison?"

"I'm looking for a job. I'm an apprentice. I can work metal, pump bellows – anything of use," Allan said. The man looked him over.

"Well, you can walk with me if you like, but I can't guarantee you any work. That would be up to the Meister, not me. I'm just the muscle." He chuckled at his own joke and flexed his arm. "Name's Drew, nice to meet you," he said pumping Allan's hand in a shake.

"Allan," he said. Drew released his hand and Allan opened and closed his fist to make sure all his fingers were still in place.

"But first, can I make a suggestion?" Drew said. Before waiting for an answer he reached out and ruffled Allan's hair up a bit, then drew the hood back over his head. "There. You won't get quite so many strange looks like that. I mean, I know you're young, but it is uncanny." Then he turned and strode off in the opposite direction. Allan had to mount Dilla to catch up with him at a trot. He didn't understand. How could they know it was he who had killed those men on the outskirts of the village? Perhaps they had scouts or guardsmen who kept watch on behalf of the King. Well, if that were the case then he had better keep a low profile – perhaps some dark corner in the forge where no one would suspect a mere apprentice smith to be a murderer.

As the market place disappeared behind them, the path widened into a copse of trees on approach to the outer circle that lead to Castle Helmstedt. In the distance, the formidable castle walls peered above the parapets of the outer keep and the reflections of the sun on the water of Lake Mariac cast shimmering waves over the brickwork. The lake surrounded the castle on three sides, acting as a natural moat, the fourth side backed by the precipitous Helm mountain range.

"We have to get through the guards at the outer, middle and inner gates before reaching the garrison," Drew said, "so I suggest you keep that face of yours well-hidden lest we create a stir amongst the locals."

An odd thing to say, thought Allan. How would the locals know anything? Besides, the watchkeepers were probably doing them all a favour, ridding them of a bunch of no good bandits who would have caused havoc in the village if left to roam. His thoughts turned sour with his anger on reflection. They had tied him to Dilla, trudged him through the woods with just a dribble of water and virtually no food for days on end to sell his own sword to a stranger for a price from which he would never stand to benefit. No. He was certainly not sorry for what the watchkeepers had done.

They crossed a small wooden bridge which was the only visible entry across the moat and Allan wondered how the watchkeepers had managed to find their way in to deliver the sword. It did occur to him that they might not be the most desirable of folk to pitch up at the inner keep expecting an audience with the King's respected guest, especially given the past diplomatic relations between the Western Isles and Arrontierre.

Drew talked to the castle guard and managed to persuade them that his companion posed no threat and they were waved through the outer gates without incident. Allan breathed a sigh of relief. Was this how it was going to be from now on? Perhaps he would have been better off going home after all.

They passed through a smaller version of the market at Canrac. Chickens ran wild across the track, chased by children. Stalls were heaving with sweet delicacies to meet the palates of the privileged. Tables were stacked high with bolts of brightly coloured patterned cloth sold in rolls. They dismounted and led the horses through the mayhem. The scent of freshly baked bread wafted across on the breeze and set Allan's stomach grumbling.

"A heel of bread for a crown?" he said, digging in his pocket and hoping he didn't sound too pathetic. Drew looked at him, then grabbed him by the shoulder dragging him towards the nearest food stall. Dilla followed in the hope of snuffling the odd scrap.

"When was the last time you ate, boy?" Drew said. He muttered a few words to the stall holder, then stuffed a hunk of bread and sliced meat into Allan's hands. He devoured it in several bites, leaving a small pile of crumbs for Dilla, who shovelled up the remains from the ground. Drew

146

pulled a water skin from his bag and handed it to him. He took a slug and nodded his thanks. The stall holder had started to peer at him, trying to look beyond the hood, then Drew snatched away his water and hustled Allan along.

Back on track, he trotted along behind Drew, who whisked them both through the middle gate and into the main castle complex. There was a practice yard, which was encircled by men, boys and knights with their squires. He thought he caught the flash of sword and several females in the mix. A semi-circular collection of outhouses surrounded the training ground, which looked like it could be the arms men's quarters. Maybe it was not such a clever idea to come to the garrison. What if he were to bump into the Countess Del'oro or the King himself, both of whom might recognise him? Despite the sweat running in beads between his shoulder blades, he pulled his cloak tighter making sure that the hood kept his face hidden. It was unlikely that either the King or the Countess would be a regular visitor to the garrison smithy. Although, they had been to Jael's forge. But then, Jael had a special relationship with the King.

A swirl of dust rose around the fighters as their boots scuffled around the dry dirt of the training area. Drew hurried him past into a cobbled courtyard and through an archway leading to the outer walls of the complex where the smithy was housed. He dismounted and Dilla's reins were snatched away from him by the stableboy.

"Don't worry, boy. She'll be taken care of until we've finished our business here," Drew said.

When they walked into the smithy, Allan instinctively pulled back his hood in the glare of heat from the forge. There were five or six men hammering, tempering the steel and working the bellows. They looked up with curiosity as Drew entered with Allan trailing behind, but dismissed him with no further surprise or recognition. Perhaps news didn't reach this far into the castle grounds. Drew must have noticed the flicker of confusion that wrinkled Allan's brow and he said, "You would have be of a certain age to remember." Before he had a chance to ponder on that remark, a grey bearded man with a hunch to his upper back appeared from a back room.

"Ah. Meister Antil, I have brought you a new recruit," Drew said, before disappearing into the workroom to contribute to the singsong ring of the sound of steel being forged. Meister Antil looked him up and down, lingering on his face for a few moments.

"Where are you from?" he said.

"My name is Allan, from Cannan."

"Well, Allan from Cannan. I once knew a famous swordsmith from Cannan. Name of Jael. In fact, it is said that even the King of Carentan favours his work above the work we do here." A whisper of resentment in his voice, but then he nodded to himself, accepting the inevitable. "Here we are churning out quantity, not quality. What do you have to offer?"

"I can work steel, handle the bellows – whatever use you might have for an apprentice,"

148

Allan said, then as an afterthought, "I have heard of this Jael."

"I should hope so, if you are as you say, from Cannan." Meister Antil narrowed his eyes. "So what are you doing here?"

"I had some... family issues," Allan said, hoping the man would not pry too much.

"Flaming youth. Think you know all the answers." The Meister snorted and shook his head. "I can pay you two crowns a day and you eat and sleep in the garrison with the rest of the workforce. Just so happens that the King is bolstering his forces and needs more weapons. Rumour is there's war brewing in the south. If it all amounts to nought, may be that I have to let you go in a few weeks."

Allan nodded. He was happy with that, it would give him time to think. Think about where his life was going and about his mother's story. All he needed was somewhere to start. So he shook hands with Meister Antil.

"Meister. May I ask you a question?" The Meister raised an eyebrow and nodded with impatience. "Why does everyone look at me with such curious expressions?"

Meister Antil looked at Allan and shook his head. "You are too young to remember King Reiner."

"King Reiner?" The previous king had died when he was just a baby. Or so his mother had told him. She told him many stories about how King Reiner had established the border controls in Carentan through the forest rangers, banned slavery and set a precedent for future generations. He had

149

died young, before his son – now the King of Carentan in his own right – had grown old enough to know his father and learn from his experience. His mother was somewhat circumspect when she talked about the Andolin family, the royal dynasty of Carentan.

"You bear a remarkable resemblance," Meister Antil said. "In fact, if you cut your hair back, like so," he reached out and lifted a few locks from Allan's face, "add a few years… one might even be forgiven for thinking that his ghost walked amongst us."

Now he understood. It had nothing to do with the dead bodies lining the path outside Canrac. He was partly relieved by this new information, although his apparent resemblance to the late king added another layer of concern.

Chapter Nineteen

Demaris turned to the three southerners as she shut the door.

"Well?" she said in her home dialect of Langan. The men at least had the decency to look sheepish. "I suppose Gilbert put you up to this?"

The men looked at each other and judging by their vacant expressions, she thought at first she might have been mistaken. The taller one with the dark hose with yellow and red panes stepped forward.

"My lady, we are watchkeepers and yes, we do work for Gilbert Amand on behalf of the Emperor of Arrontierre. We keep the peace and look for indicators of unrest between villages, towns and nations. My name is Tavorian." He swept an arm across his chest and bowed low. "And these are my companions, Abendigo and Brutas." Abendigo took off his feathered hat, placed it across his chest and bent his knee into a low bow. Brutas dipped his head with a grunt.

"I see," she said. These were the Emperor's men. She wondered what they were doing wandering about in Carentan and killing bandits along the way. She assumed they were responsible, since the scabbard had miraculously turned up at the scene. "Watchkeepers are supposed to travel incognito, remain aloof and outside of the general populace, working for the future safekeeping of Arrontierre," she paused. "You three look about as incognito as a court jester at a burial."

"Well now, I don't think that is entirely fair," Tavorian said. "When we heard that the Countess Del'oro was without her sword, we felt it our civic duty to complete the transaction."

Demaris took in a deep breath. A tiny quiver of excitement fluttered in her chest.

"Indeed," Abendigo said, "if the Countess Del'oro has need of any further assistance, we felt it most prudent to make our presence known."

"Well met, indeed," she said. "Your presence is now known across all of Carentan, alongside the messy remains of a group of bandits on the Northern Road."

"Ah. Yes, well that was unfortunately unavoidable," Tavorian said. Demaris wanted to grab their heads and bash them together. Instead, she let out a long slow breath. This was just the sort of ruse Gilbert would come up with.

"I don't want to know the details, I really don't," she said, throwing her hands up in despair. "Just tell me one thing. The smith. Is he still alive?" The watchkeepers each looked at one another, then back at Demaris.

"We sincerely hope so," Tavorian said.

The watchkeepers eventually told her all the details. They could hardly have withheld anything once the smith came into the story. She tried to hide her horror as they described the state in which they had found him, tied to his horse, half starved, with injuries to his head, wrists and ankles. Tavorian described how they had confiscated his possessions without knowing who he was or what he was doing there, on the assumption that he was likely up to no

152

good, looking like some street urchin with a sword they assumed must have been stolen.

"But he was the one who forged the sword," Damaris said.

"Yes, we know that now," Abendigo said, "but you can never be too cautious. Especially in a foreign country."

"Evidently," she said. "Where is he now?"

"Hopefully, back at our camp," Tavorian said, not sounding too hopeful.

"Or, if he has any sense, he will be leagues away from here by now," she said. The watchkeepers glanced at one another, looking for mutual support.

"My Lady," Abendigo said, "we could bring him here to you, if that might be of some comfort to you."

Comfort? She would have to be more careful. Gilbert always said that her face told a thousand stories.

"I am guessing that if he wanted to be here, he would be," she said.

"Perhaps we can yet be of some assistance to you, now that we are here," Tavorian said.

"Actually, perhaps you may be of some help," she said. Three men against a group of five bandits – not including the smith, as he was half battered at that point – were not bad odds. She could do with some muscle at her back. If she could restrain them from running off after bandits at every turn.

"I'm going on a trip," she said, "that may involve some trouble. As your countrywoman, I ask for your protection on the road and with whatever might ensue at the end of my journey." It was a bit vague and she did not know for how long she would be able to fully keep them in dark about her true intentions, but for now it had piqued their interest.

"Sounds interesting," Tavorian said, "if you might share with us the... whatever that might ensue at the end?" All three watchkeepers looked at her expectantly.

"I'm afraid I can't do that. Yet," she said, hoping that they would take her on good faith.

"What about that mess on the Northern Road?" Abendigo said.

"The only thing that could possibly be tracked back to us, is this," she said, hoisting the sword, "and that." She pointed towards the scabbard on display by the window.

"Ah, we wondered where that had got to," Tavorian said. "How very remiss of us."

"How very remiss, indeed," she said. Even Brutas withered under her steady gaze.

She bade farewell to the watchkeepers on the promise that they return in five days' time, either with or without the smith and well prepared for a journey. They were pleased at least at the notion of heading south, closer to their home, though how close to home, Demaris had not fully revealed. Apparently, they had already seen enough of Carentan. On reflection, perhaps Carentan had seen enough of them.

Demaris picked up the sapphire spangled scabbard and smiled to herself. The colour matched her eyes, although it was in dire need of a clean-up. As she tilted the tip of the sword and tried to slide it in to place, she felt a snag inside the scabbard. There was something inside that was preventing the sword from a proper fitting.

That was odd.

She withdrew the blade and peered inside. There was something stuck about half way down. She turned it upside down and shook it, but whatever it was remained stubbornly fixed to the inside. Carefully, she slid the sword back inside and worried the edge against the object blocking it. Eventually, the tip of a crease of parchment came into view and she just managed to pinch enough of a corner to lift it free of its space.

There was a neat slice down the centre of the page where the sword had met the parchment before it had crumpled enough to create a barrier. She uncurled the paper and folded it as flat as possible, holding the two separate slices together like a puzzle. Someone with a neat olden Etanese script had written on two pages and hidden it there inside her scabbard. She sat down, her curiosity piqued, and began to read stumbling over the foreign words.

***

It was time. Word had been sent and the day named. As I cast an eye out of the window and across the castle grounds, I saw the big knight, Fulk, on his horse ride out with his squire. I pondered for a moment; something was not right. The knight was wearing the colours of a forest ranger and the boy glanced oddly over his shoulder. The good breed of pony the boy rode was far superior for a mere squire and the boy's hair sat far too neatly upon his head. You see, I had been trained to assess at a single glance the meaning of a set of circumstances, however seemingly trivial. Whatever was to happen that day, this family had the curse of a wealthy man on its back.

The chambers were quiet; unnaturally so. The quiet before the storm. It was true to say that immediately preceding an event of great magnitude, there was always an unearthly stillness, like nature holding its breath.

Josselin started to cry and I released my hold, suddenly realising that I had been squeezing the child to my chest. The baby craned his body away from me, as though he sensed that something was not right. I took him to his feeding chair and gave him the concoction I had prepared earlier. He devoured the feed like his last supper and so I waited and watched as his eyes began to grow heavy, waiting to catch his little body as it slumped in the chair. I wrapped him in swaddling clothes, and hid him in a sling beneath my robes. I carried the panniers used to collect supplies from the village, placed over my clothes to hide the sling. One last check of the rooms, to make sure that all evidence of my short stay at the castle had been eliminated, then I left at exactly the same time I did each day of the week.

Outside the door, the guard nodded at me and as was my custom, I politely dipped my head in acknowledgement. Celie would return very soon to find a bundle of baby clothes in place of Josselin, at which point the alarm would be raised. I had precious little time to get into the forest and disappear before the Queen's Guard came after me. I knew that as long as I made it to the forest, they would never find me and they would never again see Josselin. That was the deal. The child had to die and his little finger would be sent to Castan's client as proof.

***

Josselin. That was the name of the baby prince who was assassinated, some sixteen years ago. Roda, the King's sister, had told her the story over and over, like a woman possessed. She claimed it caused the death of her mother, the Queen Regent, from the wasting disease some months later. Lacking the strength to fight the illness, she wasted away, inconsolable with the loss.

King Gereinte refused to accept the evidence of Josselin's assassination, stating that the grisly stub of a little finger that had been sent to the family could have come from any child. He was even known to have talked to his own children about their uncle's return to Helmstedt one day.

She read the words again with an aching pain for the family. Pain and loss that must have been suffered for over a decade. Was this written by the perpetrator and what in the world was it doing stuffed into the scabbard of her sword? It surely could not have anything to do with the smith. More likely, it had come from one those northern bandits, but now she would never find out. Not after the mincemeat that the watchkeepers had made of those men.

She should go to the King and his sisters with the parchment. Then she read the words again and a lump formed in her throat. Josselin had been assassinated and she held the proof, from whatever source that came. No. She could not do that to the family who had taken her in as their guest and treated her as one of their own. She folded the pieces into a neat square and tucked it into the bodice of her gown. Some things were best left unsaid. There was too much to do besides worrying about something that happened when she was only a baby herself.

She spent the next day packing a small bag and talking through her plans with Gereinte and his sisters. It would not do to just rush off, after all the good will they had shown her. When she was satisfied that they saw nothing strange in her travel plans, she decided the time was right to get the scabbard cleaned up and the sword polished in preparation for her journey home.

Demaris opened the smithy door and the heat from the furnace blasted her face. She looked around the modest workroom. The walls held racks of tools, tongs, hammers, chisels and in the far corner, a young man stood working a pair of bellows in front of the hearth. Four soot smeared faces looked up at her and the steady chime of hammer on steel paused for just a moment, then resumed once the men had satisfied their curiosity. An elderly man stepped into view.

"Come, come, my Lady. We can't let the cool air of morning spoil our heat," he said, ushering Demaris inside and closing the door behind her.

"Once the sun hits midday, I should think you will wish this place had no doors at all," she said. "I would like to have these cleaned and polished, if I may?"

The young man in front of the hearth turned his head at the sound of her voice and their eyes met. She held his gaze for a long while until he turned back to stoking the flames. She kept her eyes on the back of his head, afraid that he might disappear if she let him out of her sight.

"Perhaps your apprentice might be so kind?" she said, handing the sword and scabbard to the elderly man.

Chapter Twenty

For the first time in days, Allan was grateful for the heat from the hearth. It hid the involuntary flush that rose to his neck and cheeks when the Countess Del'oro came into the smithy. He knew that she recognised him the moment they locked eyes. He swallowed, trying to alleviate the dryness in his throat. He supposed he should be relieved that the watchkeepers had kept their word and delivered the sword, but he felt like a rabbit caught in a trap.

Then Meister Antil was coming towards him with the sword in its rather grubby looking scabbard.

"Look lively, lad. The Lady needs this cleaning up and polishing," Meister Antil said, drawing the sword. The Meister gasped as it made a clear chime on exit, then he stared at it, his lips parted in contemplation, as he turned, looked at the Countess then back at Allan. "You had best treat this beauty with the respect it deserves, lad," he said, laying it flat on the worktable. Allan gathered together polishing stones, rags and paste.

"I don't think we'll need a wheel for this one; it has not long been forged," he said.

Meister Antil nodded. "You are full of surprises, lad," he said, a small frown creasing his brow.

The Countess nodded her thanks to the Meister, apparently ignoring Allan, which suited him fine, then she left the smithy on agreement to return later in the day. Allan's eyes followed her exit and he noticed Meister Antil watching him. He averted his gaze. "I wouldn't worry about the Countess," the Meister said. "She can be difficult to get on with. Besides, rumour has it she is preparing to leave in the next few days."

Allan kept focussed on rubbing paste into the difficult to reach areas on the scabbard and running his cloth up and down to bring out the shine in the gem stones. It was ironic that he had only just done this some days ago. "Tell me more about King Reiner," he said. Meister Antil beamed. He did love to tell a story and Allan was an obliging listener.

Reiner Andolin was a natural born leader, like his son and heir, Gereinte. He had, according to Meister Antil, an uncanny ability to read other people. Read them in the sense of understand and empathise with them. An unusual strength, particularly in a King who was expected to be strong, assertive and bellicose in the appropriate circumstances. However, what it did enable Reiner to achieve was a unified and stable nation. That was until his untimely death, whereupon Carentan eventually descended into a civil war that threatened to rip apart all the peace treaties that Reiner had worked so hard to set up.

"He could fight, though?" Allan said, wanting so much for Reiner to be his hero, though he was not quite sure why.

"Oh aye, he could fight all right," Meister Antil said with a far-away look in his eye. "But strategy was his forte, no doubt about that. They say he and his lady wife, Queen Caitlin, had a master plan for all their children. The plan didn't quite realise its

161

original potential after Reiner's death, but King Gereinte turned out to be every bit the leader that Carentan had been promised."

Allan kept up a steady stroke on the blade, first working out the scratches, then sharpening and polishing. By the time he was finished, no one would have believed the adventures that sword had seen. Which was just as well when he thought back to the fiasco on the Northern Road.

"What happened to Reiner's second son, Josselin?" Allan said. Meister Antil's shoulders dropped and he paused, focusing on the steady rhythm of Allan's hands on the sword.

"We don't like to talk about it," he said finally. "It was a tragedy what happened to that child. The Queen Regent was never the same after that day."

Allan knew better than to push him to talk, so he just kept his own counsel and finished cleaning and polishing the Countess's sword, while the old man sat and stared into the fire.

Allan was finished long before the Countess made her appearance in the afternoon. She lingered for a while hoping, Allan fancied, that she would be able to speak alone with him. Neither of them had given any outward indication that they knew one another and he felt safer that way. No need for any questions to be asked. When it became evident that the Meister was not likely to let his new apprentice be left alone with such an important client, she placed the sword in its scabbard back onto the worktable.

162

"Please have your apprentice deliver this for me," she said. "I have a meeting to attend on the hour."

"My Lady," Meister Antil said, "I would have my most reliable man, Drew, deliver this for you." He glanced at Allan, then nodded towards Drew, who was stacking tools on the racks. Drew looked up with a *who me?* expression on his face.

"No. I would like the apprentice to deliver it to my quarters, please." The Countess turned and left the smithy without waiting for a response.

Meister Antil turned towards Allan. "Well, I did say she could be difficult. No hard feelings, eh? Just thought that she was less likely to intimidate Drew."

Allan did not feel in the least bit intimidated. He scooped up the sword and left.

As it happened, she was waiting for him just around the corner, on the opposite side of the cobbled archway, leading to the inner keep. A stableboy was saddling a mare and she had donned her full riding gear.

"I can scarcely thank you enough for what you went through to bring this to me." She took the sword and fixed it to her belt. "The watchkeepers told me everything." He was curious but kept his face impassive, wondering if they had also told her about the book. "When I heard rumours about a young new recruit in the smithy, I could not delay a moment longer to see if it was really you." She smiled at him like a young girl who had just been asked to the village dance and he looked away, flustered by her intense scrutiny.

163

"Do you have a long journey ahead, my Lady?" he said, trying to sound polite and nonchalant. She gave him a considered look before responding.

"I have a prearranged meeting with a family contact and then, I shall prepare to travel south. Back to Arrontierre," she said. His disappointment must have shown on his face because she quickly added, "but I shall return. I have some family business to attend to and then, well then I have a betrothal to see through."

A betrothal? His stomach dropped as he digested this new piece of information. The Countess looked pained. He thought women were supposed to be happy about the prospect of marriage. Of course, she was a countess. She had a duty to continue her line, to produce heirs to look after her land and estate. Why would she not be expected to marry? And there was no way in the world she could possibly feel anything for a lowly smith's apprentice.

Without thinking, he reached out and touched a palm to her cheek. His skin tingled with her warmth and then she was up close and peering into his eyes and her lips found his.

They broke apart and looked at each other. Then he looked around the courtyard. The stableboy stood staring at them with his mouth open. What Allan should have done, was to retreat with haste and hope that the stableboy would keep his own counsel. However, he had never been one to back away from a challenging situation, so with all the courage he could muster, he approached the horse and took its reins. Giving it a quick ruffle behind the ears, he led the horse back to the Countess and presented her with the reins and an offer of help to mount. She dismissed his offer and sprung into the saddle with ease. The stableboy stood gaping, then ran off towards the stables.

The Countess turned the horse and clopped out of the courtyard and into the middle circle, making her way towards the heavy wrought-iron portcullis. Just before disappearing out of sight, she turned and he caught the flicker of a smile on her lips.

It wasn't until later that day that Allan realised what she had meant by *rumours about a new recruit in the smithy*. For surely that in itself was nothing to start a rumour mill turning. A succession of visits from curious courtiers, peering suspiciously at his face left him in no doubt that word had got around.

Towards the end of the day, a woman with long dark hair and a black robe, trimmed with ermine stepped inside and strode right up to him. Her hair was pulled back from her face and held in a net, which sparkled with tiny gems. It gave her quite an austere presence, like a queen inspecting one of her subjects.

"My Lady?" he said. Meister Antil popped up beside him. How did he do that? He always seemed to appear when anyone of note entered the smithy.

"Your Highness," he said, emphasising the *Highness* in the woman's title and casting a disparaging look at Allan. "Please forgive my new apprentice, who is not yet familiar with our royal community."

The woman looked irritated by the distraction. She was taller and older than the King's sister,

Alliane, so not her twin. That only left the eldest, Roda. Who would probably be the only one who would remember exactly what King Reiner looked like, aside from what was depicted in family portraits.

"So," she said, tilting her head to one side. It was most disconcerting being under such continual scrutiny. "It is true, you do look like him. I can see what all the fuss is about. Who are you and where did you come from?" Forthright. His mother had told him that Roda was very much like the former Queen Regent, Caitlin.

"I… err, grew up in Cannan."

"I see. You have parents?"

"Yes."

"I see."

This was all rather strange. She stood looking at him for a few moments more, then with a minute shake of her head, turned and left. Allan was left watching the door shut behind her and wondering what had just happened, then the door was flung back open and she marched back in and grabbed hold of his left wrist.

"So how did you lose your finger?"

"I… err, I am a smith's apprentice. Accidents happen," he said, not wanting to admit that he didn't know. She frowned at him.

"I see," she said, releasing his hand. She gave him one last stare, then strode back out of the smithy.

Sometime later, he heard women's voices outside. The wooden door burst open anew to reveal the King's other sister, Alliane with Roda in tow.

"Don't be ridiculous," Alliane said, waving her hand in Allan's direction. "I've known that boy for years. He is Jael's son. He is the one who made the sword for the Countess Del'oro.

Meister Antil stood in between Allan and the royal sisters, his hands on his hips. He looked from Allan back to Alliane and Roda, his mouth open.

"It seems, your royal Highnesses, that this young man has not been quite as honest with some of us, as one might have expected."

Chapter Twenty-One

Demaris' meeting was held in a tavern, called the Green Ranger, just outside Canrac. Her heart had hammered against her ribcage throughout the whole journey, thumping in time to her horse's hoof beats. A faint nausea lurked in the pit of her stomach, like someone had just kicked her in the gut. Well, in fact that is how it felt after Allan had touched his hand to her face, then kissed her. It was all she could do to remain standing and not show how much it had affected her. He had nonchalantly taken the reins of her horse from the stableboy and walked the animal over to her, as though nothing untoward had happened.

It was no good. She had to forget about him. He was not the person who was meant for her, however alive he made her feel. Too many disparities between them. Their background, their status, their wealth. It was unheard of for a woman of her class to be with a peasant boy. The more she told herself this and tried not to think about him, the more he popped into her head, making her shiver with anticipation.

After passing her reins to the stableboy at the tavern, she slipped inside the lounge and made for a corner table where an unassuming middle-aged woman sat, nursing a cup of wine with her hood half covering her face. A nod from the hooded woman and the innkeeper brought over another cup and a hunk of bread with a bowl of pickles. Delyth took her hood down and Demaris was looking into a face, which looked chiselled with age and yet wise beyond years. Her dark hair was streaked with grey, but her skin was still taut and youthful. She had a glow about her, as though she understood her whole reason for being.

"He is alive then," she said, her eyes flicking towards the sword at her side. Demaris just nodded. She had the feeling that Delyth knew that already. "You have no need to fear for his safety." Perhaps a mother always knew. Demaris had watched the Queen oftentimes shoo her daughters into the training ring, when all around them, the advisers and courtiers were fussing with worry.

"I have but five days, my Lady," Demaris said. Delyth raised an eyebrow. She may not be a lady in standing but she was Lady Death and deserved the status that title brought. "Then I must leave for my home town. I want to finish this before it finishes me."

Delyth took a sip of wine and leaned forward. She was close enough that Demaris could smell the sweet, spiced scent of red wine and berries on her breath.

"A very wise man once gave me a choice. To live a short life and take revenge on the puppets who killed my family, or to live longer and learn how to take down the puppet master. What do you think I chose?"

Demaris shifted in her seat, torn between meeting the challenge in Delyth's eyes and bolting for the door. She understood then how Lady Death was renowned for striking fear into hearts of men. It was a rhetorical question, so she turned her head and lowered her gaze. Delyth had agreed to help Demaris on this mission and that was all she was interested in.

"I no longer accept commissions," Delyth said.

"But you said-"

"-that I would help you."

Demaris looked up and stared into those unforgiving eyes and though it was not her business to know how Delyth became Lady Death, she wondered what had happened in her life to make her so hardened. All of a sudden, her whole plan appeared to be crumbling around her.

"So what is the point of all this?" she said. "I might as well just go and do it myself. I have help, you know. Three of my compatriots who travelled with the smith have agreed to journey back to Arrontierre with me. If you won't come, then I'll do it myself." She was getting angry now. Not at Delyth, but at herself, to ever have trusted in the help of others. She should have done this thing a long time ago. In fact, why did she even wait for the raiders to come to her? She should have taken her own raiding party up to Klagenstill. Take the fight to her opponent. That is what Gilbert had always taught her.

Delyth was smiling. How dare she? She didn't look like Lady Death now, just an ordinary smith's wife with an amused look on her face.

"Very well," Delyth said, "but you didn't let me finish."

There was a lump rising in Demaris's throat. She felt ready to explode with pent-up emotion.

First, the unattainable smith, now Lady Death, of all people, was making a mockery of her.

"Go on," she said, "I have very little left to lose." *Except my dignity.* Delyth gave her a measured look.

"You said you have five days. Give me three and I'll turn you into an assassin far more capable of achieving your aim than an ageing has-been like me."

Demaris stared at her, her mouth hanging open.

"Yes. I gave all that up years ago when I pledged my life to my family - my beautiful husband Jael and my son, Allan. What you see before you is just an empty shell. A shadow of Lady Death." She leaned forward again and tapped a forefinger to her temple. "But the knowledge and the memory is still here."

Demaris was torn between disappointment and hope. She so wanted to be the one to take revenge. But could she really do it and would she be the same person afterwards?

"Three days? That is not long," she said.

"For what I have in mind, it is adequate. But I wouldn't count on repeating the exercise," Delyth said. "It took me years of training to become proficient. There is only so much I can teach you in three days."

"Will you come with me?" Demaris was starting to hope again. Delyth smiled and nodded.

"It would be my pleasure."

It occurred to her then that Delyth had moved in circles where people knew things and kept secrets. Secrets that were taken to the grave.

171

Perhaps she would know what became of baby Josselin. The square of parchment itched beneath her bodice, but she let it rest there, for fear of unlocking a beast that she was powerless to control. Three days proved to be more than, yet nowhere near enough time for Demaris.

Delyth took her to a small house located at the foot of the vast Helm mountain range. It was a hidden gem in a forbidding environment, surrounded by trees on the outskirts of the Forest of Dreams. She called it her safe house; somewhere she could retreat when in need of privacy.

The training room was stacked from floor to ceiling with an array of weapons from knives of every size and shape to swords, staffs, spears and weird things connected by chains.

"I used to bring Allan here as a boy," she said, her eyes glowing with reflected light from the polished floorboards.

Demaris looked around the small well-kept house, wondering at the extent of its upkeep. Over the three days, she didn't see another soul and yet everything was cleaned and painstakingly put in its proper place wherever she went.

"My housekeeper," Delyth said one morning. "She has picked up a trick or two."

The art of deception. Demaris wondered how much Allan, the smith, had picked up from his mother. If he had learnt but a modicum of what Demaris had learnt over the last day alone, then she wondered if she knew him at all.

She learnt a dozen different ways to poison a man just from plants that grew in every common

172

garden. She learnt all the locks, throws and strangleholds that would get her out of trouble if her skill with the sword should ever let her down. She learnt how to disguise herself enough to be able to blend in with those around her. To add weight to her appearance and just as easily reduce to a poverty-induced thinness simply by how she held her stance.

Chiselled into the foot of the mountain range were crude steps of rock, which Delyth marshalled her up and down at regular intervals until her thighs and calf muscles screamed in protest. The training room provided no respite, as she became so acquainted with her new Jael sword that she began to wield it as though it were an extension of her own arm.

They were outside the front of the house on day three, sitting on makeshift stools crafted from tree stumps and eating a light supper. At the height of summer, the sunlight lasted well into the evening, despite their concealed location within a glade in the shadow of the Helm.

"Why are you helping me if you no longer need the commission?" Demaris said.

Delyth just looked at her and smiled to herself as she scooped up a mouthful of garden greens with a handful of flatbread. She took her time to chew thoughtfully, then swallowed and washed it down with a mouthful of watered wine.

Despite her silence, Demaris was not deterred. "Jael's smithy does well enough. You have this place. You don't need the money."

"How do you know what I need?" Delyth said. A fleeting look, dark and dangerous glinted in her eye then just as quickly disappeared. Demaris shivered, despite the warm air. "My son likes you," Delyth said simply. "I like to help those he takes an interest in."

Demaris was at first taken aback. She had underestimated this family. If Delyth had noticed her son's interest in Demaris, had he noticed her interest in his mother?

"Your son may like me, but I have no business liking your son," she said.

Delyth raised an eyebrow at this, as though the business of young love was no concern of hers. "Besides," Demaris said, desperately wanting to justify her words. "I am betrothed to another." A chunk of bread stuck in her throat, as did the thought of marrying Colton Barra. Delyth was watching her with interest.

"How did Allan seem to you?"

"He seemed all right. Perhaps a little distracted," Demaris said. Her cheeks grew involuntarily hot at the memory of his lips on hers and she looked away, hoping that Delyth had not noticed. Who was she trying to fool?

"You know, you don't have to go along with the match. Carentan is very liberal with its customs around marriage."

"Maybe so," Demaris said, "but Arrontierre is not." She so did not want to disappoint Gilbert, as he was the closest she had to a parent. She thought about him at home on the estate and a pang of urgency made her heart skip. "We must leave."

"Rest, we have time enough. Besides, there is something I must tell you first." Delyth pulled out a piece of parchment, not unlike the one that Demaris was hiding in her belongings. She gasped and Delyth gave her a sharp look. Then Demaris realised it was just a letter and relaxed. "Yes, we do get messages occasionally when my housekeeper deigns to make an appearance." Delyth unfolded the letter. "There is a planned Klagen raid on the northern coast of Arrontierre. There may be a chance to intercept it along the way, although it may mean nothing. But we can't rule out the possibility of where they may be heading."

Demaris turned cold inside. That was it then. She might not even get a chance to try out her newfound skills, before it was time for real.

"If you ride to the port of T'sar in Tordre and take a ship to the Port of Ville de Lobo," Delyth said, "you may get there a day earlier if you are lucky and don't encounter any mishaps on the way."

"I need to let Gilbert know." Demaris stood up, dropping the last of her bread onto the grass for the wildlife.

"Peace, girl," Delyth said, coaxing her to sit. "You can probably get there faster than any message would. I take it your village has protection?"

"Some… we have the watchkeepers, of course, but three of them are here in Carentan."

"And they will ride with you," Delyth said, "as is custom for a woman of your standing."

"And you?"

"I shall be your shadow. You may not see or recognise me, but I will be there."

Chapter Twenty-Two

There were advantages and disadvantages to being an oarsman aboard the Bestla. His back ached and the skin on his hands was raw with blisters, but Wilhelm enjoyed the air with its salty seaweed tang and rush and swell of the ocean beneath the deck. They part-sailed, part-rowed their way south keeping close to the west coast of Klagenstill towards the naval waters of Sarlat. Fishing birds circled above the topmast and skimmed the water in the ship's wake, chasing their prey. Occasionally, he would catch sight of the tip of a dolphin fin, but the normally friendly grey mammals kept their distance from Klagen ships, having learnt from experience that the men on board were partial to a bit of dolphin meat if any unfortunate creatures swam too close to their nets.

The other main advantage was being hidden amongst the oars and no one, let alone Jaanta with her winsome Klagen looks, was willing to forgo the extra pulling power of one man at the rear of the vessel. So, it was a good place to be. For the moment. His main concern was his new cabin mate, Kracaw, who sat opposite him peering through a tangle of dusty hair, parted in the centre by his droopy nose. Wilhelm wondered how many fights it had taken to bend it to quite such an uncomfortable angle. When he spoke, it was all nasal grunting.

"What you starin' at?" Kracaw said.

Wilhelm levelled his steady gaze at the man. They had stopped rowing while the rigging boys, hoisted the mainsail. The cook's assistant ran barefoot along the oars, dropping cuts of meat into the oarsmen's laps, then ran back on the inside pouring a brown sludgy liquid into cups beside the men. Wilhelm tore a piece of meat with his teeth and chewed; beef or venison that was not very fresh, probably preserved in arak and was tough as a bull's hide. He sniffed at the brown sludge and grimaced; fortified ale that smelt like something they had dredged up from the seabed.

Jaanta stopped by his oar and gave him one of her smiles.

"You wanna thank your stars it is not the water. That is even worse," she said with a wink. Then she was back on her rounds. Wilhelm looked over his shoulder at her, just as she looked away and he caught her curious gaze before she disappeared behind the prow. When he turned back, Kracaw was looking at him, chewing thoughtfully around a mouthful.

"Wouldn't bother with that one if I were you," he said, spitting bits of semi-chewed meat and saliva into his lap. "She only joined the ship the other day; dead as a binge-drunk Klagen on arak."

Wilhelm raised the cup to his lips and took a tentative swallow of the brackish liquid. He grimaced and placed the cup back down with caution bordering on deference. Kracaw guffawed at him around a mouthful of meat, then picked up his own cup and swilled it back, smacking his lips and snarling behind his menacing smile.

Wilhelm straightened up, sloshed back the drink in one go, supressing the urge to puke it back

177

up again and matched Kracaw grin for grin. He really was going to have to try harder at being Lodur.

For the rest of that day, he kept his head down and tried not to draw attention to himself. This proved a little easier as the evening drew in and they swapped shifts with the night crew. Poorer light meant less likelihood of being recognised. So he picked up a bowl of stew from the ship's mess and went out on deck, finding a quiet corner to sit and eat, away from prying eyes.

"You might be fooling those idiots, but you're going to have to do better than that if Ullr or any of his warriors see you."

Wilhelm looked up, just as Jaanta dropped down beside him cradling her own bowl of steaming broth. He grunted in response and continued to shovel the stew into his mouth like he hadn't eaten properly for a week, which was not far off the truth. He wondered how much she knew or guessed.

She studied his face. "The bruising looks realistic enough though. Must have hurt some."

He stared back at her, wondering how much of a beating he needed to make his disguise realistic enough. The night sky was lit up with the moon's glow and the stars twinkled in its wake. The sea breeze had started to calm, the further south they travelled and the air was warming to southern climes. Enough to make it bearable to sit on deck at night, but not enough to cast off his furs. He wondered how soon they would leave Klagenstill waters. He looked up at Jaanta, who was looking at him through her blonde locks. The muscles were well defined across her shoulders and upper arms and he wondered how many years she had worked the oars. Most Klagen women were thickset and muscular like the men, but without the exercise of constant travel, raiding or working the ships, had a tendency toward a more curvy physique. Jaanta did not look like the average Klagen woman. She had a weathered look about her; the look of someone who spent a lot of time outdoors and there was a depth behind her eyes that spoke of untold stories and unshed tears. She may have been new to the Bestla, but she was not new a life outside the domestic norm for a Klagen woman.

"Can you get me off this ship?" he said.

Her eyebrows shot up. "I think you've come too far now."

He thought back to the burning pyre that they had left in Klagenstill and he nodded, resigned to the fact that he had effectively cornered himself and was now at the mercy of Ullr and his crew or whatever it was that Jaanta had in mind for him.

"Do you know where we are heading?" he said.

Jaanta looked at him through narrowed eyes, appraising his words, calculating her response.

"Who was it they burned?" she said.

He shook his head and looked out to sea. A school of flying fish whipped out of the water and skimmed the surface before diving back beneath the waves. The sea birds circled overhead looking for an opportune moment to feed. He imagined what those fish might feel like, daring to rise above the surface to fly free at the risk of being plucked from

179

their watery home and consumed by an airborne monster. How close to the surface was he flying?

"It was Lodur, I think."

"Did you kill him?" she said.

"Nope. Arak poisoning."

"Stupid idiot. Just shows you. He was told enough times I understand, but do they ever listen? Well, you look enough like him, but you'll only fool this bunch of Klagen misfits for so long. Keep out of people's way, if I were you."

He looked around the empty deck and shrugged his shoulders. "Well, okay. I'll give you that much at least," she said. "But even hiding out here is out of character with Lodur. He would be half cut on arak by now."

He wasn't sure if she was referring to him or the recently departed Lodur. Jaanta watched him, as though looking for signs of intelligent life behind the standard Klagen warrior mask.

Wilhelm thought back to the funeral pyre, burning on the horizon off the coast of Klagenstill. A traditional funeral pyre.

"Who do *they* think they burned?" he said. That raised a smirk from Jaanta.

"You don't know?"

He shook his head. Play dumb, best rule. How much did she think she knew?

"Only the legendary Wilhelm of the Forest. But then… surely *you* would know that?" she said. He shrugged and looked away. Only hours earlier, Ullr had threatened to tie him to the prow of his ship. Why would he then give him traditional Klagen

180

funeral rites? Perhaps it was all for show. Perhaps Ullr knew that the real Wilhelm was still alive.

"I've spent a lifetime learning to blend in," she said. "Take it from someone who knows, you may be good at blending in to the forest, but out here you stick out like chevalier's moustache."

She glanced up at the unfurled sails, which were catching the wind and propelling them through the waters, as the crew took their evening meal. She had a wistful look in her eye. "I used to climb up the rigging," she said.

Why was she telling him this?

"That was when I was a little girl, but at the time they thought I was a boy. Then I got too big and started gaining weight in all the wrong places. There came a time when I eventually had to cast off one mask for another."

Wilhelm kept his head down as he ate.

"It's about survival. And sometimes it is easier to forget," she said, looking back at him. Perhaps she had decided he wasn't worth the effort. "Give him his dues, Ullr is a cold hearted killer. But if you show him some use he is just as easily persuaded to keep you. It's all about blending in."

He wondered how far beyond blending in he had gone. His guess was that Ullr had other things on his mind than routing out his errant son, whether or not he believed he had burned the right body.

"A body can look different when it has been dragged from the river all bloated and draped in weed," he said, trying to convince himself more than anyone else. If Ullr believed him to still be alive, he would be watching his back for a very long time. He fidgeted under Jaanta's gaze, wondering what it was that she found so interesting about him. He doubted that anything on board the Bestla got past her attention. "Who are you anyway?" he said.

A twitch of a smiled played at her lips as she appraised him.

"Like you, I am a victim of circumstance. Someone who faced adversity and learnt how to blend in, escape notice." She parted her fur jerkin to reveal a long ugly scar from her neck down to her chest. It looked as though someone had once tried to slice her in two. Letting her jerkin spring back, she shook her head and her long braided hair settled into place down her front, hiding the evidence. "It was a long time ago and I prefer not to dwell on ugly times. Suffice it to say, I hold no long lasting allegiance to Ullr. It is all about survival."

It is said that the oarsmaster of a ship is often the person who hears the most, sees the most and is ultimately the one who holds the secrets of the crew. Who else was there to talk to? The oarsmaster had only one priority; keeping the ship moving. If Jaanta had the power to keep the ship moving, she had the power to bring it to a standstill. If she held the deepest and darkest secrets, she had the power to harness the thoughts and feelings of the crew. She had the power to mount a mutiny of sorts. Wilhelm wondered if that possibility had ever crossed Ullr's mind. Probably not. As she said, if Ullr found a use for you he could easily be persuaded to keep you.

"In answer to your first question, no I can't get you off this ship unless you want to swim for the

182

shore and secondly, if the reputation that precedes you holds up in reality you might want to rethink your strategy," she said, putting her bowl down and folding her arms across her chest.

Okay, so jumping ship might not be the best option. Perhaps there was something he could yet do to sabotage Ullr's latest plans.

"Only, we are heading for the northern shores of Arrontierre and there is more to this raid than you might think," Jaanta said.

Chapter Twenty-Three

Wilhelm spent the next few weeks learning to blend in with the crew of the Bestla and was rewarded by being ignored and grunted at in equal measure. The one person who he would welcome a conversation with was the oarsmaster, Jaanta. But she appeared set on ignoring him like the rest of them. Wilhelm's characterisation of Lodur had taken over the oar along with Lodur's eating and drinking habits.

He was sitting below deck in the small, cramped quarters that his crewmate Kracaw fondly referred to as *exclusive*. They were playing Capture for arak shots. Wilhelm thumped down his next stone, attempting to close off the attack from Kracaw's encroaching territory. It was a lame move, as he knew that Kracaw's line of attack would be strengthened and he had opened up the opportunity for him to capture the corner. Wilhelm played the black stones, Kracaw, the white. The Capture board was starting to look as white as a snowy mountain.

Kracaw narrowed his eyes. "Used… be much better at this game, Lodur," he said, sweeping a few more black stones off the board and reaching for the arak. He downed it in one, staring at Wilhelm and going slightly cross-eyed as the liquor hit the back of his throat.

Wilhelm was working on the theory that if he lost, he wouldn't have to throw as much of that poison down his neck. Lodur's death had been unfortunate, but he had no intention of following him to his grave.

Kracaw was starting to sway on the upturned bucket on which he sat. That was one of the disadvantages of playing Capture for shots; the greater lead you gained, the more drunk you became and the more difficult it was to maintain your lead and win the game. It was not unknown for some of the better players to pass out and forfeit their game. It depended on whether your purpose for winning was to down as much arak as possible or to actually win.

"S'what's the deal wither oars…oarsssmissus?" Kracaw said.

"No deal. She keeps out of my way, I keep out of hers," Wilhelm said.

"Huhn… thas not what you said afore. You tole me she was just playin hard to get."

Wilhelm didn't think for one moment that a woman like Jaanta would deign to spare a thought for a drunk like Lodur.

"Well, she's had a hard time of it. Doesn't hurt to give a woman some space."

Kracaw's eyebrows wrinkled as he tried to work his arak-soaked brain to understand where Lodur's new level of thinking had come from. He hiccoughed.

"I'll say… magine growin up on ships like this." He laughed with all the sexual innuendo of a Klagen drunk, which was not very much. "Good thing for her she grew wily and faster than most of the crew… they don't mess with her. So unless you have some special… thing, ah wouldn't bother."

How many years had Jaanta had to fend off hungry Klagen warriors before being able to match them for their strength? He shuddered at the thought; to be a woman in a male dominated world that held fighting, drinking and fornicating to be their most important occupations. Raiding foreign villages was merely the means to the end. The women tended to put up with this behaviour until pushed to their own limits. Then they often gave as good as they got, which was always a surprise to a Klagen warrior, who tended to think they were in control until reminded otherwise.

The ship's bell clanged to denote the hour. Wilhelm counted the bells, which should have stopped at six, but continued relentlessly as though the bell ringer himself had either fallen asleep at post or was himself drunk on arak. Kracaw belched, then his eyes slid back and he slumped onto the floor with a grunt. Seconds later, he was snoring through the noise of the bell which was sounding ever more frantic. Wilhelm was deciding that he really ought to go above deck and see what all the fuss was about, when the cabin door flew open and Jaanta stood on the threshold. She looked surprised at first to see him, then rolled her eyes when she saw the state of Kracaw.

"All crew to oars. We need to move quick. Enemy ship on the horizon." She turned and strode back out. Enemy ship? That would be interesting. This could be his opportunity to get off this sorry excuse for a Klagen ship. Wilhelm wondered who they deemed to be an enemy but remembered that they considered anyone other than Klagen to be an enemy. Well, that left the field wide open. He followed in Jaanta's wake.

They emerged on deck to a bluster of frenetic activity. The oarsmen were falling over themselves to get to their positions, the rigging monkeys were furling the sails and the captain was stalking up and down deck barking orders. Wilhelm moved towards his bench.

"Not you," Jantaa said. She looked to the horizon and he followed her gaze; there was a large war frigate, a navy vessel by the look.

"Whose waters are we in?" he said.

"Sarlat," Janta said. "We don't stand a chance of getting around it and the only way south is through it."

Wilhelm had heard stories about the size and power of the Sarlatian navy ships.

"Will Ullr fight it?"

She gave him a sarcastic look.

"As opposed to…?"

Of course, a Klagen would rather die fighting than be captured. Which rather flew in the face of their favourite sport, which was capturing and making slaves of other people. Wilhelm had no wish to return to those pens, full of lonely, terrified people just waiting to die. Fight on Ullr's ship or escape amidst the chaos? Or die trying? Not much of a choice. He glanced at Jaanta and thought about the red pinched scar running down her torso. But there was nowhere to go and now she was giving him a funny look.

"What?" he said.

187

"Nothing, you just look kind of… never mind. You have a choice. Stay and fight, or I can get you off onto a raft and you can take your chances at sea. But I can't guarantee that Ullr won't catch you before you make it any place safe."

"Do you think the Sarlatians may have got wind of Ullr's plan?" he said, his mind already made up. She shrugged.

"His influence reaches further than you might know and the world is full of spies and narks."

Either way, Ullr would go down with the Sarlatian army warship or Wilhelm would find a way to stop him before he had the opportunity to execute his raiding plans - that much Wilhelm promised himself. Or, he would die trying.

The sea was calm, but the clouds roiled in the skies ahead storming in the distance with a blanket of dense rain between them and the Sarlatian warship. Gulls circled overhead, perhaps sensing the threat of death in the air. Wilhelm took deep breaths, savouring the salty air that could be his last. Jaanta walked the oars, unconcerned by the heavy atmosphere that descended on the ship the further into the conflict zone they rowed.

Wilhelm watched the crew settle into a state of concentrated activity. They had been in this situation before and they were prepared. He noted the ballistas and crossbows, underneath the hatches, now open, on the main deck. The crew were scattered on deck, going about their business.

The warship had their weapons on deck and trained in the direction of the Bestla. The rumble of thunder was getting closer as they cut through the water on a trajectory towards the Sarlatian ship. Now close enough to see, the Sarlatians were readying themselves for battle, clad in their black and grey uniforms with Queen Fiamina's insignia emblazoned on the front, matching the flag that flew full mast claiming the territory.

Wilhelm knew that whatever the outcome of this encounter, there was one thing he needed in order to come out of this alive. He slid away while Jaanta was occupied at the oars and retrieved his spear from beneath the bunk. He strode back onto deck, his attention focussed on the ensuing battle. A few nearby Klagen glanced at him, dismissing him as just another warrior and went back to preparing to defend their ship.

Ullr was at the prow of the ship, unconcerned with the minutiae of the crew, eyes trained on the Sarlatian warship. He held a hand aloft, palm open and the crew of the Bestla waited with bated breath as the rain sheeted down and the wind kicked up a storm, driving them relentlessly forward. If they continued on that course, the Bestla would ram into the side of the Sarlatian ship. Wilhelm watched Ullr's fingers curl and uncurl with impatience, waiting for the right moment.

"Unfurl," he bellowed and the rigging monkeys let the sails go. It took moments for them to slide back down the masts and secure them to the yardarms before the wind caught the sails and the Bestla started to turn.

"Come about," Ullr roared and the helmsman wrenched around the wheel as the Bestla came around, bringing them alongside the Sarlatian ship for a full attack.

"Fire!" Ullr sliced his arm down, making a fist at the Sarlatian army crew and the deck descended into a cacophony of battle cries as the Klagen reached for their weapons and launched a blistering attack on the other ship.

On the Sarlatian ship, the front line of defenders started to crumble under the crossbow assault from the Klagens, but just as quickly as one went down, another soldier appeared in their place. The Sarlatian ship was bigger than the Bestla by at least half and they had not only crossbows in their front line, but ballistas bringing up the rear and strategically placed arbalests swinging into position to fire into the fray. A Klagen warrior only a few lengths away from him blossomed in a fountain of blood, as a crossbow bolt slammed through his chest.

The whole ship shook with a wrenching that sounded like it was being ripped in two. The Sarlatian ballistas were proving their superiority both in design and trajectory. Great holes appeared in the side of the Bestla, while the Sarlatian ship just took a few scratches and scrapes from the Bestla's efforts. Ullr had disappeared and the crew were only just holding onto their front line.

"Do something useful, or we'll all go down with this sorry ship," Jaanta said, shouldering him to one side and firing a crossbow at the nearest Sarlatian. The man crumpled around the bolt and was hauled to one side as another man popped up in his place. "Damn. They're like freaking worms; cut

190

one in half, you end up with two." A crunching explosion behind them threw splinters of wood in every direction and several Klagen screamed.

"We'll never defeat them like this," Wilhelm said. What they needed was the element of surprise. But that was all gone now, with the Klagenstill propensity for full on frontal attacks. "If I can slip out and get behind them." Jaanta gave him a look of disbelief that summed up how he was feeling; torn between defending himself and the Bestla, and fighting his way to freedom. But what if he did manage to survive, only to be captured by the Sarlatians and sentenced to death by association? They would never believe that his true intentions had been to thwart Ullr's plans all along.

No time to think.

"Come with me and bring that crossbow," he said. Jaanta fired off a few more bolts, then ran after him, waving him down.

"Don't be an idiot. Your best hope is to stay alive and get yourself captured," she said.

A Klagen warrior fell into their path, writhing with the agony of a quarrel in the gut. Wilhelm was swift to lift his spear and finish the job, skewering the man through the heart. Jaanta stopped and stood with her mouth open.

"He would have bled to death anyway," he said. She appeared to regain some composure, then overtook Wilhelm, leading him to the stern.

"Go then," she said, unfolding a rope ladder, which led down the back of the ship and into the sea. They both held on tight to the aft rail as the ship swayed and bucked with the storm and the

191

onslaught from the Sarlatians. He hefted himself over the side and looked back towards Jaanta, beckoning her forward. She shook her head. "My place is here. When all is said and done, I'll meet you on deck for a bowl of hot soup." A wry smile played on her lips. He realised then that he was on his own.

Wilhelm's hands slipped as he lowered himself into the water. The ship's stern rose up in a wave of defiance, nearly crushing him. He gasped at the cold and swallowed mouthfuls of saltwater before gaining control of himself. The sea rose and fell around him, threatening to take him off in every direction but the one he wanted to go in. But he was a strong swimmer and after battling the angry sea, he slid through the water and out onto the other side of the Sarlatian ship. He swam beneath the waves to the underside of the ship and managed to snag the end of a dangling rope ladder with his spear and drag his breathless body above the surface of the sea. His face exploded into the light and he took several great heaving gasps of air. Before having a chance to even contemplate which side to fight on, he looked up into the faces of two thin-lipped Sarlatians, who had their crossbows trained on him.

He clung to his spear with one hand and the ladder with the other.

"Friend, not foe," Wilhelm said in faltering Etanese. To their credit, the Sarlatians did not just blast him back into the water, they actually helped him up onto deck. Fighting on the side of the Sarlatians was looking rather more appealing already. They did, however, keep their crossbows levelled at his midriff.

From the opposite side of the battle, things seemed far more controlled, as though clearing the waters of Klagenstill raiders was a regular occurrence. That was one thing with which Wilhelm could readily identify. Perhaps they thought that his appearance was some kind of new Klagen trick, as they duly marched him to the captain at the prow of the ship. The captain was a tall, slim man with close-cropped dark hair and a thin smile. He shouted above the noise of the ballistas in what Wilhelm thought to be Etanese but was delivered so quickly, it could have been an altogether different language. The captain looked at him expectantly and Wilhelm shrugged. They were evidently unaccustomed to seeing a Klagen warrior split from his tribe. Very rarely did they venture out alone and never amidst a battle.

"Watch and learn," the captain said, curling his lip in disgust. Perhaps they meant to make an example of him.

Great. He had escaped being tied to the prow of Ullr's ship, only to be tied up as a Sarlatian battle trophy.

The captain raised an arm, bellowed an order and the entire front line was replaced with a fresh set of soldiers, the remainder left free to tend to the wounded. Then something remarkable happened. Remarkable and strangely disturbing.

Wilhelm was just about to throw in his lot with the Sarlatians, when the captain's eyes bulged and his mouth made a small *ohh* shape in surprise. He

193

looked down at his chest, where the head of an arrow protruded and a ring of ruby spread out, soaking the fabric of his tunic in an ever-increasing circle. The captain fell to his knees and the two soldiers looked on in complete disbelief, forgetting their weapons for a brief instant. An instant long enough for Wilhelm to gain the advantage.

A flick of the wrist and his spear shot up into his hand and with one swift move, he disabled the two Sarlatian soldiers. Their crossbows clattered to the deck just as the shaft of an arrow took first one, then the other in quick succession. Wilhelm dropped to the deck as a full-scale assault rained down around him and the Sarlatian army was reduced to a screaming wall of writhing bodies.

The head of an arrow embedded itself into the wooden deck only a finger's width from his head, the shaft twanging in the wind. He elbow-walked himself across deck to reduce the likelihood of being hit, coming to rest near the aft rail. He looked up beyond the rear of the ship at the black and white flag of a Klagenstill raiding ship.

Not the Bestla. He had completely forgotten about the second raiding ship, bringing up their rear.

On the starboard side, one half of the crew of the Bestla were leaping about cheering and waving their weapons while the others were desperately patching up holes and sloshing buckets of seawater over the side of the ship. So much for going over to the enemy side. He was back where he started.

There was an almighty boom as the hull of the Sarlatian warship was ripped apart by an explosion and Wilhelm was propelled upward, clinging on to the aft rail, before the stern of the ship rushed down to meet its watery grave. The best he could do was hold on as his face then body was plunged beneath the surface. He took a last deep breath before being filled from head to foot with seawater. His water-logged ears muffled the sound of screams from those who had survived the onslaught of arrows only to be propelled to an uncertain future. If they survived the pull of the ocean and the cold didn't kill them, then their wounds would surely bleed out under the water, leaving a litter of bloated corpses for the fish to feed on.

Wilhelm's biggest regret was having to release his spear as he let go of the rail and kicked his body back up to the surface. He may have been a perceived enemy of the Sarlatians, but the Klagen he now faced saw only one of their own. As his head burst to the surface, he took great wracking breaths between mouthfuls of water. Someone threw him a rope and he clung on, his hands cramping up with the cold, and was pulled towards the second Klagen ship. A group of puzzled looking warriors helped him aboard as he dripped great puddles of seawater onto the deck.

"Well, well," the captain said, pushing his way to the front of the crowding crew. "I swear I saw your body burn sometime back off the coast of Klagenstill." There was little similarity between Ullr and his brother; this one had more meat around his middle and his hair was streaked with grey. His beard he chose to wear cropped, but his braids still clacked with the trophy bones of his victories.

Wilhelm dropped his head to his chest, exhausted and full of defeat.

Damn these bloody Klagen tribes. Of all the bloody ships that could have picked him up, it had to be this one.

Chapter Twenty-Four

After much humming and hawing in the smithy, Allan was summoned to the castle for a private audience with King Gereinte himself. Meister Antil's attitude towards him became unduly deferent when he discovered that Allan was in fact a master swordsmith in his own right and largely responsible for maintaining the impressive Jael reputation. In fact, he seemed reluctant to let Allan go to the castle at all. One thing that both he and Allan learnt very quickly, however, was that you didn't argue with Roda.

All kinds of things were running through his mind, as Allan was escorted by castle guards, flanked either side of him, up to the inner keep. The royal princesses were visible ahead of them, every so often taking small glances over their shoulders to make sure he was keeping up.

The least of his worries was the fact that he had lied his way into a job at the smithy. His mother was an assassin. An assassin who had plotted the kidnap and murder of this royal family's own brother. If they were to find him guilty of something... anything, it wouldn't matter – misdirection, lying to Meister Antil, trying to impersonate the former king – they would likely put him in their dungeons and confiscate what few possessions he had, including the book, and that would be the end of it. Guilty by association.

The sweat trickled between his shoulder blades as he climbed the stone steps inside the keep.

Strange that they had brought him here and not to the Great Hall, where he heard the King would deal with all matters of court and petitioners. Then they were following the princesses through a set of ornate double doors and into a room that was both chaotic and strangely comforting.

A large open window looked out across the green and Allan could just see small dots which must be people moving about in the distance. The symmetry of the castle walls that surrounded the keep, made the view out of the window idyllic. On the windowsill sat two little girls playing a strange game, which involved pushing and slapping their hands together. King Gereinte, dressed in a casual robe and hose of leafy green and soft brown hues, was pacing up and down in front of the window, one arm folded across his chest, rubbing his chin with the other in deep thought. A little boy ran around him in circles making little jumps and waving his hands to attract attention. King Gereinte looked up and his eyes widened when he saw Allan.

Queen Jehanna stepped into view from behind a door leading to an annexed room. She was dressed in a flattering cotton tunic, black with gold thread that fell just below her knees. Underneath, she wore functional hose that did not detract from the beauty of her garment, just added another layer. It was an outfit you could wear to run, jump, fight, ride or... look after small children. He dropped his gaze and looked away. It was such a personal family picture, he could only imagine how they might feel about his intrusive presence. Besides, the Queen unnerved him to the point of distraction. He had only met her

198

once before when the royal family had come to Jael's smithy in order to forge a sword for her. He had only been about six, but he remembered it well; how those almond eyes had gazed at him with a mystery and curiosity that made him feel both small and at the same time, the most important person in the world. She had a dangerous glint in her eye and it was easy to imagine how she lived up to the stories people told of her former life as a mercenary.

Queen Jehanna flicked her gaze between Allan and King Gereinte, weighing up the reaction.

"Allan? I thought it was you when all the rumours starting flying around the castle," King Gereinte said. "Some people are saying you are the bastard son of King Reiner, come to stake your claim to the royal coffers. Some say you are Josselin, returned to us from the grave." He gave Allan a pointed stare and then laughed. "Don't look so worried. We have known each other for many years. I have had a long time to consider all the possible outcomes. Come and sit with me for a while." Allan took a seat beside him and Queen Jehanna joined them.

The guards dropped back and settled behind the double doors, while two serving men bustled around a trestle table and laid it with jugs of watered wine, platters of mackerel and sliced ham, and heels of freshly baked bread. Then two nursemaids came in and extracted the small boy from the King's side and hustled the young girls out of the room. The girls were reluctant to leave and managed to scramble back to the table, evading capture by their long-suffering maid.

"Allan," Gereinte said, "may I introduce my two very demanding daughters, Karla and Evgenia."

The two girls looked at him with eyes just like their mother's and Allan's pulse quickened. They looked every bit as dangerous as the Queen and doubly unnerving.

"Who are you?" Evgenia said.

"Eva," Jehanna said, "don't be rude. Allan is our guest and he is the son of one of our most treasured family friends: The swordsmith, Meister Jael."

The two girls looked at one another and nodded, which made Allan fidget in his seat, then they abruptly turned their attention back to their father.

"We want the Pygmies Tale," Karla said.

"We want, doesn't get," Jehanna said and the two girls looked at one another and smiled.

"Please may we have the Pygmies Tale?" Evgenia said, oozing charm. Those two would grow into dangerous women.

"I know that story," Allan said, forgetting for a moment that he sat at the table of the King and Queen of Carentan. The girls rewarded him with their undivided attention. "My own mother used to tell it to me. I think," he said, wrinkling his brow. He was unsure now whether it was his mother who had told him the story or someone else. "Come to think of it, I'm not sure I do remember. But it sounds familiar."

King Gereinte was looking thoughtful. "Perhaps you heard it as a boy in the village. It is a popular folk tale."

"It's about a big friendly giant," Karla said, stretching her arms wide.

"It's about a big stupid giant," Evgenia said, "and lots of clever little people."

"Are you a pygmy?" Karla said.

"I… err, don't think so," Allan said. The girls made no move to leave the room, so King Gereinte hustled them out and excused himself to attend to the duty of telling tales to young children who really ought to be sleepy but resembled nocturnal creatures. So Allan was left alone with the Queen, as he fumbled with a slice of venison.

Jehanna deftly cut herself a slice of meat with a small knife. He had never before been in the presence of someone so totally at ease with silence and once he realised that he was the only one who felt ill at ease, he began to relax.

"Gereinte is very good with them," Jehanna said. "Whereas, I have little patience."

Allan nodded appropriately.

"Except in the practice yard. Then it is the reverse. Gereinte is so jittery I have to ban him from watching, while I can spend all afternoon with them, teaching them the ways of the warrior."

"I suppose," he said, picking his words carefully, "that it is still uncommon for women to take up arms."

She shot him a look and he wished he could take back his comment. Then her eyes softened.

"Perhaps, for the Western Isles. But women rule the battlefield in the East," she said.

"I imagine you have a few stories of your own to tell," he said. She smiled with her eyes.

201

"Indeed. But that would take us far longer than the time it takes to tell the Pygmies Tale," she said. As though on cue, King Gereinte strode back in and took up a seat at the table. He scooped up some bread and several slices of meat.

The King and Queen relaxed into a comfortable silence. Apparently he wasn't going to be thrown into a dungeon, but still he felt wary of the consequences of revealing too much about his mother's connection to the assassination of Prince Josselin.

"May I ask you a question?" Gereinte said.

"Your Majesty, of course," Allan said. King Gereinte smiled a little at his deference and waved a hand as though calling him *Majesty* or not, was of no consequence.

"What led you to seek employment at Castle Helmstedt?"

He thought about that for a moment. How much should he tell the King?

"I was dispatched on a journey to deliver a sword to the Countess Del'oro," he said.

"But you didn't deliver the sword," Gereinte said. "Three of the Countess' compatriots claim to have found it and you in a rather compromising situation and then delivered it on your behalf."

Uh oh. Allan's mind flashed back to the dead bodies on the Northern Road.

"Not that I have any dispute over you working the forge at Castle Helmstedt. You have more than proven your skill. I am just rather surprised to find you hiding in plain sight."

"In plain sight, your Majesty?" Hiding. He got that right. Allan relaxed a little when he realised that King Gereinte was not going to pick up on the issue of the northerners.

"From whom do you hide?" Gereinte said.

From himself, his mother, the truth?

"I needed some time. To think," Allan said. "I have had a difficult journey."

"I should say so," Jehanna said. Allan looked at the Queen, who had that dangerous look in her eye.

"I have seen you fight, Allan," Gereinte said, "and I know you can look after yourself."

"My father taught me to fight. He says that it is not possible to forge a sword that is fit-for-purpose without having knowledge of how to wield it. He used to practise with my mother and I in the yard, but he has grown weary with age."

King Gereinte was nodding as though this was not new information and then Allan remembered that the King had often visited when he was a boy, watching in the background. At the time he had not thought much of it, as he knew no different. But on reflection, it seemed an odd thing for a King to do.

"My mother has taught me much more than fighting skills, but it seems that my face has betrayed my presence here."

"Indeed," Gereinte said, "it seems that you have created quite a stir. Even with the difference in age and hairstyle, there is no denying the likeness to my father. But then, I have seen you grow from a boy to a man. Does the attention bother you?"

Of course. It would come as no surprise to King Gereinte. Allan glanced at Queen Jehanna, who was listening but was not showing any signs of surprise.

"No, but I'm not sure if I could cope with the kind of attention your Majesties seem to draw, just by existing."

Gereinte laughed. "We all grew up knowing what to expect. But you did not."

"Will your mother and father not be missing you?" Jehanna said, deftly changing the subject.

"They sent me here on a trip to deliver the sword to the Countess," he said. He left out the part where he had been attacked, knocked unconscious, tied to his own horse then rescued by a second group of bandits, apparently attached to the Countess. Not to mention having his possessions passed from hand to hand and finally ending up at Castle Helmstedt. All told, a little bit of peace pumping bellows was about all he felt capable of doing. At least until he could get his head straight around his mother's story and what the ending meant.

"It's complicated," King Gereinte said reading his thoughts. "I understand that. Life is complicated. And to complicate it even more, I have a proposal for you."

Chapter Twenty-Five

King Gereinte's proposition took Allan back to a memory he had as a little boy. A memory, an ambition, a lost purpose. He had been just five years old when his mother took him to Canrac and they saw the King's parade pass through the village. This happened after a successful sortie in Dern and the King was bringing back more troops to bolster their defences in Carentan.

As the crowds swelled, he tugged at his mother's skirts. Legs towered around him and he had to cling furiously to her, to stop being swept along by the tide of movement following the parade. He squealed and jumped up and down until his mother lifted him into her arms so finally he could see the horses and the banners and the soldiers.

His mother was frowning as though she didn't really want to be there. In fact, they had not meant to be there at all. It was market day and for once in his short life, Allan had worn her down with his persistent requests to accompany her. And so, she had acquiesced. His heart pounded and he lifted his head as high as possible, as people started shouting, *the King is coming. Make way for the King!*

She held him tight in her arms as they watched in awe, the massive sweaty horses walking through the centre thoroughfare carrying the King and his troops home. There were men and women in black and gold tunics, mingling in amongst the King's guard with their purple banners. Alongside the King rode his Chief of Staff, Jehan Mantar. Allan had no idea who he was, but he was a soldier and that was all that mattered. He wriggled and squirmed in his mother's arms until she loosened her grip enough for him to jump back down to the ground and dodge in and out of the sea of legs, making a direct path for Jehan. The King raised his hand and shouted *halt!*, then the procession came to a slow standstill. The King dismounted, with a huge smile on his face and to Allan's utter surprise and delight, he swept him up into his arms and plonked him onto the saddle in front of Jehan Mantar. The King turned to Jehan and said something to him, and Jehan's face softened. Then he chuckled, making a soft throaty sound, despite an underlying impatience that Allan could sense.

For those few precious moments Allan was the most important person in the world and it somehow felt right. The right place to be and the right company to keep. Then the moment was gone as he was returned to his mother's arms. Her face looked like a cloud, hiding the threat of a storm.

***

The proposal was to travel with the King's men on a trip to Sarlat. As though swept up by some obscure twist of fate, he was again with the King's Chief of Staff. This time, however, Allan had his own mount and although he had not realised his ambition of becoming a soldier, the opportunity to ride out with the King's men was recompense enough.

Jehan Mantar turned to look at him, as they led the sortie across the Carentan border towards Sarlat.

"Well," he said, "you come with high recommendations."

Allan wanted to shrink away into the background. High recommendations meant high expectations. Although he had known the King all his life, he wondered how much the King knew him. It had been easy enough to accept. All he had to do was accompany the soldiers on the King's business to Sarlat. They were tasked with defusing a potentially explosive political situation.

That was it. Accompany, listen, learn, absorb and report back. Did that make him the King's messenger? No requirement to fight and he rode without a weapon. No requirements to even speak, though he had a million questions to ask, and no requirement to negotiate. Which was just as well, since he wondered who would listen to him anyway. Although, the soldiers had a strange look of deference about them whenever they came near him. Perhaps that was the new-elevated status from smith's apprentice to King's messenger. Or perhaps they still thought he looked like the old King Reiner.

Allan acknowledged Jehan's comment, as though he were in perfect control and knew exactly what was expected of him. Perhaps if he kept about him an air of quiet confidence, they would leave him alone to watch, listen and learn. It was just as well for Allan's sake that Jehan Mantar was a man of few words.

207

They were met by a welcoming committee of guards on horseback, carrying the Queen of Sarlat's banners and escorted to the capital city of Sarne, the gateway to the Southern Seas and the Green Isles. The streets were well kept, with a surprising number of official looking men patrolling public areas who looked a bit like soldiers but without weapons or the imminent threat of violence.

"Magistrate's lackeys," Jehan said, when he noticed Allan's keen regard. "They have the justice system sewn up here. Less crime on the streets means less work for the magistrates to process through the courts."

Despite the overall cleanliness, there was an underlying odour of sewage coming from the drainage system, made worse by the hot weather. The port was bursting with cargo loads and a throng of hot sweaty dockworkers.

They were escorted to the palace and met in the grandiose entrance chamber by the Queen and her consort, Darien Issoire, a Carentan noble and close friend of the King. He vaguely recognised him. Allan thought perhaps he had once been to the smithy in Cannan. His suspicions were confirmed when Darien smiled at Allan and shook his hand enthusiastically.

"Well met indeed," he said. "You probably don't remember me."

"I'm sure nobody could possibly forget you, dear," Queen Fiamina said, turning to look at Darien with a wry smile on her lips.

They were all ushered into a receiving room where they found refreshments laid out and servants to relieve them of their travel-worn belongings. Allan was handed a warm towel.

"Be careful they don't whip the clothes off your back," Darien said with a wink. "The Queen is most particular about cleanliness."

Darien shook hands with Jehan and the two men moved away towards the refreshment table, heads together in an inaudible exchange of pleasantries.

"Don't listen to my dear consort's wisdom and don't let him give you advice on affairs of the heart. That is if you ever feel the need to lay bare your heart to someone. You are after all, but a boy." Queen Fiamina smiled with a cheeky glint in her eye. Darien looked at her and wrinkled his brow.

Keep quiet, watch, listen, learn. That was all he had to do. So why did he feel the need to act or say something to fill the silence?

"Let me educate you in the way of women. We are indeed most particular about cleanliness and we don't like to be told what to do. If you want us to change, then you must have us believe that it was entirely our own idea," Queen Fiamina said.

Allan could not help but comment on this revelation. "Isn't that a bit manipulative?"

"Well, that rather depends on your own level of conviction," she said. "Something my dear consort has spent years cultivating, though I wouldn't admit to him that I've noticed." She winked at Allan.

He sighed. He didn't think he would ever get the hang of affairs of the heart. Whenever he thought about the Countess Del'oro, his heart fluttered and filled his soul with warmth. Then he remembered their respective statuses and the fact that she was betrothed to another and his stomach dropped. He wondered briefly if she felt the same way, then dismissed the idea. One opportune kiss did not overcome impossible barriers.

"Ah. I see someone has indeed caught your young eye," the Queen said with a knowing look.

"Enough banter, my love," Darien said. "To the business of sinking ships and overseas threats."

Queen Fiamina grimaced and shrugged. "We were rather hoping that Gereinte would send us more reinforcements, but I suppose you and your troops will have to do."

And so it was within a day that Allan was embarking onto a Sarlatian frigate in a convoy of warships, set to pursue two Klagenstill raiding ships enroute to Arrontierre. Jehan Mantar had stayed in Sarlat to deal with diplomatic relations following the loss of their warship to the Klagen. Darien Issoire joined them on board and although Queen Fiamina had fussed and complained about releasing her consort on the trip, she had seemed secretly proud that Darien was the favourite for extending foreign relations overseas.

Their first stop was to be the Port of T'sar in Tordre, to stock up on supplies before crossing the Southern Seas. As they left the dock, there was another ship coming into the harbour, piled high with bodies and the detritus of what looked like a sea battle gone horribly wrong; bits of wood that might once have been masts, hulls, oars and decking, bespeckled with blood and pieces of dead flesh.

Allan was given a small cabin in the forecastle, adjacent to the ship's mess. Convenient, as the salty sea air refreshed Allan's energy and gave him a roaring appetite. Some of the troops who had accompanied him from Carentan had been given shared bunks with the crew and were expected to pull their weight with the Sarlatians. No such expectation was made on Allan.

Allan and Darien sat in the ship's mess, a wooden table between them, two bowls piled high with mutton stew and a plate of bread and pickles.

"So. Tell me what really brought you to Sarlat," Darien said, fixing Allan with a hard stare. Allan gulped back a mouthful of meat and thought about the question for a moment.

"I hoped you could tell me that. Since you are so close to the King."

Darien looked steadily at him. "The King has some fantastical notion that you might be his long lost brother, Josselin."

There. It was out. Allan had more than ample reason to wonder it himself, though he was almost too scared to admit it.

"And you don't share this belief?"

Darien gave him a rueful smile. "I have to admit, it does seem almost too convenient. And I suspect that may be why the King has taken more than a passing interest in Jael's smithy and might explain your presence."

"Say, for argument's sake, it were true," Allan said. Darien raised his eyebrows, as though what he was suggesting was beyond insolent. "I'm not saying that it is. Just supposing. How would anyone know for sure?"

"Precisely. And my point on numerous occasions to the King," Darien said.

"Which is why I am a smith and not a prince," Allan said. "But if it were true, for argument's sake, don't you think I would be justified in claiming my birthright? After all these years, don't you think that my family have a right to be reacquainted with their long-lost brother?"

Darien watched him with intense scrutiny. Allan pretended not to notice, looking at him out of the corner of his eye and at the same time swallowing mouthfuls of stew washed down with watery ale.

"There is no mistaking the physical resemblance, that is for sure," Darien said at last. Then he leaned forward. "But make no assumptions based on hearsay. I and many more who are close to the Andolin family will not allow them to be held to ransom a second time." Allan looked up and met with Darien's stare. As they locked eyes, something wavered in Darien's expression. A tiny shred of doubt flickered there for a moment.

Chapter Twenty-Six

It took Demaris several days of hard riding to reach the port of T'sar in Tordre. The harbour was heaving, as she strode to the end of the wooden jetty to negotiate her passage, flanked on either side and to the rear by the watchkeepers. Seabirds circled overhead screeching and diving at any passersby who happened to carry anything vaguely nourishing. She wrinkled her nose at the scent of seaweed and sewage, at odds with one another. The hustle and bustle of people was exacerbated by workers loading barrels and boxes onto cargo ships.

The captain of a Sarlatian frigate called the Primus, agreed to take her and her companions to the northern port of Taroudant, from where it would be a few days' ride to Demaris' home town of Rotonde. In return Demaris agreed to help in negotiating passage for the Sarlatian army, which was currently chasing two raiding ships from Klagenstill that had sunk one of their frigates. She glanced at Tavorian, who was watching her carefully when the captain made his offer. She nodded, shook hands and the sense of relief not just from the captain was palpable.

She looked over the aft rail at the flotilla of warships waiting eagerly to fulfil their duty and the hairs prickled on the back of her neck. At the least she would get her trip home and a straight line to the Klagen chief who had destroyed her village and killed her parents. She might even get the opportunity to avert a war between the Western

213

Isles and Arrontierre. She wondered where Delyth was and what she was doing. It rankled that she was so close and yet still at the mercy of the decisions of others.

The watchkeepers took their quarters alongside the crew and settled in for the journey, while Demaris took a modest cabin in the forecastle near the ship's mess. It was one of three reserved for special guests, the other two of which were also apparently occupied. A cabin boy brought her a wash bowl and towels, so she set about ridding herself of the road grime she had accumulated on her ride to Tordre. Her stomach grumbled in response to the rich aroma of spiced meat coming from the mess.

On her return from Delyth's safe house, she had discovered that Allan had left Carentan on instruction from the King. Of course, a smith's apprentice was dispensable; a commoner who could act as a messenger without risking a more valuable adviser. When she had asked Meister Antil for his whereabouts, her heart lay heavy with his response. She wondered if she could live with the thought of never seeing him again.

Delyth had acted very strangely whenever she mentioned Allan, like something else of greater import was going on. Well. She should have no worries there. Demaris would act as the dutiful heir and marry her equal in status. It was what her parents would have wanted. It was what Gilbert wanted. It was what she had decided needed to be done. She wrung out the cloth and rinsed her hands and face in the bowl, the water turning a dirty grey.

Then she fixed her hair back in a net and put on a simple woollen gown.

She emerged on deck to see the watchkeepers busy unfurling sails and swinging on the yardarms, showing off their robust physiques. Brutas planted his feet on deck, pulling ropes and glaring at any crew member that looked in his direction. Unsurprisingly, they let him be. Abendigo did a forward roll on the yardarm, grabbing a loose rope and simultaneously unfurling a sail with a flourish. A small group of Sarlatian crew members were muttering about travelling circus tricks and ostentatious southerners. Demaris laughed and turned towards the stern of the ship.

Then she saw Allan.

He stood with his back to her looking out over the aft rail. His hair was untied and whipping softly in the wind. He wore a robe, belted at the waist and a tunic with the Carentan insignia. The kind of garb, you might expect of a common apprentice. But what was he doing there?

Sensing a presence, he turned and she noticed his eyes widen. Her heart took up a steady thrum, thrum within her chest.

"I didn't see you embark at T'sar," he said, then as if belatedly remembering his manners, added, "My Lady."

"It took us a while to persuade the captain to take us on board," she said.

"Us?"

Demaris inclined her head towards the rigging and Abendigo's smiling face popped up from behind the yardarm.

"You brought the watchkeepers," he said and raised a hand in greeting, looking slightly bemused. Abendigo waved back, then disappeared from sight. Demaris suspected that Allan wasn't the only one on board who was bemused by their presence.

"The Sarlatians have certainly thought up enough ways to make us pay for our passage," she said.

"They are a wily lot, these Sarlatians," Allan said. "Especially concerning foreign nobility." She thought this rather strange coming from a smith's son with little experience outside of Carentan. Then she remembered her training with Delyth. "My mother is a good teacher," he said, as though reading her thoughts.

"Yes, indeed," she said, thinking how her muscles ached in agreement.

They stood in silence for a moment, just looking at each other. She did not have the courage to say what was really on her mind, and neither she suspected did he. So many things she wanted to say, but the words would not come. She longed to be able to wrap him up in her arms and hold him. To talk to him and find out all there was to know. But it was futile. So instead she just said, "but what are you doing here?"

His face darkened. Was he thinking the same as her and that secretly they might finish what they had started? She had to force herself to show no emotion, calling into practice some of the techniques Delyth had taught her. He had to realise that there was no future in their relationship. She had hoped to put off this moment to allow more time to imagine a different future. But it was too late now that she was caught up in this crazy plan of her own making. She could only hope and trust that Lady Death would keep her part of the bargain. Otherwise, she really was on a suicide mission.

"I'm here at the King's request," he said, pulling himself taller.

"Why?" It came out a bit abrupt and more like *why you... why a lowly smith*, although she had not meant to sound so harsh. Delyth had told her that sometimes it is the words you don't say that will betray you. She had been far too distracted by the smith's presence.

He flicked his gaze away, scanning the horizon, but not before she had read the hurt in his eyes.

"About what happened before. Outside the stables," she said. His eyes darted back and she recognised the look of boyish hope. "I apologise. It was a mistake. I should not have let it happen and it wasn't fair." A sick sensation stirred in her gut as he turned away again, hiding his expression.

When he turned back to face her again, it was as though a mask had slid over his face. Calm, composed and confident. He smiled at her, no hint of errant emotion. He was good at hiding it, that much she gave him. But as he'd said, he did have a good teacher.

"In that case, I'll do my best to keep out of your way. My lady." At that, he strode away towards the mess, without a backward glance. Demaris expelled a long slow breath and let her shoulders slump. She had to focus now. Focus on getting back to her village before the raiders got there. If the Sarlatians

217

did catch up with the Klagens before they reached Arrontierre, perhaps there was a way she could get close enough to their chief to take her revenge. Those watchkeepers may well earn their keep before the end of the voyage.

In order to avoid the discomfort of having to see Allan again, she returned to her cabin and asked for some stew to be brought to her. So she sat looking out of the starboard porthole, watching the ship pitch in the waves, the only view of a clear blue horizon beckoning them into warmer climes. She thought about her plan. So many things could go wrong. As she spooned the meat into her mouth and chewed, she considered the possible contingencies should the Sarlatians outrun the Klagen. They did, after all, have a fleet of ships that were the envy of the Western Isles. But then, the Klagen were renowned for their ship building skills. Their vessels might be crude, but they withstood a battle better than any on the ocean.

The spices in the food warmed her insides and fuelled her imagination. She wished she could open the porthole and get some air into the cabin. Taking off her woollen gown, she replaced it with a cotton tunic and trews that would give her more freedom of movement and let her skin breathe. She needed to talk to Tavorian and if that meant a bit of climbing, well she was certainly not averse to physical challenges. She tied her auburn curls in a knot on top of her head and left the cabin.

She found Tavorian above the forecastle deck, out on the yardarm untying the sail ties. She climbed up, following the lead of one of the

Sarlatian sailors, stepping gingerly onto the ratlines before finding her feet, then shuffling along the yard to join Tavorian. The sails cracked and rippled in the wind, the sun bore down but she barely felt the heat with the cool sea breeze ruffling her hair and her clothes. It smelt so clean and pure. The sensation of being aloft was intoxicating. She was rocked from side to side like a baby in a crib, but with the pulsing fear of holding on for life. And all around was a vast blue ocean. The Sarlatian fleet was just a series of dots behind them.

"My Lady. Good day to you," Tavorian said, releasing the tie and letting the massive sail drop. Beneath them, the sailors caught and tied the bottom end and she felt the ship shift slightly as the wind caught the sail. "We should do well in this wind. We've outstripped the rest of the navy already and look set to catch the Klagen oar ships before they even make it to the coast."

"Yes. That was what I was worried about," she said.

"And if we do?" Tavorian unsnagged another sail tie that had caught beneath the yardarm. The ship leaned into the wind as the sailors fastened their knots below. She looked down at the crew.

"This lot don't look likely to withstand a full frontal attack from two Klagen raiding ships. The last one didn't fare too well, I heard."

"The plan is to follow but not intercept the raiders. They want to draw them out, then take them by surprise with the rest of the fleet. It is all to do with timing, my Lady."

"That's it then, isn't it?"

219

"My Lady?"

"If they catch the Klagens before they reach the coast, where does that leave me?"

Tavorian gave her a measured look.

"Safe?" he said. "That would be my primary objective. I made a promise to Gilbert. In the meantime, we shall have our fun aboard this Sarlatian tall ship." He gave a cheery wave over the top of the yardarm and Demaris followed his line of vision to see Abendigo doing his acrobatics on the topgallant yard. Good grief. Gilbert had sent her a troop of circus freaks to see her home. What did that say for her mission? Never mind. Let them do what they had to do. She was too busy cooking up a plan of her own to worry about it. All she had to do was to get onto that Klagen ship and close enough to slice the knife across Ullr's throat herself. It would not be hard to keep the watchkeepers otherwise occupied, although she worried about Brutas.

She looked down to see him hauling ropes and tying knots on the forecastle deck. As if on cue, he looked up at her. His brow furrowed. Brutas scrutinised her a little too closely for comfort. He was one she was going to have to watch while the other two indulged in their antics in the rigging.

Chapter Twenty-Seven

So, the Countess did not feel the same way Allan did. Or did she? It hadn't quite chimed true for him, the way she just brushed off that kiss, as though it meant nothing. As though it were some heinous mistake. He knew she had prior commitments. He got that. But she admitted herself that it was all just duty. It seemed to Allan that duty was just a façade to satisfy society's need to impose order on the world. Society's need to provide heirs for an estate that by rights the Countess Del'oro could probably run quite admirably by herself and had probably already being doing so. So why did she feel the need to stay true to expectations?

He said that he would keep out of her way, but he was not prepared to let it rest. What was she doing here, chasing a band of renegade Klagen raiders back to her hometown? It was unfortunate that they had not been dealt with a long time ago. Hark at him now. He was starting to sound like he had some right to a say in foreign relations. Give a boy a little hope, make him feel for one moment like he belongs and see what happens. Perhaps the King was not so random in his decisions after all.

He recalled that King Gereinte had put in place a Citizens' Charter some years ago. He guessed that no such document existed in Arrontierre, ruled as it was by the iron thumb of an emperor. Perhaps that was the Klagen plan; invade, conquer, subjugate – but he did not see how they would manage that with only two ships and a crew of blood-thirsty warriors.

King Gereinte would surely know that. Darien would have the answers. He was close enough to King Gereinte and was around at about the time the Charter was introduced. He would know where they stood with the Klagen.

Allan slipped out of his cabin and crossed to the far side of the forecastle deck. There were two other cabins. One of them would be Darien's and the other… he knocked on the door, waited a few moments before pushing it open. A quick look and he saw a long gown draped over the bunk, woven with sea blue silk and dotted with sapphires sparkling like the sun on the sea. That was definitely not Darien's cabin. He shut the door with a thud, waited outside for a few moments before curiosity overcame his wrongful intrusion and he opened the door and stepped inside.

The cabin was smaller than his and made brighter by the light casting a golden hue across the bunk from a tiny porthole. A view of the light blue horizon was visible through the window with a few distant grey streaks, reminiscent of the storm left behind.

He laid a hand across Demaris' gown, as though trying to absorb the essence of her through the fabric that had lain so close to her skin. The whole cabin was infused with her smell; light and floral like lillies. He breathed in deeply and was about to take his hand away from the gown when he noticed a corner of parchment sticking out from beneath the bodice. He gave it a gentle tug and it fell into his palm. As he unfolded it, his sense of

222

guilt was wiped away when he recognised the script.

He froze. It was his mother's writing. He turned it over. One edge of it had a jagged tear, ripped from a notebook. His notebook. His story. He slumped down on her bunk and started to read. It was an astonishing account of the lead up to tragic events that had thrown the Andolin family into a civil war that had lasted for years until King Gereinte had finally ascended to the throne, as history would tell. He was shocked that the assassin, Lady Death – his mother, had found the audacity to see the contract through to its end.

At the bottom of the page, he re-read the final words:

I knew that as long as I made it to the forest, they would never find me and they would never again see Josselin. That was the deal. The child had to die and his little finger would be sent to Castan's client as proof.

He turned the parchment over, shook it, shook the gown looking for the remainder, but there was no more. *The child had to die.* It implied that she had killed Josselin. He absently rubbed the stub on his little finger with his thumb. For the first time he began to entertain the thought that he might actually be Josselin. That would explain why his mother had written this account and why she had sent him on this journey. Although he was sure she had not envisioned quite what a fix he would manage to get himself into. He could see her in his mind's eye, shaking her head with reproof.

223

It was not just for him that she had sent him on his way and how was she to know that he would not have found this book? Rescued from the ashes of her past. The story was really for the rest of the world. For the Andolin family. So that they understood the truth of what had really happened and why she did it. He knew his mother; she could not have really killed a child. He could see how easy it might have been to kill all those rich miscreants who were destroying the lives of so many innocent people around them. But a baby? An innocent child who reminded her so much of her own beloved son that she had chosen to name him Allan. It had been Delyth's plan all along to send him into the heart of his family once he had come of age. Well, he may have turned sixteen, but he was not so sure he was ready to face what lay ahead, sailing towards a foreign coast to head off a national disaster.

Now he really had to talk to Darien. Try to make him believe he was indeed Josselin. Could the story be believed? But the ending was missing. How sure was he of the correct translation he had read the first time? It did not say what she really did with the baby. His story was incomplete, whatever he or anyone else might believe.

As he stood up, the door swung open and the Countess Del'oro stood on the threshold staring at him, a look of confused surprise on her sun-freckled face. Her eyes shifted from his face to the parchment and her expression clouded.

"What are you doing?" she said, snatching the parchment from him and folding it not once, but twice before stowing it beneath her tunic.

"Is that where you keep your secrets?" he said.

She raised an eyebrow.

"Close to your heart?"

"What do you know about matters of the heart?" she said.

He swallowed the lump in his throat. Her words stung, but they were said without conviction.

"I know what I felt when we kissed. That much, you can't hide from me."

She opened her mouth, about to say something, snapped it shut then just frowned at him.

"So what are you going to do with that?" he said.

"That is not your concern," she said. "You said you would keep away from me. Strange way to keep away by snooping around my cabin."

"I was looking for Darien," he said.

"I don't think you'll find him hiding beneath the bunk."

He gave her a sour look and reluctantly stood to leave. He wanted those pages back, but he was not willing to reveal his story to her. Not yet. She looked like she wanted to say something, but he could not think of any compelling reason to stay, so he opened the cabin door and was just about to leave when she said, "Wait." He turned and looked at her pained expression. "Your mother was concerned about you."

"My mother? When did you see my mother?" He stepped back into the cabin, shut the door and leant against it. There was doubt in her eyes now, as if she had said too much.

"She is helping me. With a personal mission," she said.

So this was the commission. He was sent one way, while his mother interfered on another level. Misdirection; classic Kali. What was Lady Death up to now? Curiosity turned to concern as he had a sudden fear that the Countess might be involved in more than just a trip back home.

"Why did you pick this particular ship to return home? It wouldn't have anything to do with the Sarlatian mission?" he said. She looked away and he noticed little circles of flush on her cheek bones.

"Your mother may be a good teacher," she said, "but I just don't seem to be able to hide anything from you."

He stumbled forward. "Countess... my Lady," he said.

"Oh, stop all of that nonsense," she said.

He swept up her hand and held it in his palm. She felt warm and it felt right.

"I may be just a smith's son, but that doesn't make me any less worthy of a girl's affection." There. See how she liked that. He was rewarded by a deeper red blush on her cheeks. He ran his finger across the back of her hand and she shivered and pulled her hand away.

"Damn you," she said, rubbing her cheeks with a fury.

"Is that your secret, then? This personal mission that my mother is helping you with?"

"You're very familiar all of a sudden," she said.

"You let me kiss you and don't change the subject. My lady."

Her fists clenched at her side and the muscles twitched in her jaw. But, she kept calm when he tried a cheeky smile. "Huh... you are infuriating."

"The mission?"

He could see conflicting emotions running across her face, but she relented and sat down on the bunk with a resigned *harrumph*. Her airs and graces had disappeared and she looked just like a peasant girl in her tunic and trews.

She told him about how she lost her parents, and the perpetual threat to her village from raiders in the north. For many years she had not known where these raiders came from, then a few years past, news had reached her of a wild kingdom in the north of Carentan called Klagenstill and she had vowed that one day, she would take her revenge on the Klagen.

"I hadn't expected to have the fortune to be sent to Carentan for a marriage proposition, only to discover that two Klagen ships were heading to northern Arrontierre." She looked a little sheepish when she mentioned marriage, but her face dropped and her eyes darkened when she talked of the Klagen.

"You can't take on two ship loads of raiders by yourself," he said. What was she thinking? He felt almost sick at the thought of her throwing herself in the path of danger and could not quite believe that his mother had anything at all to do with this ridiculous plan.

"I won't have to. If I can just get close enough to the chief – that is all I want. They say that if the chief falls, the clan falls. I can put an end to all this raiding. For good." She looked up at him with eyes round and innocent.

"All they will do is appoint a new leader, surely?"

"It is the clan chief of chiefs who is on that ship. Ullr. Kill him and the whole barbaric structure falls apart. The only way to replace him is for one of his own people to fight a duel to the death. Assassinate him and they are left without a leader." She folded her arms across her chest like a stubborn child, then smiled, daring him to contradict her logic.

"You don't mean to get on board that ship and assassinate him yourself?"

She did not say a word, but her eyes responded to his question and his heart sank. "You can't. Whatever my mother has taught you won't make up for the years of experience she has." Something just did not add up. Why would his mother send a young woman into such danger? However good a fighter she was, she was no match for the clan chief of chiefs of Klagenstill. "And anyway, how do you know for sure it was the Klagen responsible for your village?" She dropped her head into her hands and rubbed at her forehead and cheeks, as though trying to erase an invisible stain.

"Because," she said, raising her head in defiance and looking him in the eye, "they left behind a few reminders. A legacy of their debauchery. Only they hadn't anticipated that the

228

women of my village were quite as hardy as they are. Or perhaps they didn't really check whether everyone was dead. I have spent the last eight years concocting suitable stories for the children of these raiders, so they didn't feel and weren't treated like outcasts in their home."

"I can't let you do this," he said.

"You can't stop me doing this," she said. "Either help me or keep out of my way. But whatever you decide, I will find a way."

Chapter Twenty-Eight

The ship's bell clanged four times, paused, then clanged four times more in quick succession. Allan and the Countess exchanged a look, then she leapt up and craned her neck out of the porthole. Without waiting for further clarification, he stepped out of the cabin at exact the same time that Darien stepped out of his own cabin next door. Darien glanced at the Countess' door, then gave him a measured look. Allan shrugged.

"I needed to talk to you," he said.

Darien raised his hands. "I can't help you there," he said, nodding at the Countess' door. On the deck above, the bell continued to burst out with short staccato notes in sets of four.

"What does it mean?" Allan said.

"We have probably caught up with the Klagen ships, is my guess," Darien said.

Allan followed him up onto the forecastle deck. Crewmembers were running back and forth. The captain was at the prow of the ship, surrounded by his advisers, navigator and the boatswain. They were looking into the distance with a viewing glass and alternately pointing at maps. The crew had uncovered their ballistas and were busy loading them up with ammunition while the watchkeepers sharpened their swords.

Allan's heart lurched to his throat.

"They mean to attack? Are they mad?" He squinted into the distance over the aft rail, but the remaining Sarlatian army had not even reached the horizon. His first thought went to the Countess and he jerked around, just about to run back to her cabin when Darien placed a restraining hand on his arm.

"Just precautions. We are too far away yet, but in these winds we could be on top of them before we reach shore. The crew need to be prepared."

The boatswain ran across deck and started shouting commands up into the rigging. The sails on the portside were unfurled and the ship started to lean into the wind, slowing its progress through the water and keeping them at a respectful distance from the Klagen ships.

Darien nodded and smiled to himself. "It would be embarrassing, not to mention suicidal if we caught up with them ahead of the navy. What was it you wanted to talk about?"

"I'm concerned about the Countess Del'oro," Allan said. Darien gave him a sidelong glance and raised an eyebrow.

"So I saw."

"No, I mean these raiders. Do they have no obligation under the people's charter? The one King Gereinte introduced after his coronation."

Darien looked taken aback. "You know your history, then. No, they don't. Klagenstill was left to its own devices after the introduction of the charter. It was thought that if we made an example of the raiders, they might eventually behave themselves. In hindsight that was a little optimistic."

"Then, there is no other option, but to chase them down and risk a declaration of war between the Western Isles and Arrontierre?"

"That is why we are fortunate enough to have the Countess on board. We were rather hoping she might act as a mediator between our two nations."

"And me? What use do you have for a lowly blacksmith's son?" Allan lifted his chin a little, daring Darien to challenge his assumptions. Darien just looked at him and shook his head, his lips twitching in a smile.

"Well, if you want to play it like that then we have plenty of work for a travelling smith when the navy disembarks and we take to the road. The Sarlatian fighting force has its needs. If you are as good with horseshoes and arrowheads as you are with swords, we'll be fighting fit by the time we catch up with the Klagen raiders. Look."

Allan followed Darien's line of vision. The wind made the sails shudder and snap, leaning the ship just enough to set it off towards a coastline that crept into view on the horizon. The Countess Del'oro was on deck, leaning against the starboard rail. She looked out towards the Klagen ships, which gradually disappeared from view, heading in a different direction. He couldn't see her face, but her body and stance was tense.

"If we make good time into Taroudant, by the time the rest of the ships catch up with us, we can be ready to ride across to cut them off before they even disembark." Darien looked pleased with himself.

The Primus sailed into the port of Taroudant and the Klagen ships slipped back into the distance. Allan went below decks to gather what meagre belongings he had. His hand hesitated over his mother's notebook, before burying it at the bottom of his bag. Perhaps the final pages were with the Countess, or perhaps she was no wiser than he as to the ending of his story. He wondered if his mother had left it deliberately open to interpretation. After all, his true story had barely begun. If those final words were indeed lost to the world, all that remained was to confront his mother to find out the truth. Although, now that he knew she was involved in the Countess's plans, he was less inclined to trust what she had to say.

As they approached the port, Allan could see Taroudant Castle, looming larger the closer they moved towards the docks. It looked as though it had just leapt out of a children's storybook, with its red and mauve turrets. The castle was built on a promontory that overhung the harbour and created a neat row of caves, hidden by the rocky coast. A smugglers' paradise.

The ship came to a gradual stop and Allan felt the pull and bump of the vessel against its moorings, as men rushed back and forward tying the ropes. He was relieved when he disembarked to see the Countess talking to the harbour master. It gave him more reassurance to see the watchkeepers, hovering in the background. Darien was next to her while she presumably translated his words of negotiation. All the while, the harbour master, a brown-skinned southern man, was staring out to sea beyond the Countess with a worried expression. It wasn't every day that a national fleet of ships descended on a small harbour town.

The Countess negotiated lodgings in the town for them until the Sarlatian ships caught up. The crew slept aboard the Primus and would wait for their back-up to arrive before moving out. She managed to secure enough horses and provisions to supply her own party on their journey across land. Not without ample monetary persuasion from Darien, Allan noted. The southerners might appear willing and friendly on the surface, but they weren't that different from the Sarlatians when it came to striking up a bargain.

The inn was just a short ride from the port; a modest dwelling and Allan was given a room to share with the watchkeepers. The Countess had a small room of her own above the stables, which concerned Allan. Especially when he saw her expression as they told her where she could stay; a flicker of vulnerability, then a steely determination set into her face.

"Are you sure that the Countess will be all right, alone in her room?" he said, as they sat on makeshift pallets with straw-filled mattresses and grubby blankets. Not that they needed much in the way of blankets, as the heat in the room was stifling; no windows, no air vents – it was almost as though they had been given an empty pantry to sleep in. Tavorian had a troubled look on his face. "What are you three really doing here?" Allan said.

Tavorian continued to look dark and distracted, Abendigo looked away at the walls and Brutas cleaned his fingernails with a pocketknife. Allan let the question hang for a moment.

"It wasn't just coincidence that you happened upon me on the Northern Road in Carentan, was it?"

Tavorian looked back at him. "Coincidence, perhaps not entirely. We were sent by Countess Del'oro's sergeant-at-arms, Gilbert Amand. To keep her safe on her return journey."

"I think perhaps the Countess has other ideas," Allan said, wondering how much they really knew about Demaris and her intentions.

"She can be strong minded," Tavorian said.

"But she will comply with Amand's wishes," Abendigo said, turning his attention back to the conversation. Allan thought about the Countess' story and the way in which she described her father's sergeant-at-arms; the man who had saved her life and brought her up. Something didn't quite sit right with him. Why was it so important to bring her safely back when she wasn't given a chaperone to bring her to Carentan in the first place? Tavorian still looked concerned and Allan knew there was something they were not telling him.

He spent a sleepless night, thinking about his last conversation with the Countess.

"Either help me or keep out of my way," she had said. Then he imagined her lying alone above the stables, perhaps in a hayloft with all the sounds, smells and memories of the night her parents died. The more he thought about her, the more he sensed her agitation. He tossed and turned, but could not get comfortable. Eventually, he drifted into an uneasy sleep and woke very early with a sense of panic. It was then he decided that he must help her.

He had no other choice, as he could not bear the thought of never seeing her again.

He threw on some clothes and left the watchkeepers snoring in their sleep. He made his way down to the stables and swung open the door deliberately letting it crash against its frame to warn her of his presence. He half expected the door to the room at the top of the steps to creep open and her face to appear in curiosity, but it remained resolutely shut. The only noise was the soft whickering of the horses in their stables. Perhaps she was asleep. He felt a little ridiculous but forced himself to go up the steps to the door, making stomping noises as he went. His light knock on the door was followed by silence. Then he swung open the door on an empty room. Empty, in fact it looked as though no one had been there at all.

The Countess Demaris Del'oro was gone.

There was a moment's hesitation before the truth hit him, and panic spiked through his body making his nerves buzz. He raced back down the steps and out into the courtyard, rousing the stableboy and promising him an extra coin if he would prepare four horses in double quick time. It took a bit more than the promise of coin to rouse the watchkeepers.

"But… it is your duty to keep her safe. What kind of watchkeepers are you?" he said. Brutas blinked sleepily at Tavorian and Abendigo rolled over and went back to sleep. "Get up, you idiots – she has gone off on her own… we have to help her!"

Tavorian perked up. "We will have to track her carefully," Tavorian reasoned. "If we go haring off after her in the wrong direction, how is that helping anyone?"

"Wouldn't it be better to stay put and wait for the rest of the Sarlatians?" Abendigo said.

Brutas blinked, then squinted at Allan.

"You'll never catch her like that," Allan said.

"What do you know?" Tavorian said. At least he seemed a bit more together than the rest of them.

"I know that she is chasing the Klagen ships. She is more interested in a confrontation with the chief of chiefs than allowing you three to chaperone her back to her estate."

Brutas stopped blinking and Abendigo rolled up to a sitting position, rubbing his eyes.

"Or whatever it is that your man Gilbert Amand has charged you to do."

"Right," Tavorian said, slapping his thighs and standing up. "I presume you need coin for the stableboy and some provisions." He flipped a silver at Allan who snatched it out of the air. He bowed his thanks, then retreated to the inn and the stables.

Within the hour, they were on the road, with provisions hastily procured from the kitchens. Allan belatedly wondered whether he should have left some kind of note for Darien, but then shrugged it off. That would have been another person to spend too long persuading that they needed to go and the Countess was already one night's ride ahead of them. He had to stop her. Could he even stop her? Help her or stay out of her way, she had said. There was only ever one choice.

Chapter Twenty-Nine

From the prow of the second Klagen ship, named the Kraken, Wilhelm watched Ullr roar and shake his fists in the air with triumph as they took a course on towards Arrontierre, leaving in their wake a slew of bloated Sarlatian bodies and the splintered hull of their ship.

"Well," the captain of the Kraken said. "This will piss off my little brother no end."

"Are you hoping for the chance to challenge Ullr when we get to dry land?" Wilhelm said. The captain, brother to Ullr, whose name was Njord, looked at him through his matted grey hair and tutted so all around could hear his disapproval. Wilhelm did not believe it, of course. It was well known that Njord cherished a long-held ambition to usurp his brother's position.

"What are you suggesting? Of course I am. What else was there to do when I heard of this raid? This is what we do. We raid, we fight, we raid again. It is our way." Njord looked satisfied, as though his words explained everything. There were a few grunts of approval from amongst the crowd. "Can't let Ullr have all the fun now can we?"

Wilhelm supposed it might serve as a useful distraction, while he himself sneaked up behind Ullr with his own dagger. It might prove difficult if Njord killed Ullr before Wilhelm had the chance to intervene. That would just replace one bad leader with another. Not much of an improvement.

238

"Actually no," Njord said. "You're going to fight him. And then, I'm going to kill you." A tumultuous cheer of approval surrounded them and the Klagen warriors began to stomp their feet on the wooden deck. Ah. Wilhelm could see how that might complicate his own agenda.

Wilhelm wondered if Ullr had even noticed that he had burned the wrong man, then let the right man first of all help row his ship out into southern waters, then escape unseen to the other side only to wind up on his brother's ship.

"And if I refuse?" Wilhelm looked up into a sea of blood-lusting Klagen faces, laughing at the very thought that he even had a choice.

"Well now. That's not very Klagen of you, is it? See over there?" Njord pointed towards the flurry of activity on the deck of the Bestla. "They are busy preparing your second funeral pyre. This time we'll give you the send-off you deserve. But not before you have done this little favour for us." Njord grinned through blackened teeth and Wilhelm thought about his spear, sinking to the bottom of the ocean along with his dreams and his plans for a better future, a better Klagenstill.

The warriors took up a chant in time with their stomping, surrounding Wilhelm in a circle of dirty boots and scraggy tangled beards. The bones in their hair clacked in time to their Jarvic chant, which loosely translated to mean, 'rape, pillage, rape, raid' over and over. It sickened Wilhelm to the core, but he kept his counsel as they tied him to the nearest yardarm with a rope that cut into his wrists and

239

made his arms burn with the loss of bloodflow to his limbs.

After they finished their Klagen ritual, the crew left Wilhelm to reflect on his future task and went about the business of setting sail after the Bestla, which had already moved some way ahead. With the wind behind them it was easy enough to catch the other ship, but they kept a comfortable distance. It wasn't unheard of for one Klagen ship to turn on another and there was certainly no love lost between Ullr and Njord.

The Bestla's oars were in and the sails unfurled as it was propelled through the water by the wind. Wilhelm squinted into the distance, trying to see the flat boyish figure of Jaanta running up and down the oars, but he could not see her.

Every so often, Wilhelm saw the formidable Ullr rush to the aft rail and wave a fist in aggressive challenge at the Kraken, although it seemed as though it was directed specifically at Wilhelm himself. Hard to tell. Ullr huddled amidst his group of advisers, probably plotting how he was going to kill Njord as well as Wilhelm and everyone in any village in northern Arrontierre who happened to get in the way.

The skies grew a lighter shade of blue and the heat intensified the closer they crept towards the coast. After a while, the crew on both ships started agitating and rushing up and down the decks, pointing to the horizon. Wilhelm craned his neck and was just able to make out a speck in the distance. Gradually, the outline of another ship took shape. A tall ship with many more sails than the

240

Bestla or the Kraken put together. It could be coincidence, but Wilhelm doubted that. There was no nation in all the Western Isles that would let a navy ship be subjected to such an attack by the Klagen and let it lie. He wondered how many more ships were bringing up the rear.

As the day drew to a close and the curtain of night drew itself around the Kraken and its crew, one of the warriors strode past Wilhelm and threw a bucket of dirty water over him. He licked his cracking lips and tried to slake his thirst, but it was not enough. Other crew members, catching on to the idea of a bit of fun started throwing things at Wilhelm; cups of drink, left-over food, then just empty jars and plates. At least during the food and liquid onslaught, he was able to scrounge the odd mouthful of something bland and gooey and the water dripped down his forehead in a steady stream, so all he had to do was lift his head and drink the remnants. Dignity was not a word that existed in Jarvic.

Cold, sore and wet, Wilhelm was too exhausted to let his discomfort stave off sleep. He fell in and out of sleep, disturbed only by the slap of waves on the hull of the ship. Awoken by something tapping his head, he lifted his chin and a seabird squawked and flew off, carrying a morsel of something edible that had been hiding in his hair. Elevated slightly above the deck and hanging like a limp puppet from the yardarm, Wilhelm was in a perfect position to watch as the crews on the Bestla and the Kraken worked in tandem to turn their ships. His relief at the sight of land turned to dismay when he realised they were being diverted away from the fast approaching port to follow the coastline.

The day wore on and somewhere between the coastal port of Taroudant and the northern-most tip of Arrontierre, he lost sight of the tall ship. Wilhelm wondered if it had been following them after all. Perhaps they had been mistaken.

The rigging monkeys climbed up above him, pausing briefly to step on his sunburnt head with little fear of consequential damage. One day, they would make fine Klagen warriors indeed, Wilhelm thought with bitter regret. He heard the rippling sound of an unfurling sail just before it hit him on the back. His imprisonment to the yardarm was complete as the sail was tied and he felt like he was being stretched and pressed against some ancient instrument of torture.

The ship leaned to the left as the wind took hold of the sail and with the combined force of the oarsmen, they ploughed through the water towards the northern coastline and the small promontory that must be their final port of call.

The sun dipped down towards the horizon as evening drew the light behind a curtain and the temperature dropped. It was small comfort that he had been protected from the worst of the sun's rays during the day by the sail. The lack of food and water gnawed away at him and sunburn was the least of his worries.

Wilhelm let his head drop and he fell into an uncomfortable semi-conscious state between sleep and wake; not quite getting the benefit of the sweet pain relief that sleep would bring but enough to dull his senses.

When he came to, the Kraken had anchored a short distance from the Bestla. The port was dark but there was vague movement on shore. The ship swayed in its mooring, seemingly empty and abandoned. Water gently slapped the sides of the hull and the deck was bereft of crew, save for the odd drunken groan from the aft rail on the starboard side.

There was a splosh of water on the deck, then the soft pad of footsteps too light to be a Klagen warrior. Then a moonlit shadow loomed above him with a two-handed sword raised over a head of blonde locks and sturdy shoulders.

That was it then.

He was destined to die on that ship.

His dreams of living to create a better world were about to be cast aside.

"I'm sorry, Arianne. I have let you down. I have let down the memory of you and our girls who were sweet and good and could have forged alliances between the worst of people. I thought I could make this a better place for us all to live; get rid of the pens, the raiding, the suffering. But all I have done is create more suffering." His words were whispered almost to himself and as though Arianne had returned from the grave, he heard a female voice say,

"I don't know who Arianne is or was, but I do gather that you owe her and all of us who have suffered at the hands of Ullr some kind of reckoning. That hour of reckoning has come."

Then the sword came down, the voice grunted and the ropes tying Wilhelm to the yardarm released him with a thump to the wooden deck. For a moment, he just lay there wondering in his delirious state whether he was alive or dead. A pair of rough hands hauled him up by the scruff and he staggered to his feet, blinking bleary-eyed at Jaanta, the oarsmaster of the Bestla, standing in front of him sheathing her sword. "Come on," she said, "before anyone realises you're gone."

They slipped over the edge of the ship and Wilhelm half swam and was half dragged by Jaanta towards the shore. He rolled onto his back and let the water wash over him, wincing as the sting of salt cleaned his wounds.

Chapter Thirty

Allan and the watchkeepers were half a day's ride out of Taroudant following the coastal road before they caught sight of Klagen sails billowing in the wind. At their current speed, they would not catch up with the ships unless they moored up en route to Countess Del'oro's village and estates. That was Allan's worst fear. By his current reckoning, though, the Countess had at least a day or a night's lead on them.

Tavorian rode up beside Allan with Brutas and Abendigo trailing at the rear.

"We will have to stop and rest the horses," he said, "and this coastal road will not be safe come nightfall."

Allan knew that the words made sense, but was overwhelmed by an irrational fear.

"No. We have to catch up with the Countess."

"The horses will not make it beyond the next village if we continue to drive them at this rate," Tavorian said, sounding annoyingly rational. Allan cursed under his breath. He knew the truth of it. "And unless the Countess has a mare sprung from fairy tales, then I suspect she will have to do the same."

So they turned off the coastal road with its sandy track and clusters of pine trees, and headed towards the nearest village. Allan was itching with frustration, not being familiar with either the land or the people. They passed a travelling merchant who they bargained with for a fresh canteen of water and some grain for the horses. Tavorian and Abendigo babbled in their own language while Brutas glared and the merchant cast curious glances at Allan.

The village, which Allan was reliably informed by Abendigo was named Attora, consisted of half a dozen small establishments, an inn with a stable and a rambling market place which was just packing up for the day when they rode into the village square.

The rooms in the inn were all taken, so they negotiated a corner of the stable for a price that included due care of their horses. So there was nothing much else for Allan to do but sit in the public room with the watchkeepers, take a drink of ale and worry about the lack of progress they were making.

It was similar to the kind of inns found in Carentan. It had largely stone exterior walls, only here they were adorned with colourful tapestries of emerald and ruby threads, depicting scenes with heroes and stories of sea fights and castle vistas. The noise was different though and brought his attention back to the moment. The Arrontierre villagers liked to vocalise their mood, as much as their taste in clothing lit up their personalities. The Carentans by comparison seemed positively staid.

There was a minstrel in the corner strumming a lute and joyfully fulfilling requests that fed the wine-induced merriment of the patrons. After a little while, even Brutas was tapping his foot and nodding his head in time with the repetitive refrains. After picking at his pot roast, Allan supped some ale while Tavorian and Abendigo did a little jig in time with the music.

A dark man in a tattered green and red tunic with age-old stains that could have been blood or wine, sat down on the bench. The stench of unwashed hair and latrines wafted under Allan's nose and made that pot roast sit heavily in the bottom of his stomach. The man looked at him through rheumy eyes, leaning to one side as though trying to stop himself from sliding back off the bench. He muttered something unintelligible to Allan, then frowned when he got no response. From the other side of the table, Brutas gabbled some words in his own tongue and the man's eyes widened.

"Oh," he said, "So is eta... etan... enta-"

"Etanese," Allan said. "Yes, I speak Etanese."

The man mumbled something else and Allan looked at Brutas, who shrugged.

"He say... bloody foreigners... or something," Brutas said in broken Langan.

"Charmed I'm sure," Allan said.

"You is welcome," the man said with a hiccough. He downed the remaining ale in his mug and slammed it down on the wooden table. "If you is pay, I tell you secret." He burped.

"Don't take any notice of that man," the innkeep said in Etanese over the din. "He has just returned from a prolonged detainment at the Emperor's pleasure and is spouting nonsense about foreign plots to overthrow the Empire of Arrontierre." He made a shaking motion with his hand to intimate that the man was more than slightly unstable of mind.

247

Still. Allan had nothing better to do with his time than listen to the man rant over a mug of ale, so he flipped a coin to the innkeep, who filled both of their mugs. The man smiled to himself, as he looked into his mug of ale.

"That's worth a special story," he said. Allan glanced at the innkeep who rolled his eyes in response and waited as the man guzzled and burped. "Once 'pon a time in a land far, far away in somewhere called... now, what was it? Caren... something. Anyways, it was a foreign land." He gulped some more ale and slammed down his empty mug with a loud belch. "There was this king of the foreign land who right royally pissed off the Emperor of Arrontierre." The man nodded at his mug and Allan sighed as he tossed another coin to the innkeep. This was going to be an expensive waste of time.

"That is all you are getting from me, my friend," Allan said, "unless you make it worth his while too." Allan nodded at Brutas who bared his teeth in a grin that looked more like a grimace. The man gulped back a mouthful of liquid. He coughed.

"Well now. Let us see. Yes, I do recall there being something of interest for your err... friend. Associate, let's say." This last he said in broken Langan, at which Brutas perked up and leaned forward to listen. The man leant back, and looked as if he was pretending to adjust his seating posture on the bench. Allan immediately thought he was hiding something. "The Emperor once sent a batta... battal... lot of chevaliers to this foreign land like a, what is it called now... kind of a trade delegation.

248

But... it didn't quite work out as planned and they returned, depleted and with no leader. Beat on all sides by the foreign king and his eastern allies."

Allan reached over and took the man's mug away, sliding it across the table top to his side. "Tell us something we don't know. This is common knowledge to anyone who knows their history."

Brutas nodded his approval to Allan and the man looked longingly at his ale mug.

"What you might not know," the man said through slurred Langan, "is that after denying all knowledge of this supposed plot, the Emperor started his own plans on how to bring down this foreign king and his allies, 'cos one thing you don't do is embarrass Arrontierre or its Emperor."

"By bringing the war to Arrontierre?"

"Well... it wouldn't do to disgrace his chev... chevaliers again now, would it?" The man looked away, as though realising that he had probably said too much but was beyond reproach.

"And if it all went wrong again, he could always just blame it on a conspiracy," Allan said. He realised a bit too late what he had said when several people stopped what they were doing, including the innkeep, and gave him a long hard stare. Okay, so there were more people here that understood Etanese than he thought. Lesson learnt. You did not disrespect the Emperor of Arrontierre. In the Western Isles, Allan was used to candid conversation about their rulers and notions of a fair society. Brutas shook his head and muttered a few words, at which the onlookers 'tssked' and went back to their business without further remonstration.

"I still don't see what this has to do with us," Allan said, although he was starting to feel uncomfortable about the Sarlatian forces that were about to dock on southern land, despite the very valid excuse of chasing down two Klagen raiding ships. And now, they were without their principal translator, the Countess, who was galloping off to an uncertain destiny, even as he sat there listening to this unkempt storyteller, an escapee from the Emperor's dungeons.

"Signs of unrest are already upon us," the man said, making a surreptitious play for his ale mug. But Allan just slipped it further out of reach. Tears smarted the corners of the man's eyes and he dribbled a little spittle down his chin.

"What signs?" Allan said.

"Well, I wouldn't want to worry you, kind sir, but beings how you're a foreigner, I would be watching me back if I was you."

Allan raised an eyebrow, then slid the mug a little closer to the man.

"Only the other day," the man said, "I overheard two chevaliers talking about some plot to marry off a local landowner to a foreign dignitary just to incite outrage on her estates. They don't like foreigners around here, you see." Yes, Allan was beginning to see that now. "And there was that woman on horse-back only yesterday," he said. Allan sat forward and pushed the mug of ale back into the man's hands, who scooped it up to his lips and swigged it back and then smacked his lips together with satisfaction.

"Tell me more about this woman," Allan said.

250

"The way she rode, I thought she might be an escapee from the Emperor's dungeons herself, if not for her fine clothes."

Allan was impatient to get back on the road and gallop off after the Countess, but he knew it would be foolish. They had to allow the horses to rest if they didn't want to disable them before they even reached the Countess or her estates. That was supposing she was heading home. So he sat back and watched Tavorian and Abendigo cavort with the locals, singing, dancing and flirting with the only woman in the establishment who although appearing bored by the attention, took it in good humour.

He sat back and closed his eyes for a moment, letting the laughter and the music and the clashing of mugs wash over him. When he opened his eyes, the man was looking at him, cross-eyed. Allan leaned forward.

"Tell me more about the Emperor's plans," he said. When the man just stared at him with no expression, he added, "and I promise not to reveal your identity, such as it is, or your whereabouts." It was enough reassurance any drunk needed, whose desire to have someone listen to him overcame any loyalty to a nation that had left him to rot in an imperial dungeon.

Chapter Thirty-One

Wilhelm was dreaming of forest rainfall and the blasting heat from the hot coals of a roaring campfire. It was the screech of hungry seabirds – not quite belonging in the forest – that drew him back to consciousness. He opened an eye to the realisation that the heat was the blaring southern sun and the drip, drip of rainwater, was in fact Jaanta attempting to clean his wounds. He batted her hands away, grimacing at the sting of salt water.

He lay on a beach in a cove, sheltered by rocks and away from the direct view of the small harbour. In the distance, he could just make out the topsails of the two Klagen ships.

"What now?" he said, voice croaking and his throat constricted by thirst.

"Here," Jaanta said, dripping water from a canteen into his mouth. He sucked and rolled his tongue around his lips, desperate not to spill a drop. It was not enough to slake the thirst he had acquired whilst tied to the yardarm for the last two days.

"Steady on," Jaanta said. "Little and often is the only way to recover. I've bound the worst of your wounds." He looked down at the rags tied to his ankles and wrists, then back at Jaanta.

"You didn't answer my question," he said.

She looked wistful. "Now, we sit, we wait, follow, then choose our moment." So. She had chosen her future too. "There is an army chasing us down."

"From Carentan?"

"Sarlat," she said.

Ah. That made sense. "And when they catch us?"

Jaanta shrugged. "We pick sides. Who are we to stand in the way of justice?"

Wilhelm smiled. It was a plan. Of sorts. But not quite what he originally had in mind. Although the idea of staying put and resting for a while was most appealing to his half-starved, weather-worn body.

He crawled into a small alcove to shade from the sun, whilst Jaanta declared she was going to acquire some food and water for them both. Before she left, she laid something heavy and slim by his side. He reached out and felt the reassuring cold touch of his spear.

"You found it," he said. She looked back over her shoulder and nodded once as though he never had the need to doubt her. "Thank you."

She turned and left, scouting around the outline of the rocks on the shore and keeping as much out of sight as was possible.

It seemed like an age before Jaanta returned, and the sun had long since disappeared beneath the horizon. In Wilhelm's half-starved dehydrated state, he had begun to hallucinate, thinking he was being attacked by native forces. Every so often he rolled onto his knees clutching his spear like an old friend, afraid to use it, afraid not to. Each time, he ended up looking out upon an empty dark beach, nothing but night creatures scuttling about. The waves gently lapped the sand like a giant's tongue and the moon cast a blue hue across the night sky.

He slumped back into the shade of the cove just as Jaanta sprang over the top of a rock, dumping a sack into their hiding place.

"Come morning, they'll be on the move," she said, tossing him a canteen of water and a hunk of bread. "We'll have to follow, otherwise we lose the opportunity and any small advantage we may have." Advantage? He wanted to laugh out loud at that. The only advantage he had at that moment was not being tied to a yardarm. Besides, he was going nowhere until he had emptied that canteen and the contents of the sack.

Jaanta sat and patiently watched while Wilhelm devoured the best part of three loaves of bread, two large hunks of cheese, a side of cooked venison and a long thin sausage of meat that had a tough white rind. It tasted good, salty and meaty, but it was tough on the jaw. He guessed you were probably supposed to slice it but was far too impatient to satisfy the gnawing ache in his stomach to even acknowledge the small skinning knife that Jaanta proffered. Instead she cut one end off and proceeded to slice it into delicate pieces for herself.

They settled down to get as much sleep as possible before morning. It was not particularly restful, but at least the visions had stopped. Come first light, Wilhelm was anxious to get onto the road and finish this.

"Are you sure you want to do this?" Jaanta said. "Once we start, there will be no going back."

There was no going back for Wilhelm either way. "I am. Are you?"

She nodded.

"Right. Let's go," he said, grabbing his spear.

Jaanta looked him up and down. "I got you these," she said, chucking a handful of clothes at him. The garments fell into a heap at his feet. He looked down at his tattered undershirt and trousers, gestured for Jaanta to turn around and when she stood there with hands on hips, he glared at her. "It's nothing I haven't seen before. I've been oarsmaster on various ships for over ten years. Think I've never seen a naked Klagen?"

Wilhelm felt a flush rise up his neck. "I'm not a Klagen. Well, not quite."

"Far as I'm concerned, a Klagen is a Klagen is a Klagen," she said turning her back. He ripped off the remaining shreds of his clothes and pulled on the fresh trousers and jerkin that she had found for him. The fit was a bit tight, but it would do. It gave him enough freedom of movement to run or fight. And then they were on the move, striding side by side across the sandy beach and onto the coastal road, following the tracks of the Klagen. The raiders were some hours ahead of them. If they kept up their current pace, they would catch them just before they made it to the next village, before returning with their bounty to the well-concealed ships. He wondered how many times before they had done this. And if they timed it just right, they could be away before the Sarlatian ships following them had even docked and been granted permission to disembark.

As the sun climbed up to its zenith, they stopped to gain their breath and take some of their precious supply of water. Squatting in the shade of a dune, Wilhelm handed the canteen to Jaanta and wiped a sheen of sweat from his brow.

"I don't suppose you have a plan," he said. Jaanta took a mouthful and with puffed cheeks, shook her head, then swallowed.

"Somehow I thought you maybe knew what you were doing," she said.

"I do. Kill Ullr, take over the Klagen as his successor and put an end to all this."

"As easy as that," she said.

"I just need to get close enough to…" he caught a flicker of movement in his peripheral vision.

"What is it?"

He placed a firm hand on Jaanta's arm and flicked his eyes to the left from where he saw the movement. Her eyes followed his movement, then in one swift motion, she dove on top of a row of shrubs bordering a large pine tree. There was a loud *oomff*, then she rolled out from the undergrowth, arms and legs wrestling with a large Klagen warrior. Damn. They had sent a scouting party back, just in case their errant oarsmaster and her bounty showed up. So they were expecting them to follow. Unusual for Ullr to actually think before he moved out.

Wilhelm sensed movement behind him and gripped his spear. He lowered his head, keeping his gaze down where his peripheral vision could detect movement behind him. He kept still, breath slow, heart beating out a steady rhythm, supressing the adrenaline pumping through his veins. It all seemed to happen so slowly for him, as though he could see and move one step ahead of everyone else. He saw the bulk of the warrior approach from behind, he waited until the moment before the warrior struck, then flickered into action, thrusting his spear in a straight line behind him.

The impact sung down the length of his spear as he slid it free. It had not lost any of its edge, despite being neglected on this journey. Wilhelm stood and turned, watching the look of disbelief on the Klagen's ugly, hairy face, as he slumped to the ground blood pouring from his stomach wound. The sand around him turned a rusty brown.

He turned to help Jaanta, just as she head-butted her opponent. Then with a swift upward kick with her instep, she flipped him onto his front and twisted his arm at an impossible angle. Wilhelm heard an audible 'pop' and the man started to scream. Impressive upper body strength, he thought, then his attention was distracted as three more warriors rushed him at full pelt.

The first, he picked off easily with a spear thrust to the throat. That Klagen joined his friend on the ground, hands clawing his throat trying to hold himself together. Before he had a chance to reassess, the other two were upon him. He could only keep the spear close to his body and use it to block the blows that now rained down on him from their war hammers.

They were determined, he would give them that. Then again, who wouldn't be when returning to Ullr in defeat was like writing your own death sentence? He ducked as a mighty blow missed his head by inches, then thrust a fist up into the body. The Klagen doubled over, Wilhelm only just withdrawing in time without being dragged to the ground with him. He pulled back just as the other one glanced a blow off Wilhelm's arm, temporarily deadening all feeling.

Never let it be said that Wilhelm of the Forest could not manage with only one arm; one arm and two perfectly good legs. He stomped on the first warrior, still supine on the ground, and swung the spear around just missing the second man. The man sailed past to join his comrade, but sprang back up while the other nursed a sore head. Why didn't these bastards just die?

Wilhelm dodged back, twirling his spear to keep the distance, not allowing the Klagen to close the space between them. They were stupid, but not stupid enough to run onto a waiting spear. Out of the corner of his eye, he could see Jaanta engaged in some fancy locks and holds, spraying sand all around her. The screaming Klagen beneath her body stopped screaming and lay still.

He maintained a steady circling of his spear as his opponent fruitlessly looked for an opening. All the while, Wilhelm was aware of the fight going on to the side of him. Jaanta lifted her weight ever so slightly and the body beneath her lay still. Do not let him fool you, woman, he thought keeping his eyes trained on his opponent, but his mouth shut. These men would use any distraction to their advantage and sometimes it didn't matter how many joints you popped and bones you broke, they kept on going. Just as she shifted her body clear of her opponent, the Klagen she thought dead swung a meaty fist, which caught her just below the ribcage. Jaanta doubled over and the man whipped out a hunting knife. Wilhelm twisted into a low stance and launched his spear, then turned just as his opponent barrelled into him. They tumbled to the ground in a fountain spray of sand and he just caught sight of Jaanta's opponent with a spear sticking out of his chest, as Jaanta prised the knife from her opponent's hand and flicked it in Wilhelm's direction.

The Klagen on top of Wilhelm lifted his head in surprise as the knife thudded into his back. His eyes rolled up and back, then a searing pain spread from Wilhelm's upper arm, across his shoulder and down into his chest, as the hulking inert form of the Klagen warrior pinned him to the ground. A black fog seeped around the edges of his vision and all that food he had scoffed before coming on this journey threatened to come back up. So this was it. End of the road. Again. At least Jaanta was alive, for now. There was small comfort in knowing that in the end.

Then the massive bulk that was weighing him down shifted. Surely the Klagen could not be still alive? Wilhelm was surely finished now. That is if he didn't bleed out before the man could do his worst. The body rolled off and Wilhelm turned his head to look at the knife sticking out of the back of the dead man's neck. Jaanta's face appeared above him.

"Are you going to lie there all day?"

He took a long slow swallow of relief.

"I think I've broken my arm," he said.

A shadow loomed behind Jaanta, the grisly face of a half-dead, half-crazed Klagen staggering towards them both swinging an axe. Jaanta hadn't seen him, hadn't anticipated any of them were still alive and was about to turn right into the path of his axe. His body roared in pain, as Wilhelm reached for the knife, plucking it from his opponent's neck just as the Klagen screamed. Jaanta turned, ducked, then he heard another scream, this time higher in pitch, then the sound like a scythe cutting grass whistled on the wind and the Klagen's snarl froze on his lips. His head tilted to one side as though in quiet contemplation, then slid from his shoulders. A young red haired woman looked at Wilhelm with murder in her eyes, from behind the hilt of a supremely sharp sword.

Chapter Thirty-Two

A myriad of thoughts ran through Demaris' mind as she raced away from Taroudant in the fading light of the evening. Would Allan ever forgive her for running out on him? At least this way, she had a head start should he mistakenly decide to follow. Besides, she knew these roads so well that she could ride throughout the night with a blindfold and still find the short cuts. Someone less familiar with the terrain would be slowed by the unpredictability of the ground and the lie of the land. She rode through the town of Attora and a few curtains at the windows twitched when she galloped as if a demon were in pursuit of her.

She estimated that the Klagen would likely find a secluded cove in which to disembark on their final leg towards Rotonde. Somewhere like Trethla, which was only a few hours ride away from Attora. If she kept up the pace, she could arrive ahead of them, take a short rest, then wait for an opportune moment. The only thing she had on her side was the element of surprise. That and her beautiful Jael sword.

She stopped just outside of Trethla and sure enough, before the sun sunk below the horizon the Klagen ships sailed into the small port. Port was rather too grand a word to describe Trethla. It was more like a few mismatched shacks in a rocky cove with a building that looked like an outhouse, which laughingly described itself as the Fisherman's Inn. She knew the owner, Messr de Queval, who would likely be scarpering to the hills with as much of his hidden wealth as possible. She watched the crew disembark.

Demaris tied her horse to a tree with enough slack to allow it to graze on the sporadic tufts of grass and drink from a nearby rock pool. She took a catnap, hugging her sword to her chest and keeping an ear open for any movement around her. It wasn't restful sleep, but enough to keep her going for a while and long enough to allow the Klagen to moor their ships, disembark and settle down for the night. She did not dare sleep longer knowing that they would be up and out by dawn, hoping to catch the villagers of Rotonde unawares. Early morning raids were a pattern that had followed the length of this part of coastal Arrontierre.

Once, she had petitioned the Emperor for help and his response had been so reassuring, affirming that he would put resources in place to protect the northern villages with chevaliers at their disposal. She had held out with hope for two more years before she realised that he had no intention of helping the villages on her estate. That was when she had decided to take matters into her own hands.

After a quick meal of dried salt-beef and cheese, Demaris slipped through the night with the sand softening the sound of her movement. She took the sword with her, leaving the gaudy scabbard in her saddlebags. A quick peek into the outhouse revealed a few snoring lumps, illuminated by the moon through an open window. She followed the snores, hiding in the shadows of the room. There was a large Klagen warrior sitting in an upright position. The watch, perhaps. Although on closer inspection his head lolled to one side and he dribbled saliva down his beard, so slipping past him was no problem. She guessed that most of the crew had slept on the ships, which suited her purposes just fine. But where was the Chief? Should she just guess which lump was Ullr? Was he the largest one in the corner that snored the loudest? If she stabbed that one, what if the rest of them woke up and it wasn't Ullr? There was no way she could take on all of them at once. Her success hung on finding the right Klagen, killing him swiftly to retreat and watch the rest of them descend into disarray. Getting captured, raped and murdered was not part of the plan.

She heard a faint scratching noise near the window and retreated into the shadows to watch and wait. A figure dropped through the window and landed soundlessly on all fours. Another Klagen. What was another one doing sneaking around their own camp? But then the figure straightened to his... no, her full height - too slight for a Klagen. She had long blonde rat tails, threaded with shells which she held still as she moved from one sleeping Klagen to another and with practised sleight of hand, started retrieving items from the sleeping warriors. A canteen of water here, a handful of coin there, some wrapped up foodstuffs, some rolled up clothes; not enough to raise an alarm in the morning, but sufficient for her apparent needs. She stuffed them all into a backpack and took a final look around the room. Her eyes rested for a moment on the corner where Demaris hid and for a brief moment it seemed as though she were smiling at her. Then she climbed back out of the window with the ease of someone who spent a lot of time on the move.

Demaris sat still for what seemed like hours before she crept out of the corner and peered at the sleeping warriors. The one nearest to her snorted, then appeared to stop breathing. Was he awake, listening to the presence in the room and waiting for a moment to leap up and rip the head from her shoulders? Then he let wind with a *purrpt,* loud enough to wake the heaviest of sleepers. Demaris winced and waited for the whole room to explode into action. She wrinkled her nose at the fetid smell of undigested meat. Then the man resumed snoring. The room remained silent and she let out a long slow breath.

This was not the time to go around stabbing sleeping Klagen in the hope that she might find the Chief. But her curiosity was piqued by the female thief. She retraced her steps out into the summer chill of the Arrontierre night. She took the long way back to her horse so she could study the tracks in the sand. They disappeared as soon as she came close to the water's edge where the tide had washed the beach clean. She returned to her horse with no choice but to hunker down for the rest of the night and continue her pursuit in the morning.

Before the dawn broke, the Klagen warriors were up and moving on. Demaris left her horse at the bottom of a tall pine and shimmied up, using knotholes and branch stubs as hand and foot holds. She peered up above the canopy to watch the raiding party strike out towards Rotonde. They took the more direct route along the coastal road, which although more difficult terrain to navigate, would bring them out at the northern end of the town. Perfect for sneaking up on unsuspecting quarry. Her cheeks flushed beetroot and her body quivered with outrage. No one would have chosen that route if they didn't know where they were heading. Most self-respecting citizens would have taken the more stable road which lead to the southern end of Rotonde.

She was just about to shimmy back down to her horse when she caught a flicker of movement on the beach. They had left one of their own behind. A Klagen with a much leaner physique was changing his clothes. A bit strange. He must have known he had missed the rest of his party's departure and why was he changing his clothes on the beach? And then Demaris saw her. The female thief, standing with her back to the man. Okay, so now she got it. Some people had other priorities. But then, why was she standing with her back to him? He looked ragged and injured, like he had already been through a raid and come out the other end, perhaps not as favourably as one might expect for a Klagen warrior. Then the two of them picked up their sacks and starting trotting out, presumably to catch up with the raiding party, although she doubted they would catch up with Ullr and his men, judging from the way the man was limping along using his spear as a running aid.

Demaris, on the other hand, had the advantage of her horse. She climbed back down and led her horse to a nearby stream. Rummaging through her

265

saddlebags, she pulled out some apples and shared a meagre meal with the mare, before continuing with the pursuit. Careful to maintain a distance so as not to alert them to her presence, she turned onto the coastal road. She thought about Allan. If he had decided to follow her, she calculated he would be only a couple of hours behind now, even accounting for a night's rest. Oh well. She had no control over what he would do. He would either help her or keep out of her way. Beyond reason, she hoped he had not chosen the latter.

She didn't rate the chances of the two Klagen misfits, given the apparent injuries of the man. But it was when she saw a group of five Klagen warriors steal away into the undergrowth in an attempt to cut them off, that her curiosity was piqued. She dismounted and tied her horse to the nearest tree before continuing on foot, her sword held in a guard position in front of her. She was careful to keep a distance. Besides which, the five warriors looked far too intent on their quarry to be concerned about any additional distractions. It turned out, she need not have worried.

As she crouched behind a crop of bushes, she watched the first warrior go in for a wrestling match with the woman. Her impressive ground fighting gave her the advantage despite being of smaller frame and stature. Demaris winced as she saw the woman headbutt her opponent before twisting and breaking his arm. After such a poor display of combat from their associate, the other four took no time in going for the injured Klagen with the spear. That was it, then. Four on one and injured to boot, he didn't stand a chance. It looked as though the man was immobile one moment, then the next he sprung into life, whipping that spear around with devastating alacrity. Demaris slowly stood, confident now that no one would be paying the slightest bit of attention to her. She backed away, keeping her eyes trained on the fight and the bushes around her. Klagen on Klagen; what was going on?

Beyond all belief, the injured spear-man pulled the fight back and then the one remaining warrior was on top of the man and he looked to be squashed beneath that hefty body, then the woman threw a knife to the back of the big man's head and he slumped to one side. The advantage switched again. Demaris didn't fancy her chances with those two, so she kept sneaking back, hoping to make it to her horse before they noticed her skulking about in the bushes.

But then, just when she thought they had conveniently dispatched the last Klagen, one of them appeared to rise up from the dead, swinging an axe. Gods, what did it take to kill one of these warriors? Something switched in her brain at that point. All the memories came rushing back; the screaming, the butchering, the total lack of mercy for any innocent being, it all came crashing down on her in a wave of anger. Demaris ran into the clearing and with a high pitched battle cry and a well-executed slice to the Klagen's head, she ran her Jael sword through his neck. The Klagen stopped mid-swing and his head slid neatly from his shoulders and his body slumped to the ground. A spray of blood splattered across her face and down her front.

She held her sword in front of her and stared into the eyes of the spear-man, his expression one of total surprise.

Chapter Thirty-Three

Allan and the watchkeepers rode out of the small village of Attora, impatient to close the gap between them and the Countess.

"We ride at a canter," Allan said, picking up the pace. Abendigo glanced at Brutas, who shrugged and shot Tavorian a knowing look. They rode the horses at a canter, exchanging barely a word between them, before Tavorian called them to a halt.

"We cannot keep up this pace without taking a break," he said dismounting and tethering his horse to a tree. Brutas and Abendigo followed suit and Allan found he had no alternative but to acquiesce, since he would find it impossible to locate the Countess and her estates on his own. Despite the overnight rest, hearty evening meal and a hasty breakfast of porridge oats, the anxiety returned to gnaw at his insides with renewed vigour.

"I don't understand why you are not more concerned about the Countess," he said, slumping down beside the watchkeepers and accepting a canteen of water and a small piece of honey cake. "After all, weren't you sent to Carentan to protect her?"

"Ostensibly, yes," Tavorian said.

"But she has never been in any real danger," Abendigo said around a mouthful of cake. He then mumbled and coughed, as though choking, although whether it was the honey cake or his words on which he choked, Allan was not too sure.

"Real danger? What do you call those barbarians at sea that just blasted a Sarlatian ship to smithereens along with most of its crew?" The watchkeepers looked blankly back at him.

"Our chevaliers make them looked like oversized bears," Abendigo said. Allan wasn't convinced that he would even want to fight an oversized bear, much less two shiploads of them.

"You're sure the Countess will have returned to her estates?" Allan said.

"Of course. Where else would she go?" Tavorian said.

Allan thought back to the conversation he had had with Demaris on board the Sarlatian tall ship and her mission to assassinate the Klagen chief of chiefs.

"I think we should get going," he said. "At best, we'll catch up with her before she catches up with the Klagen, at worst we might be there in time to pick up the pieces."

Tavorian frowned. "Young man, don't be such a pessimist. What makes you think the Klagen mean harm to our beautiful Countess?"

"It wasn't the Countess I was thinking about," he muttered half to himself. The watchkeepers looked at one another as if to say *he's foreign, what more can you expect?* then they reluctantly got up to prepare for the last leg of their journey. Allan was almost beyond hope that they might now catch up with Demaris.

They rode at a steady pace, so many conflicting thoughts worrying around the edges of Allan's mind. After riding hard for a short while, they dropped back to a trot and he edged his horse up to ride between Tavorian and Abendigo. Brutas still brought up the rear.

"Tell me about this fellow who works for the Countess, the one who suggested the marriage."

"Oh, you mean Captain Amand?" Tavorian said with careful enunciation.

"Yes, that one."

"He is a man who cares very dearly for his master's charge."

"Master's charge?"

"The Count's daughter, Countess Demaris Del'oro." Tavorian frowned at him.

"But the Count is dead. Didn't he die when she was young?"

"In a raid on their village, yes. Along with his lady wife, the former Countess Del'oro."

"In which case, correct me if I'm wrong, the Countess Demaris Del'oro is his successor and current owner of the lands?" Allan found this southern attitude towards women and their rights quite baffling, having been brought up under the Citizen's Charter of the Western Isles.

"Technically yes," Abendigo said. "However, under southern rights, a female can only inherit when she comes of age. Demaris Del'oro is just sixteen."

"In Carentan, a young person comes of age at sixteen. Our own king ascended to the throne at seventeen."

"A fact that did not go unnoticed in these parts," Tavorian said.

"Enough to wage a war?"

"Now, see here. That little historical faux pas was instigated by a renegade chevalier who was renounced by the Emperor."

"How convenient," Allan said, thinking back to the old drunk's story in the inn. "How many times can an emperor wage war and deny it before his country finds a new emperor?"

The watchkeepers looked warily at one another. "That's not how it works here," Tavorian said. "You are young and inexperienced. You'll learn."

Allan swallowed his indignation. "That aside, you haven't told me much about this Captain Amand. Why would he want to marry the Countess to some foreign lord?"

"To secure her holdings. A woman's ability to hold onto land in Arrontierre is routinely brought into question," Tavorian said.

"Have you seen the Countess fight?" he said.

"Well... not exactly. We only met her recently in Carentan," Abendigo said, looking sheepish. Allan kept his counsel. Lord, but these men were in for a shock if they did manage to catch up with Demaris. What was it that they were not telling him?

"What kind of agreement was made?"

Tavorian and Abendigo looked at each other, then avoided Allan's glare. Tavorian whistled under his breath and Abendigo pulled his hat a little further down on his forehead. Frustrated Allan looked over his shoulder at Brutas who stared back at him with an uncharacteristic frown. Oh well. He wasn't so young and inexperienced that he couldn't smell a rotten corpse of a lie.

272

They rode on for a good few hours, before the coastal track they followed narrowed and Tavorian put up a hand to still the party. He dismounted and looked carefully at the ground, tracing his finger along an arc in the sand.

"She came this way," he said after a while. Allan was about to dig his heels into his mare when Tavorian took his reins. "We move carefully. Don't forget, my troubled young smith, there is a very good chance that we are not the only ones who have caught up with the Countess."

They skirted the edge of the next village to avoid unnecessary encounters with the locals. As they turned on the track towards Demaris's home town of Rotonde, Allan saw the tips of the masts of two ships, moored just off the coast, peering through the pine trees. His fingers itched to snap the reins on his horse and dig his heels in for speed. As though anticipating his reaction, Tavorian raised a hand and they plodded on. The track became sandier and less defined as it veered towards the coast and the horses' hooves slipped and sank at regular intervals slowing their progress to the point that Allan thought it might be better to get off and walk.

"It won't be like this all the way," Tavorian said, as Allan's horse struggled to gain purchase on the ground. "In fact, just around this bend," his voice trailed off as they walked their horses into the scene of an abandoned bloody battle. It was the colour of the sand Allan noticed first. Stained to a rusty red and congealed in clusters, looking like someone had just had a fight with a redcurrant bush.

Then, in a small copse of young pines, they saw the bodies. Five large bundles of hair and fur that could indeed almost be mistaken for brown bears. These monsters had been quite thoroughly dealt with, their throats neatly speared and left to bleed out and gather flies in the burning heat of the day. There was no way the Countess had managed this alone, even with her Jael sword.

"You don't think," Abendigo said, looking rather pale and staring at the pile of Klagen warriors.

"I think she is no longer alone," Tavorian said. Allan hoped it were true and that she had met with an ally along the way. Then again, if there were people with her capable of this, what would they do with the Countess when they discovered the rich treasure of her estates? The thought did nothing to reassure him.

"Search them," Tavorian said. "Take anything of use, including some furs. We may need them if we end up having to sleep outside tonight." They dismounted and allowed the horses to graze.

Brutas systematically ripped the furs off their backs and gave the dead a cursory search. He found a few knives and Allan watched as he slipped them into his saddlebags, dropping the bodies where he found them. One of the knives was big enough to serve as a small sword for someone of Allan's stature.

"Just in case," Allan said in Langan, nodding at the knife, as Brutas tried unsuccessfully to hide it in his bags. "Besides, it won't fit in there and I have a belt where it will fit just fine." Brutas looked to

Tavorian, who held Allan's gaze for a moment before nodding at Brutas. It didn't bode well if their local guide was spooked enough to agree to giving a weapon to a foreigner. Allan took it and slipped it into his belt hook before Tavorian changed his mind.

Abendigo scouted ahead, coming back to report that there were at least three sets of different footprints and the hooves of one horse, imprinted in the path ahead. Looking up at the sun, then pulling out his shadow clock, he calculated that whoever made those prints could be as little as an hour ahead.

They headed out and pushed the horses as hard as they dared without forcing lameness upon them. Just one mile out from the town of Rotonde, they trotted through a dense patch of sandy pines and into a clearing that was out of sight of any travellers, thinking it a good place to rest before exploring their options. As they huddled in the centre of the copse and dismounted, Allan felt exposed, as though being watched by something in the trees. He twisted around, scanning the undergrowth and saw a flicker of movement and then a figure blurred out of the trees and ran at them full pelt. He pulled out the Klagen knife and held it in front of him like a poor man's long sword. Steel from a far superior weapon clashed with his blade and sent shimmers of pain up his arm. The look of surprise on his opponent's face did not compensate for the fury of blows that rained down on him as he dodged and weaved using his speed and agility as his only defence.

The horses scattered to the edges of the copse and in his peripheral vision, he saw the watchkeepers engaged in combat with a mismatch of assailants. Allan's opponent was getting frustrated every time he swung his sword only to slice at thin air, until he started to anticipate Allan's movement. This didn't work out too well for him either, when Allan noted the faint tells in his sword arm that showed him where the cut was likely to fall. The more frustrated his opponent became, the easier it was for Allan to pick him apart. A quick dodge and a weave brought Allan on the inside of a killing thrust, which he met with his own counter. The little knife-sword sunk deep into the man's stomach, resulting in a blossom of blood as the man sank to his knees.

When he turned to help the watchkeepers, he saw a scattering of bodies, then the trees around them burst into an array of ruby, green and opal tunics as an army of chevaliers erupted from beneath the sandy ground. One of them stepped forward and started bellowing something in Langan, then the watchkeepers stopped and their opponents fell back. Tavorian placed his bloody sword on the ground and held his hands aloft, Abendigo and Brutas following suit. Allan kept a tight grip on his weapon until Tavorian turned to him and spoke in Etanese.

"Yield, my Carentan friend. Yield. These are the emperor's troops."

Chapter Thirty-Four

Demaris stood still and watched the startled Klagen spear-man, ready to anticipate his next move. When finally he did move, it was slow and measured. Her breath caught in ragged gasps and her hair was plastered to her forehead by the splatter of blood from the dead man's head. Gods but she had never anticipated how easily her sword would slice through bone and sinew. She held the sword in front of her, at an angle that would facilitate a quick cut to the throat if the man moved too quickly. She thought he sensed this too, by the worried look in his eye. She could never trust a Klagen, whoever he was and whatever his motivation. She took long slow breaths, in and out, trying to still her thumping heart. Then she remembered the woman. Where was the woman?

"We need to move quickly if you want to catch them before they decimate your village," the woman said, moving behind the spear-man so that she was in full view. She ignored Demaris and continued to bind the man's arm while he winced in pain. Demaris lowered her sword, keeping it drawn and ready. The woman seemed not to see her as a threat. The man cast a confused glance at the woman and it was only then she realised that the Klagen woman had spoken in perfect Etanese. The man uttered a few garbled and guttural sounding words. The woman shrugged. "You learn a lot when you sail across the lands, raiding and taking captives from many different isles."

"What do you know about Rotonde?" Demaris said.

"I know that you have a massive problem in the form of a Klagen raiding party about to descend upon it," the woman said. Demaris thought about this for a moment. Were these two a threat to the Chief, or just opportunist renegades? It was a gamble.

"Will you help me?" Demaris said.

The woman did not look up, but continued to set and bind the man's arm with strips of leather and fur from a dead Klagen's jerkin. They had given her no good reason to trust them, other than sharing a common enemy. Perhaps that was enough.

"When the time comes, it must be Wilhelm who kills the Chief," the woman said. Her tone was firm, uncompromising. Wilhelm. That was a strong Klagen name. For many years, Demaris had dreamed of looking the Klagen chief in the eye and watching his life drain away. "People always believe that vengeance is sweet. But it rarely ever is. It won't bring back the dead. And it doesn't make you feel any better, believe me."

"How do you know what I want and what I feel?" Demaris said. They might be useful, but she could certainly go on without them if needs be. The woman looked up, caught her eye and Demaris gasped in recognition; indeed – they had met before.

"I can read it in your eyes, my girl. My name is Jaanta." She proffered a hand and they shook, the Klagen way, forearm to forearm. The spear-man, Wilhelm, looked on in slight bewilderment, then

278

jumped to his feet, holding his spear with his good arm.

Demaris sheathed her sword and marched off into the undergrowth. "I know a shortcut," she said without looking over her shoulder to see if they were following.

Letting her horse loose, Demaris led the Klagen misfits on foot through the woods, keeping away from the coastal track. They slipped into the village from the northern end, keeping well out of sight and crouched behind a large wooden shack that was normally used to pen animals. On the other side of the yard, Demaris' pulse quicked at the sight of the new barn. It had been rebuilt after the fire years ago, but never ceased to elicit a flutter of nerves in her stomach.

The village seemed quiet, empty. Had they already been given a warning? Had the raiders been and gone? No, impossible. They could not have reached the main entrance before Demaris without the advantage of her knowledge of the paths. Then she heard a low moan from inside the wooden pen. Jaanta looked around at her, raising an eyebrow in question and Demaris beckoned them to follow, lifted the locking bar and slipped into the pen.

The walls were lined with grim looking figures; about eight girls and boys in grubby tattered clothing, looking as though they had been abandoned with no access to food or water. She noted the look of shock on Wilhelm and Jaanta's faces as they registered the look of the children. Strangely large for southern offspring, with thick full foreheads and curly tangled hair, hands and feet too big for their growing bodies. Half southern, half Klagen. A legacy of the raids that had killed her parents.

One of the figures launched itself at Demaris, knocking her to the floor in a bear hug. In a flash Wilhelm drew his spear and was about to launch it when Jaanta stayed his hand.

"Gods, how we have missed you," the child cried and was surrounded by the rest, all hugging each other and pushing to get a look at Demaris.

Then Demaris was crying, her throat constricted and unable to speak as she hugged them all and tried to wipe their tears but only succeeded in smearing the dirt across their faces in grubby finger trails.

"Where have you been?" they cried, multiple voices tumbling over each other.

"Away, but I'm back now. Don't worry. Somebody tell me what is going on? Greta, Vicktor?" A girl and a boy stepped forward and tumbled into her arms. Greta looked a bit like Jaanta, but without the sinewy muscles and the seashells in her hair. Vicktor could have passed for a young version of Wilhelm, albeit with a southern coloured nut-brown skin.

"They put us in here two days ago," Greta said.

"They, who? Where's Gilbert?"

"I want my mum," Greta sobbed. It was far worse than she thought. How had the Klagen managed to get ahead of them?

"It was Gilbert who put us in here," Vicktor said, "and he sent the others away."

Wait. That was not possible. Why would he do that? "What about the bad men?"

The children looked confused. "What bad men?" Greta said, wiping a sleeve across her snotty nose. The pieces of the puzzle locked into place. Gilbert had been her world; always there for her after her parents had been killed. She looked to Jaanta.

"Come on," Jaanta said. "We need to get moving. Tell the children to stay here and hide."

"I can't believe Gilbert would betray me. Why has he put the children in here?"

Jaanta looked at her with impatience. "Bait?"

"But what does he stand to gain?"

"Take a good look at your estates, Countess," Jaanta said.

Demaris realised too late how she had been played. "I can't leave them here," she said.

"We can't take them with us. They will be safer here, as long as we move now and put an end to this."

Demaris knew that what Jaanta proposed made the most sense, but the children wailed louder than ever and she had to prise their fingers from around her arms and legs, promising to return quickly if they kept quiet and remained hidden. She tried not to look at them as they left the pen and slipped the locking bar back into place behind them.

They made it as far as the village square before the perimeter of the village boiled over with Klagen warriors. Demaris and Jaanta drew their swords and took down two warriors ahead of the pack, while Wilhelm kept another at bay, flicking his spear out

281

and back as a rabble of warriors fell at his feet, clawing their sides and throats with the stab wounds.

There were many still who flew past their poor excuse for a front line, rushing into houses, extracting screaming people, hacking doors to splinters with their axes and bellowing like bellicose giants with all the strategy of a group of wild boar on the rampage.

The Klagen spread out through the empty village, finding only the old and the very young which enraged them even more. Demaris' sword cut through flesh with disturbing ease, but she had no time to feel sick at the thought of what she was doing. The sweat dripped into her eyes, making them sting and temporarily blurring her vision.

Then fires sprang up across the square. First a house in the middle of a row over the other side of the village, then one of the hay lofts and before long a set of little smoking pyres were spewing out smoke and noxious fumes. The sword seemed weightless in her hands and the thrust and parry of her technique gained a rhythm of its own, as though the sword was moulding itself to her will.

Jaanta and Wilhelm held their own, weaving in and out of opponents, cutting and thrusting and spearing with alarming skill. How the spear-man managed to keep the warriors at bay with only one arm, was the stuff of which legends were born. But the raiders kept coming and they kept slipping through and Demaris wondered if their contribution was just a pin-prick in the side of the Klagen party, like the buzzing of a fly in your ear.

Her body flagged and her nose and throat constricted with the acrid smoke, just as her eyes watered and her vision faltered. She was caught off-guard as an ugly brute with a short stubby nose popped up and sliced across her left guard, cutting a long strip of flesh from her upper arm to her elbow. Her sleeve blossomed in red blood and it took a moment before the sting of the blow registered in her mind. But she could not stop and let it get to her. She would continue to fight if her arm were hanging off. She still had her right arm and her sword still moved of its own volition despite the savage pain running down her left side.

A distant bell clanged and clanged like the day her parents had been buried and the entire estate had mourned their dead. Although she registered the sound, it seemed like a world away. She ran her sword through the snub-nosed Klagen and watched him drop to the ground in a great hairy heap, no feeling attached to what she was doing, only a relentless thirst to right the wrongs that had been heaped on her people.

Demaris looked around her at the carnage. Raiders were running everywhere, in and out of buildings, ransacking and dragging whatever plunder they could find, human or otherwise. Some of the raiders were dragging their booty off in the direction of the coastal road.

Her head was dizzy, her vision blurred and it seemed as though someone had cast a veil over the scene. The cries of pain, the shrieks of vengeance and the roar of fire faded into the background with the village bell, which kept on clanging as though the day would never end. In the centre of the square a platform had been hastily erected in front of the bell tower, which held a wooden structure that she could not quite understand. Was that a rope that hung from the pole?

Then the back of her head burst with pain, sending her spinning to the ground. She landed on all fours, dropping her sword and turned to face the perpetrator of her attack, but a black curtain drew across her vision, her head spun with dizzy nausea and she lost all consciousness.

Chapter Thirty-Five

Allan stepped away from the chevalier in front of him, who clutched at his side with ragged breath but still alive. About forty men formed a circle around them. Already, the watchkeepers had their weapons down and their hands raised, so Allan followed suit. He could not hope to outrun them, so his best defence was to stick with the watchkeepers.

Words were exchanged in their local dialect and while the watchkeepers were permitted to sheath their swords, Allan had his weapon confiscated. More talk and then the chevaliers relaxed and bustled into action making camp. He appealed to Tavorian.

"What are they doing? Don't they know that there is a raiding party of Klagen warriors on its way to one of their local villages?"

Tavorian looked away. "Oh, they know."

"Then why aren't they doing something? Chasing them down and stopping them?" In Allan's mind, the Klagen had already reached Demaris' estates and Demaris was there, fighting a threat that no one person could ever hope to contain on their own. "Why aren't you doing anything?" He paced back and forth, like a caged animal.

"Still. Be still," Abendigo said, laying a hand on Allan's arm. "The Countess was never really in any danger."

"How the darkness would you know?" Allan's angry words carried across the camp and a few chevaliers looked over at them.

"We have Gilbert's best assurances," Tavorian said.

"Gilbert? You mean the man who sold her off to the highest bidder like a piece of property?"

"It is not like that," Abendigo said.

"Then what is it like? Please tell me, because from where I am, it seems a lot like that."

"Gilbert has her best interests at heart," Tavorian said again.

"Then why are the Emperor's troops here?" Allan said.

The watchkeepers looked at one another.

And then a thought locked into place, as though it had been looking for a fit ever since he heard the old drunk's story in Attora.

"They are not here to stop the Klagen, are they?"

Tavorian looked away and Abendigo looked at the ground and scuffed his feet in a pile of sandy pine needles.

"What have you done?" Allan said. "What deal has been made with the Emperor?"

"You weren't supposed to go haring off after her," Tavorian said.

"And I suppose that she wasn't supposed to ride off into the night on her own either?" Allan said. The watchkeepers looked at one another. "You knew she would do that, didn't you?"

"Gilbert did warn us of her… impetuous nature," Abendigo said. "But he reassured us that she would come to no harm. The Klagen raid is just a decoy and once they have crossed the line, the chevaliers will spring their trap and take them down."

"Starting a war in the process," Allan said.

"A slight complication that could well be appeased by a fair trade. After all, the Countess' estate is a rich piece of land in Arrontierre."

"Like I said, selling her off."

"To avert a war."

Allan wanted to punch Tavorian through his dense southern head.

"Like a piece of property!"

"A cultural distinction," Abendigo said.

Allan wanted to scream and smash their heads together. He looked over at Brutas, who was watching him carefully, a curious look in his eye.

"How is any of this right, by any account?" Allan said in Langan as he walked past Brutas and off towards the trees. He was stopped by an armed chevalier who waved him cheerily back towards the camp. He gritted his teeth and sat down by a group of chevaliers engaged in sharpening their weapons, not even able to bring himself to speak to anyone.

Tavorian and Abendigo joined their compatriots in the preparations to make war on the Klagen, while Allan quietly seethed, trying to work out how he could get out of there and help Demaris. Brutas stood between the two groups, looking from his compatriots and over to Allan, a frown creasing his brow. Then resigned, he came to sit beside Allan, offering his sword and a sharpening stone. Allan did not much feel like helping any of these chevaliers, but having nothing much else to do with his hands, took the sword and began the rhythmic strokes up and down the blade. Brutas earned himself a few harsh words from the group of chevaliers, but he just glared at them in his inimitable fashion and they thought better of interfering. After a while, he commandeered another sword and began sharpening the blade alongside Allan, taking turns by following the smooth sweeping motion that characterised Allan's steel work. He nodded and smiled to himself.

"Never trusted that man," Brutas said in broken Langan.

"Who… Gilbert Amand?"

Brutas nodded. The soft sweeping of the two swords up and down was calming Allan's anger, giving him space to think.

"The horses?" he said. Brutas nodded to a cluster of pines behind Allan. He looked over his shoulder and could just about make out a chestnut head dipping down to nibble at the ground. "How far?"

Brutas continued with the up and down, up and down of steel on stone as though no one had spoken at all. Just as Allan thought he had not heard or understood, Brutas murmured something, keeping his eyes trained on the sword work.

"Within the hour, if we move fast. They will allow the raid to happen, then move in to clean up." Brutas looked up and caught Allan's eye. His gaze was sharp and made Allan's spine tingle.

"How could he? He's supposed to be her guardian," Allan said.

"Political," Brutas said. Then with the casual ease of someone who had been part of that troop for

288

his entire life, he stood, sheathed his sword and strolled over towards the horses. Allan rose with the smooth alacrity of a chevalier, casually donned a cloak that had been discarded and followed Brutas with a sense of belonging he did not feel. Testing times for all, but clearly the chevaliers did not see the watchkeepers and their odd looking companion as a threat to their mission. The perimeter guards just waved Brutas through, making no attempt to stop Allan who followed, his heart hammering against his ribcage. They mounted their horses with ease. Allan stowed the sharpening stone and slipped the extra sword through his belt.

As Allan and Brutas thundered down the coastal road towards Rotonde, Allan noticed that a good many large-footed individuals and horses had already passed that way. The ground was freshly marked and great clods of sandy earth lay strewn across the path. They neared the northern-most village and drew to a steady walk in anticipation of what lay ahead. Brutas looked sideways at Allan.

"Why her?" he said.

That was a very good question, Allan thought. Why her indeed? Every time he closed his eyes, her image was imprinted on the insides of his eyelids. Every time she was near, he felt an overwhelming desire just to hold onto her and not let go. Because he could not bear the thought of never seeing her again.

"She has something of mine," he said. Brutas raised an eyebrow as though he did not believe a word of it. "Something of great importance to me."

"A piece of your soul?" Brutas said with a wry smile.

"Something like that," Allan said to himself.

"Foreign and of low birth," he said. "No chance."

"As long as she is safe, that is all that matters to me," Allan said.

After a while, Brutas slowed to a stop holding one hand aloft and then placed a finger to his lips. In the distance, the roaring of the ocean ebbed and flowed interspersed by a different kind of roaring. The smell of something burning wafted beneath Allan's nostrils and filled him with a queasy sense of unease. A grey curl of smoke rose up above the trees to their left and the woods gave way to a crop of outhouses. The northern perimeter of Rotonde. "We're too late," he whispered.

The horses skittered and tossed their heads. Then Klagen warriors burst out of the trees. Riding in a tight arc, Brutas drew his sword and cut down three in one go with an almighty slice that took the first one in the stomach, the second across the chest splattering blood in his face to finish at the throat of the third. All three dropped to the ground, to be replaced by more Klagen who clambered over their felled compatriots, snarling and swinging their axes.

Allan whirled his horse around, drawing his sword and jerking the reins so that the animal took him to the rear of the group that had just crowded around Brutas. Two of the Klagen broke away, anticipating his move and tried to cut him down before he reached the rest of the group. Their axes were too low to reach Allan, but one swipe to his horse's legs and it crumpled to a bloody heap, forcing Allan to leap to safety before being crushed by the animal's weight. He landed on unsteady feet, tumbling into a shoulder roll, which sent his sword flying off in the opposite direction.

One of the Klagen was not so quick to get out of the way as the horse landed on top of him, pinning him to the ground. The other Klagen used the two bodies as a stepping-stone to launch himself at Allan, throwing something long and thin through the air. Allan scrambled to all fours as a round spiked ball thudded to the ground beside his feet. It was attached to a long chain, which the Klagen pulled sending the ball careening back to its owner. Allan ran for the nearest tree, making a lunge for his sword in the process. He missed the hilt by inches, then felt a sudden pressure wrap around his ankle. He looked down just as he was jerked off his feet, head whacking the ground, then dragged foot-first back towards the Klagen. His nose and mouth filled with sand, and pine needles pricked his skin as he tried in vain to grab at anything to halt his progress; branches, tree stumps, rocks… anything. But there was nothing to hold onto except the smooth sand that ran through his fingers like water.

A rough, giant hand grabbed his ankle. Allan grabbed a fistful of sand, twisted his body and threw it into the face of the Klagen who stood poised with his axe swung back, ready to take off his head. The Klagen blinked, sneezed and shook his head, spraying sand all around while Allan struggled to get free of the chain around his ankle. The axe fell, but it fell far short of hitting Allan. The point of a broadsword peered out at Allan from the Klagen's chest, before he jerked to one side and tumbled to the ground to reveal Brutas standing behind him, a snarl on his face.

Allan looked around at the carnage. Brutas put his foot on the Klagen's back, and withdrew his sword with a grunt.

"Bloody Klagen," he grumbled. "All furs and no brain."

Allan wanted to laugh at the big man's assessment. There was something indeed to be said for the garish southern garb and feather-like armour. Speed being the more obvious.

"There'll be more if we don't get into hiding," Allan said, releasing his foot and rubbing the bruising around his ankle. He picked himself up and retrieved his weapon.

They skirted the perimeter of the village, keeping low and hidden by the trees and the undergrowth. As they came closer to the centre buildings and the source of the smoke, Allan's nose began to close around the acrid stench of burning flesh, and the back of his throat tickled. From the shelter of the bushes, they peered at the deserted village square and saw a single figure dangling from a noose attached to a makeshift platform in front of a bell tower. The body swung to and fro, as flame licked up from their toes to their torso. The bile rose from Allan's stomach and he pitched over the bushes and retched.

Chapter Thirty-Six

Allan lifted his head and wiped the spittle away from his chin. Despite losing his breakfast, he still felt a grinding nausea in his gut and a rising panic at the sight of the burning figure in the centre of the village. It was hard to tell at that distance, but the figure looked female.

"No, no, no..." Allan started forward, but Brutas grabbed his arm and held him fast.

"Don't," Brutas said, nodding to the figure that swung on the end of its rope. "It is a trap. Look how empty the village is. Whoever that was, you can't help them now." Allan gazed at the carnage. It looked as though someone had just abandoned the scene in mid-battle. You would have expected at best to see the winning side tending to their wounded or worst, plundering the dead. But the place was deserted and smouldering as though a curse lay on Rotonde.

Allan shook himself free of Brutas' grip and ran headlong into the centre of the square. He drew his sword and with one swift cut to the rope dropped the body to the ground. He took off his cloak and rolled it around her, dousing the flames. He dared not lift his cloak for fear of seeing her face, so he knelt down and tried to find some sign of life, but it was as Brutas had said; whoever this had been, he could not help them now. Brutas knelt beside him.

"We have to go," he said. "I don't like this at all."

Then a single pair of hands clapped out a slow rhythm across the eerie silence, as though applauding a particularly bad circus performance. Allan looked up at a figure in a flamboyant red and green jerkin leaning over the parapet of the bell tower. He had one of those droopy moustaches like Abendigo and a forest green beret with a long tawny feather flopping down over his ear.

"Gilbert Amand," Brutas said, his voice growling under his breath. Allan pulled the young female body closer to him.

"What have you done to her?" he called up to the man in the bell tower. "She was your ward." Gilbert looked down on him, his expression guarded.

"Oh. You don't think that is the Countess do you?"

Allan realised then that the body he held was the wrong shape for Demaris; more flesh, less height, though it was hard to tell through the cloak. Still he held on.

"Where is she?"

"Oh, she is safe, don't you worry. Although the same may not be said for you."

There was an almighty crunch and a wooden door flew back on its hinges and hung limp from its splintered frame. From the interior of some kind of barn, a screaming woman flew towards them followed by a motley bunch of bewildered looking youngsters, blinking in the daylight.

Allan barely recognised her, coated as she was from head to foot in blood, a fresh wound in her arm spilling more blood as she ran. Her face was wild with anger and for a moment it seemed directed at him. Had she been armed, she might have run him through without a second thought. But she stopped when she recognised him and saw that he held the bundle with tender care. Tears streamed down her cheeks and she knelt beside him.

"Greta, Greta, Greta… nooo…" she wailed. Allan felt her pain as keenly as though it were his own; a tidal wave of despair washing over him. It was one of the children she had told him about.

Demaris uncovered the body and held a shaking, bloody hand to the disfigured face. One by one, the other children came, teary eyed and with weary looking limbs. They patted Demaris as if to console her and laid hands on the girl that had been Greta. A young boy with thickset Klagen features came and took the bundle from Allan and cradled the body.

"You bastard!" Allan stood up and drew his sword, pointing it up at the bell tower where Gilbert looked on. "How could you do this?"

Gilbert raised his hands. "This was not my doing, young man… whoever you are. It is an unfortunate product of circumstance. This is a war. That man," he pointed at Brutas, "only had one simple task. To bring the Countess safely back home, at the appropriate time. With her betrothed. You boy, hardly look like a Carentan lord to me."

"You lied to me," Demaris shouted up at the bell tower. "You said you would keep them safe. You said you would keep Rotonde safe, but you opened its gates to the very monsters that killed my family."

"Huh. Well that's interesting. Unless my eyesight is failing me, didn't you just pitch up with two of the enemy clan? And look at you now, consorting with the offspring. I thought you would thank me for ridding the village of the reminders. As soon as this situation is resolved, I am sending you straight back to Carentan to be married to that lord."

Demaris stood up and hooked her arm through Allan's in defiance.

"This is Lord Barra and this is the man I intend to marry," she said.

Gilbert frowned, but he did not look half as confused as Allan felt. Out of the corner of his eye, he caught two figures sneaking out of the wooden pen. They looked Klagen, but moved like sneak thieves, flitting across the square and behind the bell tower. He turned his head just a fraction towards the Countess and she responded by squeezing gently on his arm in warning. He kept his gaze focused on Gilbert, who was twitching and wringing his hands.

"Whoever, whatever," he said. "You need to go, my Lady," Gilbert said.

"Where did the raiders go?" Allan said, in an attempt to distract Gilbert's attention.

"Back, back to their ships… I don't know," he said, waving his arms towards the back entrance to the village and the coastal road. "But you need to move on. Get to the outskirts of town. There are a group of Chevaliers in waiting, who will keep you safe." Something about his urgency to move Demaris on, was making Allan feel uneasy.

"Why do you care what happens to me?" Demaris said.

"I have had enough of this," Brutas said, striding forward towards the bell tower. "How do you get into this place? You will answer for your crimes. His plan was to sell you off to Carentan and take the estate and the Emperor's favour for himself." Demaris released Allan's arm and stood between Brutas and the bell tower entrance.

"You knew," she said, her voice icy with accusation, "and you still brought me here?"

"My Lady," Brutas said kneeling before her. "The plan was to keep you safe. Not bring you here. And that was before I even knew. Before your... the boy worked out the truth himself." He nodded at Allan. Demaris swung around to look at him, her mouth open, about to say something. But then a wave of Klagen warriors erupted from the undergrowth surrounding the square, all screaming and racing towards them.

Brutas felled the first attacker to reach them and Allan drew his sword, stepping in front of Demaris and the children. Demaris bundled the children back and urged them towards the bell tower. The door to the tower flew open and a man raced out, carrying a spear and screaming in Etanese. Allan was so surprised that he missed a parry and one of the attacking Klagen almost took a chunk out of his shoulder with his axe, cutting through his tunic and grazing the skin beneath. The axe rose, then Allan deciphered what the spear-man was shouting through his thick Jarvic accent and he ducked, just as a spear whistled over the top of his head and sunk into the attacking warrior's chest.

The warrior stopped mid-swing and looked down at the shaft protruding from his stomach, blood soaking his furs. His expression was one of disbelief as he clawed at it in vain, then fell forward. The lithe, but solid spear-man leapt over Allan and yanked his weapon from the body, a look of manic delight on his face. Allan stared at him without moving for a moment. This must be the enemy clan Gilbert had referred to. He looked over his shoulder wondering where the other one was and just caught a flicker of commotion from the top of the bell tower before he was confronted by a fresh Klagen wielding an axe.

Allan fought back to back with the spear-man as they circled and struck forward, driving the Klagen back as a string of enemy bodies collapsed amidst the chaos. He was impressed and relieved in equal measure that this strange hybrid warrior was fighting on his side.

Despite the spear-man's help, they were slowly being corralled backwards toward the bell tower and the centre of the square. It was as though the moment they dropped one warrior, another one popped up in his place. Did they have a never-ending supply of raiders, hell-bent on taking their fair share of the killing? Very soon, there would be nowhere to go and nowhere to run. Brutas was doing his best to hold them off from the other direction, but they were surrounded and the enemy would soon be able to close off the circle, leaving the three of them trapped and outnumbered.

The wound in his shoulder flared up with red-hot anger and Allan's sword arm faltered. The Klagen facing him found his weakness and swung his axe with uncoordinated fervour. Allan dodged on the inside of the swing, using his sword as a shield, but miscalculated his distance, his shoulder ramming against the flat of the axe-head and pulsing with pain. He crumpled forward, opening up his head and neck to the next blow, cut short by a spear through the throat of his enemy.

The spear-man now had a large knife in one hand and a determined Klagen hanging onto his back. His other arm hung limp at his side. Fighting through the agony shooting down his arm from his shoulder, Allan turned and thrust his sword through the neck of the enemy, who released the spear-man and flailed to the ground clutching at his throat. The spear-man at once leapt over the body and retrieved his spear, nodding to Allan as though it were all in a day's work.

Brutas edged closer to them from the other side until the three of them were almost back to back, all exits cut off and sealed within the centre of a melee of warriors that stretched too far for any sane chance of breaking their way through.

It seemed hopeless, but Allan continued to parry every attack that came in, thrusting and weaving and turning and stabbing in some vague hope that all was not lost. His body moved of its own volition as though his limbs belonged to someone else. In the distance, he could hear shouting and screaming coming from the direction of the bell tower and he hoped that Demaris would

299

get her vengeance somehow, and that in some small way he had helped. It was the best he could hope for; perhaps her other new-found friend would help her. He had a numb sensation running from his shoulder down his arm and although he still wielded the sword with some kind of precision, his arm could have belonged to someone else.

Nausea and dizziness overcame him. So much so that he swore he could see the Klagen ranks ripple and undulate towards them. Then he caught glimpses of brightly coloured cloth - jade, azure and crimson, flashing intermittently. He closed his eyes and let the world rush over him.

Chapter Thirty-Seven

Demaris ran into the bell tower, pulling the children around her and urging them through the open door. The Klagen were no longer her concern, now that she knew who was really responsible. It was up to Wilhelm and Jaanta to finish off the mess that Gilbert had started. She was more worried for Allan. What was he doing there? Then there were the children. She shepherded them into a ground floor room for safety, and they cried and clung onto her clothes when she tried to leave them, which just stoked her anger.

"Vicktor, you are in charge now. Look after your brothers and sisters." Vicktor stood up tall. Then he gently laid the cloaked bundle in the corner.

"What about Greta?" he said.

"There is nothing we can do for Greta now, she is at peace. Look after the little ones." Before they had time to dispute, Demaris darted out of the door and began climbing the spiral stairs. She had some questions for Gilbert. Her head throbbed with the aftermath of the blow and she had only just managed to shake off the disorientation enough to free herself and the children from the pen. She reached the top of the stairs and paused for a brief moment, watching Gilbert as he leaned out shouting instructions to someone amidst the chaos below.

Demaris slid behind the bell, which was bigger than a Klagen's midriff, hoping to close the gap between them. She lost sight of him for a split second, then there was a sword levelled at her chest and she was looking down the shaft of her own blade and into the eyes of the man she had trusted her entire life.

"The sapphires in the hilt match the colour of your eyes so well," he said. "It must have been a most observant person to have crafted such a unique weapon."

"Why have you done this?" she said.

"It's not personal, my sweet. It is political. I never could get you interested in the wider consequences of looking after the estate."

"I don't understand. You practically own it all in everything but name. What do you stand to gain?"

His thin smile made him look unsure and he shook his head. "It's complicated. Your parents never understood either. This village has always been a target for raiders. This time, I chose to take control for the good of the nation. Look," he nodded over his shoulder, then nudged Demaris forward so she could see out into the square. There was a circle of Klagen warriors moving in against three figures. A stab of panic rose in her chest as she located Allan, right in the middle of the mayhem. "Where did you get him? And don't think I believe for one moment that he is Lord Barra. Where would a Carentan lord learn to fight like that?"

"Oh, you would be surprised," she said, thinking of Princess Alliane and her sword fighting lessons. "You didn't have to kill Greta," she said, her throat constricting around the words.

"The Klagen were not satisfied because I wasn't prepared to sacrifice the whole village. Greta was collateral. It is a war, after all. Someone is always going to get hurt."

"It is a war you started." She spat out her words as they were the only weapon at her disposal, but Gilbert just pressed closer with the sword in warning. "So you're going to kill me too?"

"Not yet," he said. "You are too precious to me. I have devoted a lifetime to you. You will cement relationships across nations. It was always your destiny, even if your parents had survived."

"You let them into our village... after all that happened." Demaris' words trailed off into a sob. "I came to kill the Klagen leader, but really it is you I should kill."

"I think you are on the wrong side of this debate," Gilbert said, twisting the sword as if to make a point. A small slit opened beneath the blade on the front of her blood-stained jerkin and Gilbert pulled back a fraction.

"Before you sell me off to Carentan, you can at least tell me the truth about what happened that night when my parents died."

Gilbert tilted his head to one side and sighed. "I suppose I owe you that much. I'm not a monster you know," he said. Demaris snorted with derision. "Look... the chevaliers have arrived." He took a look over his shoulder, then settled his gaze back onto Demaris. He had taught her all the sneaky tricks to get out of situations and must have been well aware that she would try them at the first opportunity. Over his shoulder, Demaris could make out streaks of colour in amongst the Klagen. The fur-backed warriors began to fall, though she could still make out Allan, Brutas and Wilhelm back-to-back in the centre of the fight.

"What is it you need to know, my sweet?" Gilbert said.

"Don't call me that." Demaris could not hide the hurt in her voice. Gilbert's eyes narrowed, making the wrinkles on his face pinch inward. "I want to know if you were responsible for that first raid eight years ago?"

Gilbert thought about it for a while. "Yes… and no," he said. His face looked grey and tired. "You know my allegiance has always been to the Emperor. Eight years ago, the Emperor was having difficulty maintaining his position due to opposition leaders blaming him for action taken by one of his senior chevaliers, which lead to a brief and embarrassing defeat in Vermondie. His forces were crushed by the combined might of the Western Isles and their Eastern allies."

The story was well known. But what was better known was how the Emperor had dealt with that embarrassment, disclaiming all knowledge and having any poor soul who spoke of it thrown into his dungeons. It was typical of the current ruler to take all credit when something goes well, but he was quick to apportion blame when things did not turn out to be quite as successful.

"You sacrificed my village for the Emperor?"

"No, it wasn't like that. It was fortuitous that the raid came at a time when the Emperor needed to build a case."

304

"So why did it take so long to do anything about it?"

"Well, they're hardly the brightest bunch," Gilbert said, nodding over his shoulder without taking his eyes away from Demaris.

"So you helped the Emperor to start a war in order to finish a war that the Western Isles didn't start in the first place? Sounds to me like we need a new ruler," Demaris said through gritted teeth.

"How very libertarian of you, my sweet. It seems that your Carentan friends have had more influence on you than I anticipated. I might have to rethink that alliance."

"Forget your alliance," she said. "If I ever marry, it will be on my own terms and to the person I want."

"Really? You can't possibly mean that ill-prepared boy you tried to pass off as a lord, do you?" Gilbert laughed with exaggerated contempt. "Can't think what use he will be to you."

"Oh, you have no idea," she said, glancing nervously at the Jael sword levelled at her chest. "That night…"

"I wasn't expecting your parents to be caught in the midst of it, but they were as impetuous and ardent as their daughter is now."

"But you were hurt too, I saw it with my own eyes. I thought you were dead." Despite herself, she welled up as the memory came flooding back. When all hope had been lost, the thought of the one remaining constant in her life lying lifeless in the square had brought the eight-year-old Demaris' world crashing down around her ears.

His hand shook as he held the sword, and he looked very much like an old man at the end of his road. Perhaps she was mistaken and he had not meant for her parents to be killed. Was that a glint of hope in his eye? Then his grip on the sword strengthened and she knew she had lost. She had lost the fight for her estates and she had lost her fight for reprisal.

"Yes, you're right. I was hurt. But you see, it had to look convincing."

"You tried to save them."

"I did. And I'm truly sorry that it ended the way it did. But as I said, my loyalty has always been to the Emperor. This is his war, not mine. I am but an instrument in far greater battle."

Demaris saw a shadow flit across the room out of the corner of her eye, then disappear. In the distance, she could now see the colours of the chevaliers moving in and out of the Klagen and taking them down one by one. Then the fighting seemed to slow and a large figure was running through the crowds, leaping from the backs of the Klagen and using the dead bodies first as shields and then as stepping-stones to reach the centre of the crowd. This new force made a straight line for Allan, Brutas and Wilhelm.

"Spare my companions, at least," she said, her throat constricting as she saw Allan fall to his knees. She was gripped by a sudden dizzy nausea.

"Casualties of war, I'm afraid," Gilbert said.

"Or perhaps not," she said as the circle parted and a large Klagen with long matted hair entwined with the bones of his enemies stepped to the fore.

306

She saw Wilhelm step forward to meet the hulking warrior, who must have been at least twice his size. A dim ray of hope lit Demaris up inside as she picked out Brutas, dragging Allan to the side. She levelled her gaze at Gilbert.

"Well? Are you going to use that? It would be a shame to put such a fine piece of work to waste," she said. Gilbert looked down at the sword pointing at her.

"Don't fret, my sweet. A remarkable sword like this will find the home it truly deserves. I will take good care of it, of that you may be assured."

"Yes. It is indeed a remarkable sword. Quite dangerous in the wrong hands," she said.

"Don't make idle threats. Remember, I taught you everything you know," he said, light glinting in his eye.

"Not quite everything," a soft voice behind him said. A shadow loomed up behind Gilbert, then Demaris saw the flash of a blade and he dropped the sword and grasped both hands to his throat. His eyes popped open in surprise as the blood dripped from between his fingers and ran down his arms. Then his look softened as he gazed at Demaris with a fondness reminiscent of her childhood and her unconditional love.

"No…," she let out a small, strangled cry, knowing it was futile and knowing that her dream was all wrong and her trust so badly misplaced.

Gilbert slid to his knees. Standing right behind him with the knife in her hand was Jaanta.

307

Chapter Thirty-Eight

Wilhelm was prepared to die there on the battlefield. He expected to be the one to protect his comrades-in-arms, strange though it seemed to be fighting alongside both a southerner and a westerner. He also expected to be the last man standing, if it took all day to flush Ullr out of his hiding place. Then, Ullr appeared. Like a cloud of foul-smelling air, descending upon them from the gods-knew-where, stepping on the fallen as if they meant nothing. The dead had families too. They had lives and purpose before this warped regime put them to work and then put them to death.

He did not know who the southerners answered to, but they gave Ullr a wide berth, as he cut an opening through the melee, making a straight line for Wilhelm. At least they had the good sense to get out of the way. Any unfortunate Klagen in Ullr's path was either slashed by his circling axe or stomped on by his great Klagen boots. This was why Ullr was the Klagen Chief of Clans; undefeated in combat, unchallenged in years and wearing the trophies of his conquests plaited into the long beard that swept from side to side as he lumbered into the circle. He straightened to his full height and loomed above Wilhelm, circling his axe in an easy rhythm.

"I should have put you down as a babe," he barked in Jarvic. "You're like some annoying fly; buzz, buzz, buzz." Spittle flew from his mouth. "Look at you. Some half-breed weakling, unfit to lead our tribes, unfit to carry on the traditions."

"I am flattered that you rowed your ships all this way to tell me that," Wilhelm said with a wry smile.

"Perhaps this time you'll have the decency to stay dead," Ullr said, swinging his axe. "And you can take that hybrid woman with you. Don't need no jumped up oarsmaster sneaking off behind my back." For the first time since the fighting began, Wilhelm wondered what had become of Jaanta. "I could get ten of her kind at half the contracted price in Klagenstill." Wilhelm did not have time to wonder what he meant before Ullr gave a bellowing battle cry and wheeled in with a bone smashing swing to Wilhelm's head.

Wilhelm reacted in just a flicker of a moment, leaping on the inside of the massive swing. The attack was wide and slow, leaving Ullr's right side open. Wilhelm cut down the distance, using the spear to block the huge man's arm and just managing to avoid losing a couple of fingers in the process. His limp left arm dangled and dripped blood. Ullr eyed him up like a hungry wolf getting ready to snack on a wild rabbit. He was still fresh, while Wilhelm shuddered with exhaustion.

He steeled himself, as Ullr broke away and circled, readying himself for another punishing swing. His moves were easy to read, telegraphed in huge preparatory twitches, but even though Wilhelm knew when it was coming, the force of the attack was enough to shatter what little strength remained in his bones. He whirled away from the axe strike this time, making enough distance to take a shot with his spear. It had better be a clear one and strike true, because if he lost the spear and Ullr remained standing, he had lost the fight on one fool move. He stood still, but did not take the shot. It was too much of a risk to lose his weapon so early in the fight.

Ullr came crashing forward, his axe swinging just in reach of the spear, and attempted to hook the weapon from Wilhelm's hands with the angled axe-head. Wilhelm withdrew the spear bringing it beneath Ullr's swing, and lengthened his stance aiming for a headshot. Despite his bulk, Ullr danced out of reach and grinned at him.

"Oh, you're going to have to do better than that, my son," he said. "If only you had trained with me, we could have made a fearsome duo, father and son."

Wilhelm wheeled backwards, using the spear shaft to deflect the axe as it came crashing back down towards his head. Did he not just call him a half-breed weakling?

"If you agree to change your ways, we still could," Wilhelm said. "We could lead together in a new era for Klagenstill. Yield now or the regime will die with you."

Ullr pulled back his axe, readying for another strike. "You, lead? Never." As the axe came down, Wilhelm stepped in, using the shaft of the spear to block the attack and push the axe over his head. Ullr adjusted his stance, released one hand from the axe and grabbed Wilhelm's spear with the other. They tussled there toe-to-toe in a stand-off of who had the strongest grip, until Wilhelm twisted the spear free and used the momentum to take a stab at Ullr's unprotected side. The spear slid easily between his furs and Ullr just looked down as though distracted by an irritating bee sting. Wilhelm could not even be sure if he had hit flesh beneath the layers of clothing. A single drop of blood dripped from the tip of his spear as he pulled it free and still Ullr grinned beneath his matted beard. "Buzz, buzz, buzz," he said, eyes widening and face lurching forward with menace.

Wilhelm staggered back, his one good arm straining with fatigue and almost as useless as his broken one. He knew then that he would not be able to keep up the pace and he had to finish it quickly or not at all. Then without giving him time to recover, Ullr was driving forwards once more with both hands on the shaft of the axe, swinging up and down with rage in his eyes. Wilhelm dove to his left, ducking under Ullr's swinging arm, was about to take aim for a thrust beneath his armpit, when his foot slipped and he went down onto his back, skidding to a stop beneath Ullr's feet. His spear clattered uselessly to the ground several feet away.

Ullr took full advantage. He dropped the axe and slumped the weight of his body onto Wilhelm, pinning his arms to the ground.

"Now, I have you," he growled. They were face-to-face, too close for comfort. Wilhelm screamed in agony as Ullr ground his knee into his broken arm. For one fleeting instant, the pressure on his good arm let up enough for Wilhelm to inch his hand down to reach into his boot. Bending his knee to extract the knife, he rolled his body, using Ullr's weight to tip him over. Ullr was grinning at the agony he was causing, then his eyes widened as his imbalance toppled him to the side and then Wilhelm was on top.

"Now *I* have *you*," Wilhelm said, then butted Ullr between the eyes on the bridge of the nose. Ullr's nose exploded in a spray of crimson and Wilhelm's forehead stung with the force of the blow. Gods, but that man had a nose of stone. Wilhelm drew the knife up, going for the neck, but Ullr was too quick and took hold of his wrist. With one hand caught in the grip and the other too useless to use, Wilhelm was stuck. No momentum for a stab or a throw, no leverage to release the hold. Ullr's thumb dug into his wrist and pain shot up his arm, making his fingers involuntarily release their grip on the knife, which dropped to the ground.

Then Ullr was scrabbling in the dirt for the knife, his huge body trying to find purchase on the dusty, pebbly ground. They both found their feet and sprang up to face each other. Blood oozed from Ullr's nose and he blinked, trying to clear his dazed vision. Wilhelm's good arm screamed in agony, but he pushed the pain aside and concentrated on the Klagen chief who circled him now with his own knife.

Ullr bared his teeth in a snarl, blood dripping from his nose staining his mouth and teeth in a scarlet grimace. Forces around them were swelling, as though for every dead warrior another two popped up in their place. He kept his eyes trained on Ullr, his only target in the moment. If he died there that day, as long as he took the Klagen leader with him, he would die a fulfilled man.

312

They circled each other, Ullr looking for an opening, Wilhelm reading his opponent's body language and waiting for the inevitable lunge. He knew Ullr could not afford to leave it too long, could not afford to allow Wilhelm enough time to recover. His left arm twitched, as it led his body into the attack. But then Ullr did something unusual; he switched legs as nimble as a dancer, then barrelled forwards on his right side going for a high neck stab.

Wilhelm shifted his body at the last moment, blocked the knife attack then locked Ullr's arm into a hold. Ullr looked surprised, then confused when Wilhelm lifted himself up and wrapped both legs around his body. For a moment he just hung there; the man was as immovable as tree trunk. One twist on the locked arm caused Ullr to move his body, adjusting to compensate for the pain just enough to topple himself.

He went down with a thump and Wilhelm gave the arm one last twist. He felt the bone crunch and grind from its socket, then Ullr screamed like a hog on the end of a spear. The knife dropped from his grip and Wilhelm swiped it up and with one last effort, thrust it into Ullr's neck. A spray of blood spewed out, splashing across Wilhelm's face and Ullr twisted himself free enough to reach up towards his neck. Before he had a chance to pull free the knife, Wilhelm delivered a palm heel strike to the base of the knife hilt, driving it deeper into Ullr's neck.

Wilhelm lay back, panting, unable to move as his right leg was trapped beneath the great hulking

313

bulk. The Klagen Chief drew rattling breaths as he bled out, his breathing getting slower and slower.

"My... son," he said and then was silent.

Wilhelm closed his eyes, vaguely aware of battles raging around him. He no longer had the energy to fight, so he just waited for the next Klagen to step into the fray. By all accounts, he was now the Klagen Chief of Chiefs – who wouldn't want to challenge that? He wondered why no one attacked him as he lay there. Perhaps they thought he too was dead? And then he realised that the fighting had stopped and he opened one eye.

The ugly snarling Klagen face of Ullr grinned above him with an axe raised above his head. It wasn't possible. What did it take to kill this man? In his semi-lucid state, Wilhelm wondered at how quickly the man's nose had recovered, before he realised he was looking into the murderous eyes of Njord, Ullr's brother. There was a flicker of hesitation before the axe fell. Then the tip of a sword sliced through the Klagen's chest from back to front and Njord's eyes opened in surprise. The axe fell harmlessly to one side and his body slumped to the other, landing on top of his brother. Standing in place of Njord was the Carentan fighter, who had kept Wilhelm's back throughout the battle. He too looked about ready to fall over.

Wilhelm nodded. "Thanks, soldier," he said.

The boy looked at him, puzzled for a moment. "I'm not a soldier," he said with a wry smile. "I'm a smith."

Chapter Thirty-Nine

Demaris was weak with fatigue and her head pulsed with pain, spreading from the lump and radiating out to her temples. She unfastened her cloak and laid it over Gilbert's inert body, closing his staring eyes gently with her fingertips. She looked up at Jaanta, who was watching the fight below in the square.

"Allan," Demaris said with a strangled cry, tumbling over Gilbert's body in her haste to get a better view.

"He is fine, don't fret," Jaanta said. "His mother taught him well."

"It is you, isn't it?" Demaris said. "How did you...?"

Delyth pulled the blonde hairpiece from her head revealing her dark, straight hair beneath. "People often see what they think they want to. What gave me away?"

"Your eyes – something about the way you looked at me."

"Ah, I see. Yes, you are like him in that respect," Delyth nodded down to the square where Allan stood, propped up by Brutas. "You might make a suitable couple, after all. I'm sure you would rather have a prince than a lord." With that, Delyth smiled and slipped out of the narrow exit.

"What do you mean?" Demaris started after her, but by the time she reached the exit, the winding staircase was empty. Following her would have been futile, as she knew she would not find her, so she crept back to the balcony. She noted with relief that Tavorian and Abendigo had joined up with Brutas, making a human wall in front of Allan and picking off any Klagen opportunists.

But it was not over as long as the Klagen Chief still stood and his men continued to fight. She glanced over her shoulder at the bleeding body that was once Gilbert and shuddered. Then the Klagen Chief was down and Wilhelm scrambled on top of him. Both weapon-less now, both scuffling for a knife that lay a few feet away from their heads. Ullr got there first and Demaris held her shaky breath as both fighters sprang to their feet. The odds were all but impossible; Wilhelm was half his size, fighting with only one arm and weaponless. Then in a blur that hardly seemed real, Wilhelm had the huge Klagen in an arm lock that made her wince with imagined pain, then they were down again and the next thing she saw was the life leaking out of Ullr, a knife sticking out of his throat.

Demaris pressed her hands together as though in prayer and whispered to herself.

"That is for Ma. That is for Pa. And that is for the suffering you visited upon my home and my estates. May it never be repeated by you or yours from this day on." She closed her eyes and took a deep shuddering breath. She opened them just in time to see Allan fell an enormous beast of a Klagen who loomed over the dead Chief, swinging an axe in Wilhelm's direction. She held her breath until she was sure the beast was dead and watched Brutas help Wilhelm to his feet.

316

She looked back out into the square and Allan was staring up at the bell tower, his face a picture of battle-ridden fatigue and angst. When he caught sight of her, she noticed his shoulders drop, releasing their tension. Brutas looked to where Allan stared and gave Demaris a short salute with the tips of his fingers. Abendigo did a little shoe-shuffle dance with his feet, then took off his feathered hat with a sweeping bow in her direction. Tavorian looked at the pair of them and shrugged an apology in her direction. She looked again for Allan, but he was gone. Dropping her head to her hands, she let out a shuddering breath.

She watched a wave of armoured guards from the Sarlatian army, which had finally caught up with their quarry. It was like a silver-black wave of destruction, flowing in and out of the Arrontierre troops to take down the Klagen one by one. The advantage shifted quite suddenly as the chevaliers worked alongside the Sarlatians to subdue and finally bring to a stop the carnage that had been unleashed by Gilbert and the Klagens.

"Don't ever do that again," she said to herself.

"I'm sorry," a voice behind her said.

She started and turned. His emerald eyes sparkled, though he limped towards her looking ragged and weary. Blood seeped from his wounds, but he still smiled at her.

"You're hurt," she said, offering her arm for him to lean on.

"So are you," he said, reaching out with his free hand and cradling her aching head. She moved her cheek to meet his touch and it felt warm and safe beneath his trembling palm.

"Why are you sorry? You did nothing wrong except being in the wrong place at the wrong time," she said.

"I wanted to protect you, but all I did was play into their hands."

"I don't know, you killed a fair few Klagens yourself out there," she said looking down to the square. They peered together over the parapet to watch as the Sarlatians and Chevaliers cleaned up the mess, rounded up the remaining Klagen and saw to the walking wounded. Darien Issoire was riding through the melee, issuing orders and directing the Sarlatians who jumped at his command. She wondered if they were more afraid of him or the thought of reproach from his wife, the Queen of Sarlat. Allan followed her gaze and smiled to himself, as though he knew what she was thinking.

"I think we have all been tools in someone else's fight," he said.

She glanced back at Gilbert's corpse and let her head drop to Allan's chest, opening the raw emotional wounds and letting her tears wash bloody streaks down her face. Allan wiped her face with the tip of his thumb and noticing the stub on his little finger, she picked up his hand and inspected it with curiosity. "How did you lose your finger?" A strange tingly feeling itched down her spine. His cheeks blushed.

"I… don't remember," he said. "Haven't we had this conversation before?"

318

She sensed his discomfort. "I suppose it must be a dangerous occupation, making swords," she said, thinking to put him at ease.

He wrinkled his brow. "I suppose. But I have been forging swords for as long as I can remember and I think I might have remembered if I had lopped off a finger." He smiled ruefully.

"Oh." There was that dizzy, strange feeling that she had missed something. "Why did you chase me all the way out here?"

He sighed. "You told me to either help you or stay out of your way. I couldn't stay out of your way, so I had to try and help you. I'm sorry I wasn't much use."

"You were more than some use," she said. "I can't believe you are still standing."

He shrugged. "I had help."

She rolled her eyes at him and he just smiled annoyingly. Together, they peered out over the square and watched the curious ceremony that was going on. The remaining Klagen prisoners were kneeling before Wilhelm and shouting in their guttural Jarvic tones. Then Wilhelm emerged from the centre of the crowd. With his good arm, he swung an axe up high into the air and brought it down with a sickening crunch. Demaris winced, as she watched Ullr's head elevated onto the spike of Wilhelm's spear and pillared into the ground like some ancient warning to anyone deemed foolish enough to challenge him.

"I was worried that you were going to try and take him on," Allan said.

"Well lucky for me I met someone more suitable for that task on my way here," she said.

"I don't blame you for your intentions," he said. "I would have done the same if it were my family and home."

"I don't think I'll keep the impaled head, but I certainly appreciate the gesture," she said. She closed her eyes, exhausted and he held onto her as they both slid down to the ground, keeping their arms circled around each other. She rested her head on his shoulder with no energy to do anything much but sit and rest.

"May I ask you something?" he said.

She sensed his nervousness. "Hmm?"

"If I were a lord and not a smith's son?"

Her eyes snapped open. He looked worried. "Yes. I would, whatever your question. A smith's son or no." What if she had read him wrong? "Was that a hypothetical question?"

"No. But if it were," he said. She mock punched him on the upper arm. "Ow... ow... axe wound," he said.

"Sorry, sorry," she placed a hand over the spot and put pressure on it.

"Better," he said with a mischievous glint in his eye. His gaze turned serious. "If you will consent to be my wife, I'll take you back to Carentan and seek permission from my parents. Would it disappoint your loyal subjects if you married a smith's son?"

"You're forgetting something," she said. "If I consent to be your wife and we marry, you will be a Count."

"Oh. I had never thought of it like that. But there is something else we are forgetting."

"Lord Barra," she said. He nodded, looking faintly disturbed. She glanced at Gilbert's body and he followed her gaze. "That was a marriage of convenience set up by a man who abused my trust. I will appeal to King Gereinte of Carentan to annul the betrothal."

Allan's whole body relaxed beneath her touch as though a knot inside him was gradually unwinding. "There is something else that I need your help with," he said.

"Oh?" She looked up into his emerald gaze.

"I have a personal puzzle to solve."

Chapter Forty

Allan and Demaris stood side by side in the Great Hall at Castle Helmstedt; a smith's son, beside a foreign Countess, petitioning the King to overturn her betrothal to his kin. Allan was tense with nerves, though he kept an open and confident expression. Demaris took his hand discreetly and squeezed it in her own. He felt her nerves too, compounding his own though she hid it well.

It was early evening and the King had all but concluded his court for the day when they had arrived and asked for an audience. Lord Barra was at court and so surprisingly was Allan's mother, who watched from the gallery and smiled at him with irritating confidence as if she knew how this was likely to end. Only she had the last piece of the puzzle.

Around the edges of the hall, a few onlookers and courtiers had just been ready to disperse when they had been announced and now sat waiting for something interesting to happen. In fact, as the King was concluding matters from the preceding petitioner, a steady stream of people began to fill the hall. They were looking at Allan with that strange expression that he had encountered when he first arrived in Carentan only weeks ago. Even more unsettling was the reappearance of the King's sisters, Roda and Alliane, who both sat at the front of the hall looking out toward him, the weight of expectancy in their expressions. What would happen if his story proved false? Banishment was the punishment for treason. A small frown creased the Princess Alliane's brow as her eyes flicked between Demaris and himself. Princess Roda looked perfectly serene.

Allan and Demaris had travelled back to Carentan with the Sarlatian forces and what was left of the Klagen clans. The Klagen had gathered themselves around their new leader, Wilhelm of the Forest, who despite nursing major injuries had organised them into some semblance of a functioning community. His companion, the Oarsmaster Jaanta, had mysteriously disappeared but no one, other than Allan, seemed in the least bit surprised.

The Arrontierre Chevaliers had declared a victory over Klagenstill and come to a reluctant alliance with the Sarlatians, who after all was said and done, had come to their aid. The Emperor claimed it as a victory over the Western Isles and denounced all involvement with the purported rumour of an Arrontierre master-at-arms taking the protection of his estates to dangerous political extremes.

Allan took a step back allowing Demaris to approach the dais where the King sat.

"Your Majesty," she said, but King Gereinte held up one hand and she stopped.

"Why are all these people here?" he said, looking around the hall. He frowned at his sisters, as though just noticing them for the first time. "I was led to believe this was a simple petition to overturn a betrothal." Roda glared at her brother and gave a curt nod in Allan's direction. "Ah, I see. The smith returns. All well and good. Am I also to expect a report on recent occurrences in Arrontierre?"

"Your Majesty," Darien Issoire said, standing up from his seat in the gallery. "That is most certainly forthcoming. I have the report for you, but I think there are more pressing issues here to be resolved." He smiled in that annoyingly charming way that Allan wished he were able to replicate. The King nodded, and the corners of his mouth twitched as though he was trying hard not to smile.

"So. This betrothal," he said turning towards Demaris. "It is not to your liking?"

"Your Majesty," a strangled voice cut across the hall and Lord Barra pushed his way to the front of the crowds. "I really must object. This was a perfectly legitimate arrangement, made by your good self and the Sergeant-at-arms of a most respectable family in Arrontierre; a long-standing servant of this young lady's family and ratified here in Carentan. It is not my wish to overturn this arrangement. It is a most suitable match of two families of repute and a bonding of nations that I am sure you will agree is most fortuitous, given the current political situation."

Allan let his mouth hang open. He could not possibly let her marry this lordly fool.

The King turned his attention away from Lord Barra. "My Lady," he said. "That is certainly true - I did agree to this arrangement. How would your guardian and mentor react if I were to overturn it?"

"My guardian, Gilbert Amand, is dead, your Majesty." There was hushed rumble of muttering across the hall. "I am sure that your compatriot,

324

Darien Issoire, will furnish you with the details in his report. Suffice it to say, I have no appetite for such an arrangement."

The King looked surprised. "Oh. I see. A lord is not good enough for my Lady?"

Demaris smiled. "A lord would be perfectly fine, your Majesty. But I would rather have a prince." She glanced into the gallery and Allan saw his mother smile.

"Interesting," King Gereinte said. He tapped his fingertips on the arms of his chair and made a play of looking around the room. "It seems we are all out of princes. Unless playing building bricks and making mud pies with Edwyn is your kind of thing." His eyes sparkled with mischief.

"I beg to differ," Demaris said and she pulled out Allan's notebook with the two missing pages tucked neatly back into place, then approached the King.

"What is this?" King Gereinte said. He took the book and flicked through it before settling at the first page. He read a few words, then snapped up his head. "Everyone out! Not you, or you... or you." He pointed first to Demaris and Allan, then to his sisters and finally, to the gallery where Allan's mother and Darien Issoire sat. The rest of the hangers-on and court entourage reluctantly shuffled out leaving an empty, echoing space in the hall. Allan could hear the muted mutterings of Lord Barra as he was hustled along with the crowds. King Gereinte did not say another word, just read page after page after page, without even looking up when his sisters leaned in and read over his shoulder.

Allan's limbs were aching from standing still for so long, his bandaged injuries throbbing and making him sway on the spot. Demaris stepped back to join him, looking just as travel worn and exhausted as he. They propped each other up as best they could, waiting for the King to finish. Darien Issoire remained in the gallery, watching with a keen look in his eye. Allan's mother had disappeared into the shadows.

When King Gereinte finally reached the last two torn pages, he held them up one after the other, allowing Roda and Alliane to follow the familiar flowing script. The princesses gasped in unison. Roda covered her mouth with her hand, and tears filled her eyes. Then the King stopped, frowned, and turned over the final page flapping it about as though expecting another hidden page. He looked up at Demaris and then caught Allan's eye and quickly averted his gaze. "But where is the rest of it? The story can't end there."

"Your Majesty," his mother said, moving into the light.

"I should have you seized and locked up in the dungeons for what you have done. For what you have kept from us," King Gereinte said. Princess Alliane was sobbing, her head buried in her sister's shoulder. Roda stood staring at Delyth, stony-faced.

"Please," Delyth said, "I have done a lot of things in my life that probably deserve to see me locked up in a dungeon, but believe me when I say that this was not one of them."

326

"Explain," Gereinte said.

"Look in front of you, your Majesty. Look how much he resembles King Reiner. I could no more have killed him than I could my own son," Delyth said. Gereinte pursed his lips and settled his emerald gaze on Allan. He should have felt uncomfortable, intimidated even, being so scrutinised by the King of Carentan. But all Allan saw were his own eyes staring back at him. A lump pushed up in his throat and his breath quickened.

"How do I know that this isn't some kind of Kali trick?" Gereinte said without taking his eyes off Allan.

"My mentor, Castan, was dying," Delyth said. "Somewhere along his travels he had picked up the wasting disease. I had seen the symptoms before and often watched the victims slowly waste away and die." Roda let out a cry and the two princesses hugged each other.

"Our mother died of the wasting disease," Gereinte said. Allan felt a sudden heaviness in his chest. She was his true mother too. Delyth nodded and paused before she continued.

"Castan had insisted that I continued with the assignment at Castle Helmstedt sixteen years ago. It was some six months later that I returned to Castan's house with a babe in arms screaming with his own pain and loss." Delyth glanced at Allan and he instinctively rubbed the stub on his little finger with his thumb. The King's eyes flicked down to Allan's hand, then back up to his face.

"Castan knew that I would not let him down and he said as much to me, but I didn't understand. I

327

had failed to complete the job. I cut off the baby's finger with my skinning knife and gave it to your enemies, as instructed. I took their money and kept the child. I deceived everyone."

There was another shocked gasp from Roda and a cry escaped from Alliane.

"Continue," Gereinte said. Delyth nodded.

"Instead of taking an innocent life, I had given life to a child. I had to wonder why Castan had insisted that I take that job when it went against all of the principles we had lived and worked by. Then I understood. He knew I wouldn't do it and he used me. I wanted revenge, while he needed political leverage. He stared at me through his rheumy eyes and in those dying moments bequeathed to me his house in a village near Lake Mariac, not far from the Port of Killanin. He told me to take the child and bring him up as my own and to never tell a soul and never let him out of my sight. One day, I would know that what I had done was the right thing. He gave me his blessing."

King Gereinte looked at Delyth with a steady gaze, one arch of an eyebrow raised in question. He turned the book over in his hands and frowned.

"It looks like someone didn't want us to know the truth," he said, picking at the burnt corners.

"You know that Allan… Josselin, is a gifted smith," Delyth said. Allan's face flushed at the sound of his given name. "There is no one quite as skilled to continue the Jael tradition. My husband's reasons were not all selfish; he wanted to protect Allan more than anything. As it happened, Allan's curiosity has always got the better of him. I had

328

hoped once he reached Castle Helmstedt that he would be in a position to make his own decisions. However, circumstances took an unexpected twist." His mother took a sidelong glance at Demaris.

There was a profound silence in the hall.

Gereinte stood up and walked slowly over to Allan. His heart thumped against his ribcage as the King held out his hand. Allan took it and Gereinte turned over his palm and looked at his left hand. He smiled to himself with a small shake of his head, then looked up into Allan's eyes. Then he took Demaris' hand and laid Allan's palm on top of hers.

"It appears we have sixteen years to catch up on," he said. "Well met, little brother."

The End

Acknowledgements

Many thanks to Charlotte Laval for her undiminished enthusiasm for this final book, her encouragement in getting it written and her dedication to reading drafts, suggesting changes and edits.

Thanks also must go to the Orbiter #5 of the British Science Fiction Association, who are; Susan Oke, Terry Jackman, Mark Bilsborough and Pam Baddeley. You have painstakingly read through every chapter with suggestions, comments, line edits and bigger picture edits. Your input has shaped the final story.

I have to also thank my family, friends and supporters for all their pestering (in a good way!) for me to complete this book. Special thanks to Billy, Will and Damien for putting up with my mind being in another world for large chunks of time.

Finally, I would like to thank you, my dearest readers, for joining me on this journey into the world of Carentan. If you would like more on the background of the Western Isles and information about the authors, please see: www.carentan.co.uk

www.ingramcontent.com/pod-product-compliance
Lightning Source LLC
Chambersburg PA
CBHW011457170626
46814CB00008B/2941